BLACK

is

The New

Black

Russell Blake

First Edition

ISBN: 978-1494974152

Published by

Reprobatio Limited

Books by Russell Blake

THRILLERS

FATAL EXCHANGE

THE GERONIMO BREACH

ZERO SUM

THE DELPHI CHRONICLE TRILOGY

KING OF SWORDS

NIGHT OF THE ASSASSIN

RETURN OF THE ASSASSIN

REVENGE OF THE ASSASSIN

BLOOD OF THE ASSASSIN

THE VOYNICH CYPHER

SILVER JUSTICE

JET

JET II – BETRAYAL

JET III – VENGEANCE

JET IV – RECKONING

JET V – LEGACY

JET VI – JUSTICE

UPON A PALE HORSE

BLACK

BLACK IS BACK

BLACK IS THE NEW BLACK

NON FICTION

AN ANGEL WITH FUR

HOW TO SELL A GAZILLION EBOOKS

Prologue

Peals of laughter drifted over the pulsing disco beat in the ballroom of the Peninsula Hotel. A cross section of New York's beautiful people wiggled and shook to the band's spirited rendition of "Play That Funky Music." The singer leered in all the appropriate places, his white Angel Flight slacks and red satin shirt shimmering in the rippling light from the overhead disco ball as he did his best Mick Jagger rooster strut for the crowd.

Three tall young women on the dance floor ground their hips with the enthusiasm of strippers, twerking their equally statuesque and stunning partners, each one the lucky recipient of exceptional genes and youthful enough so any signs of debauchery hadn't begun to show. One of the dancers, a thin black man wearing a too-tight yellow T-shirt that highlighted his bleached silver dreadlocks, threw back his head and grinned as the Ecstasy he'd taken a half hour earlier finally hit like a body slam to the mat.

Daria disengaged from her partner, a twenty-something hedge fund manager who'd invited her to his mansion in the Hamptons an hour after meeting her, and ran a hand through her ebony locks. He was nice, but insufferably full of himself, she thought as she raised a regal finger at a waiter. In spite of the man's money, she'd already decided to blow him off – she could pick and choose rich admirers, and had been linked to some of the wealthiest bachelors in the world, so this again was just more of the same.

She gazed around and sighed. The whole party was a bore. After three years as one of the most sought-after models in the business, she'd attended more wrap parties than she could remember, and the novelty had long ago worn thin.

She'd come a long way from her native Venezuela, where she'd been discovered at fifteen by a scout from an American agency; her sultry look was an intoxicating blend of the lascivious and the pure, according to the gushing spotlight features in a spate of magazines the following year. Now, at nearly twenty-one, she was nearing middle age in her career, with a bloated bank account, two small dogs, and more frequent flyer miles than a diplomat to show for it.

The tables ringing the floor were sparsely occupied now that dinner was a memory and the fashion shoot finished. The crew took this opportunity to let their hair down along with the models, the music and dim lighting a great equalizer, everyone a rock star on this celebratory evening. Tomorrow would bring hangovers, flights back home and regrets after waking up with strangers, but for a few short hours it was prom night, and booty shaking was the order of the day. High-powered Wall Street bankers chatted with models half their ages from Milan and Paris, a pop diva held court with a fawning entourage, and a film star with a bad boy reputation was driving home an earnest point to a male star of the New York City Ballet who sipped theatrically on a martini, doing his best Marlene Dietrich with a forbidden cigarette smoldering in an ebony holder.

The band segued into KC and the Sunshine Band's "That's The Way" and the dancers woohooed like the singer had tossed hundred dollar bills into the air. A steward moved like a wraith through the assembly, balancing a tray laden with champagne flutes and Perrier bottles with the practiced dexterity of a juggler. The band worked the chorus, the bass player, a dead ringer for Bootsy Collins, hamming it up as he shucked and jived. A young woman clad in a painted-on black sequined dress, all chocolate skin and neon red hair, joined the singer on the refrain, and the crowd went wild – an hour earlier she'd been taking a final bow before a sold-out crowd at the Apollo.

Three days of grueling photo shoots in the Bowery and a host of distressed locations around the city were finally over, and the fall collection for one of the world's top mediocre designers had been commemorated with smoldering urban angst, featuring cadaverous women from runways around the world and a cast of male counterparts with brooding glowers and come-hither pouts. Hundreds of thousands of dollars had been spent to get just the right look: steam rising from early-morning manhole covers framing barely legal ingénues with impossibly long legs and smiles that promised paradise.

Daria took another sip of champagne. The Veuve Clicquot the caterers were serving tasted like ambrosia, and she lifted her long waterfall of hair off her neck so the air could cool her. It had been an odd night so far, but that was nothing new in her whirlwind life. A wave of disorientation washed over her and then receded. She closed her eyes for a moment and got her bearings, and then took another sip from her glass. Daria liked her booze and her pills a little too much, but on the last blow-out following a big campaign she felt entitled to a little relaxation – after all, she'd more than earned it, a star in a glowing constellation of the fabulously beautiful.

Her new suitor moved to her side, and she spent the next five minutes and another glass of champagne apologizing for not taking him up on his generous offer, promising to look him up when she came back to town after another shoot in Prague the following week – a promise she had no intention of keeping. His arrogant face darkened at the rejection, albeit artful, and she saw the flash of spoiled petulance of someone used to getting what he wanted, which gave her enormous satisfaction as she strutted away. As she crossed the floor she glanced at her watch and realized that she was running late – she'd committed to a rendezvous for midnight, and it was already a few minutes past the hour.

With smooth efficiency, the elevator whisked her to the sun deck terrace high above the bustle of the streets, traffic still heavy even at the late hour on a Thursday. Daria pushed through the tempered glass doors and a cool breeze greeted her, carrying with it the familiar smells she associated with the city: exhaust and the unique odors of the river and the park, all fresh-cut grass and dewy trees rustling in the moonlight.

She extracted a cigarette from her slim purse and lit it with a delicate gold lighter – a gift from a Saudi prince who'd been enamored of her charms, she remembered vaguely. One day tended to blur into the next for Daria on a treadmill of shoots around the world, long flights dulled by chemicals, and a loneliness so massive that at times it felt as though its weight would crush her. She blew a long plume of smoke at the stars. The skyscrapers around her glowed, and Fifth Avenue stretched below her with its neon parade of vehicles jockeying for position like a living organism fueled by the impatience of the privileged.

Her chocolate eyes took in the parade with impatience, and she checked the time again. The meeting had been an odd request, but she'd been intrigued, so she'd agreed. Being sworn to secrecy only added to the allure. But her time was valuable, even if she was slightly tipsy – the half a Dilaudid she'd swallowed on her last trip to the ladies' room intensified the effects of the alcohol with a welcome rush of warm well-being.

Downstairs, a taxi pulled to the curb and a couple climbed out, laughing, their soirée at the theater having been topped off with a nightcap at a trendy bar. The man took his mate's hand possessively and pulled her to him. She smiled as she nuzzled his neck, and was standing on her tiptoes to kiss him when the cab's hood suddenly crumpled with an explosive crash and a shower of broken glass: Daria's body had reached nearly terminal velocity before slamming into the vehicle.

The driver swung his door open as traffic screeched to a stop, horns blaring, Daria's ruined form a bloody mess on the street next to the car.

The police arrived six minutes later, and the cruiser double parked, shielding her mangled corpse from oncoming vehicles. Her sightless eyes stared in wonder at the heavens, her earthly concerns no longer an issue, still beautiful even after the brutal finality of death had ended her worldly stay. One of the two uniforms approached with a blanket and paused before draping it over her.

"Damn shame, huh? She looks like she's barely out of her teens," he said to his partner, a stubby officer with a fireplug physique already going to fat.

"Yeah. Takes all kinds, though, huh? Probably high as a kite, thought she could fly or something. Or life was too hard – maybe she broke a nail this afternoon and couldn't go on?"

They exchanged tired glances far older than their years and waited for the coroner's van, waving traffic around the crime scene. Rubbernecking drivers slowed as they crept past, causing a chain reaction that would be felt for a mile.

The next day an article on the second page of the *Times* would bemoan the sad untimely death of one of modeling's top stars, two networks would rush specials chronicling Daria's meteoric rise to the air, an entertainment channel would feature a half hour of tearful commentary from her colleagues and family, and her last shoot would propel sales of the talentless designer's collection to giddy heights. The cab driver would go on to sue Daria's estate for emotional trauma, and her agent and peers would organize a candlelight vigil in Central Park, where one of Broadway's hottest stars would deliver an *a capella* rendition of "Hallelujah" that would be the most downloaded video on YouTube for a month.

Chapter 1

Black hated when the Santa Ana winds blew the dust, pollen, and pollution from the Riverside basin into Los Angeles, seemingly targeting his allergies to maximize his misery. He knew that the seasonal weather wasn't specifically designed to torture him, but as he sat behind the wheel of his Eldorado, eyes red, itching, and watering, it might as well have been personal. It was bad enough that he'd been up for two nights in a row on a stakeout, living on energy drinks, Snickers bars and convenience store coffee. The Santa Anas kicked that up to a whole new level of unpleasant, and he was now firmly entrenched in his own box seat in the seventh circle of hell.

He shifted, trying to get comfortable, his ass asleep from innumerable hours watching the dilapidated ranch house on the wrong side of the East L.A. border, and a partially drunk cup of tepid coffee spilled onto the seat from where he'd propped it before promptly forgetting it.

"Gah–" he exclaimed, cursing the universe as he strained to raise his cheeks from the red leather that would now be a diarrheic burgundy after the java had soaked in. He edged from behind the wheel and groped around on the passenger-side floor for the entertainment magazine he'd brought to pass the time, fishing between the wrappers and empty cans until his fingers found the cover. Fortunately for him the pages were cheap stock and absorbed far more than would expensive, glossy fodder. Most of the coffee was sopped up between announcements of films recently optioned or stories chronicling which starlets were in rehab again.

Satisfied he'd done everything he could, he resigned himself to sitting with a wet backside in a graffiti-covered armpit of Los Angeles, watching a tired stucco crackerbox for signs of life in the wee hours of the morning. Another gust of wind blew a cloud of dust and trash down the street, and the cloth roof of the convertible shuddered like a vagrant with the DTs.

A light went on in the house, and then off again – probably someone going to the bathroom. Black's quarry was a man by the name of Ernest

Crabtree, who'd never held a job longer than a year, and whose latest occupation had been working at a small hot dog shop that Black's friend and confidante, Stan Colt, co-owned with two other cops. Ernest had slipped and fallen three months into his employment, and was now suing the partners for the pain and suffering he'd been forced to endure as a result of the mishap. He was drawing disability in the process, and Stan had asked Black to take a hard look at him, believing that it was possible Ernest was being less than forthright about his injury, for which he was getting daily massages, physical therapy, and apparently anything else he could think of, regardless of cost.

Black had agreed to do Stan a favor and had spent the last two evenings watching the house. Stan had opined that Ernest might be working an off-the-books night job to make ends meet – he'd apparently had similar gigs in the past at the airport and at the docks in San Pedro, loading cargo for a C-note at the end of a six-hour shift. Black had done some research into his background and found three prior injury claims over the last decade, lending some weight to Stan's suspicions about him milking the system.

"The damned attorney is saying to settle with him," Stan had said over a beer three days earlier. "Said it would cost an easy fifty grand to defend it through trial, so we'd better off cutting a check for that now and sparing ourselves the grief."

"Ouch. Those are expensive hot dogs."

"Tell me about it. The problem is nobody's got that much lying around – we dumped most of our spare cash into the business."

"Did you try making him a lower offer?"

"Not yet. I'm telling you, I think the guy's a wrong one. He's got that shifty dirtbag look, you know?"

"I see it every time I look in the mirror," Black had affirmed.

"I'm not kidding. I didn't hire him – Tommy did. I should have known better than to let him handle that, but I had a full caseload at the time, and…you know how it goes."

"Tell me again why you thought a hot dog business would be a great investment?"

"The location's killer, with a bus stop right in front, and we're selling two hundred dogs a day during lunch. We clear about a buck per dog after expenses, and with drinks…it's a money-maker."

"Right. Tubes of mystery meat. Empire building. But you didn't factor in Ernest, huh?"

"Exactly. Come on. Do me a favor. It's not like I haven't done you enough of them. I talked to the guys. We'd even be willing to throw some cash at covering your gas, a few meals, you know?"

"Well, I'm awfully busy…"

"You told me it's been a week and a half since your last case."

"Did I say that? I must have been drunk. Or disoriented."

"It was nine in the morning. On a Sunday."

"That explains it – must have been the Rapture."

Stan had slipped two hundred bucks across the table, clinching Black's fate for the foreseeable future. In truth, he would have helped out anyway, but with earnest money on the table, he felt more committed.

"I'll do what I can. I need to keep my days open in case clients want to meet."

"Suit yourself. Anything's better than being bled to death by this parasite."

The first amber glow of dawn was illuminating the sky when the lights snapped back on inside the house, and this time, stayed on. Black sat up. The street was quiet now, the wind having died down an hour earlier, leaving the asphalt dusted with a coating of sand blown west from the desert. He sank below the level of the dash when the front door opened. Out stepped Ernest, wearing a whiplash collar, a pair of sweat pants that did nothing for his rotund frame, and a white T-shirt that struggled to cover his belly. Black watched as he made his way to his car, a Ford Taurus from the mid-nineties, gingerly slid into the driver's seat and started the engine.

Black followed the car to a twenty-four hour market, which Ernest entered while Black sat across the street. He emerged a few minutes later with a loaf of bread in one hand and a bulging plastic bag in the other, and returned to his house. Black took a few photos, but knew as he did so that Ernest walking into a store meant nothing in terms of his claimed disability – he hadn't claimed to be wheelchair bound, only that he'd injured his spine.

Black frowned and rubbed a tired hand over his face. Ten hours of surveillance for shots of Ernest with breakfast. Not exactly a home run.

His eyes burned, and he caught a glimpse of himself in the rear view mirror. He looked like a hobo, with a pallid face, dull unwashed hair, and the beginnings of dark circles under his eyes. Black felt an almost overwhelming desire for a cigarette, but quashed it – he'd managed to avoid smoking for several months, and wasn't going to wreck the streak now with a weak moment.

Black settled back in, watching, and two hours later checked the time, the street now bright with morning light. He needed to get into the office, and traffic from East L.A. would be a bear. It would be a small miracle if he made it in less than an hour, putting him at his building about the time Roxie usually sauntered in at nine-ish.

The big V8 roared to life and he pulled away from the curb. At least he'd reassured himself that, whatever Ernest's faults, he wasn't moonlighting on the docks, so he could scratch that off his list. Which wouldn't really help Stan, but facts were facts.

He wheeled to the end of the block and onto the artery that led to the freeway, where he was greeted by a sea of brake lights. Waves of heat shimmered off hoods as the great unwashed waited for their chance to crawl their way to work. Black punched his stereo on and tapped his fingers to Aerosmith's "Love in an Elevator," Tyler's bawdy wail cutting through the screaming guitars like a testosterone-driven bird of prey. The car next to him held two Latinos with gang tattoos pumping whatever the latest rap noise was; the atonal stuttering of the rapper bemoaned the trials and tribulations of keeping his bitches in line and fending off hoes who wanted a piece of him.

Black considered dropping the top but decided against it, as the residual Santa Anas were still gusting, carrying with them enough allergens to make Black's face swell like a Shar Pei's. He debated popping another Benadryl, but thought better of it given how sleepy he already was, now forty-eight hours since he'd started the nocturnal surveillance with no more than cat naps each day for a break. If it had been anyone but Stan, he would have been charging two grand a day for his time, easy, but friends were friends, and he didn't have anything better to do – certainly no clients beating down his door.

Which was fine. There was money in the bank, for the first time since he could remember, from a series of jobs that had been thrown his way by satisfied customers. So he wasn't worried. Yet. Although he knew it could turn on a dime, and just because he'd had a good run didn't guarantee it would continue.

The drive into downtown was worse than he'd feared, and by the time he made it to the office it was half past nine. There were no parking places on his block, and he had to walk what seemed like miles from his eventual spot to his building, tired, unshaven, bleary-eyed and un-showered. He mentally steeled himself for a scathing reception from Roxie as he swung the downstairs entrance open and tromped heavily up the stairs, his limbs feeling like he was swimming through molten lead as he made his way toward a truculent, obese cat that despised him and an assistant who tormented him for sport.

And that was the good part.

When he pushed through his office door, Mugsy, the porky feline bane of his existence, cracked one sleepy eye and took him in with a look of disapproval before going back to sleep. For a brief instant Black envied the cat, but shook it off as an odor like an open sewer assaulted him.

"I see Mugsy's digestive problems aren't preventing him from on-loading his body weight in cat chow per day. Can't you open a window or something? It smells like a camp latrine in here," Black said by way of morning greeting.

Roxie didn't look up from her monitor. Her hair was dyed purple with black tips and her forearm sported a new tattoo of the cartoon character Speedy Gonzalez slathered with Vaseline. "Morning, boss man. Why don't you just kick him while you're at it? Start the day right?"

"I'm just saying that if I was a client, I'd turn around if that hit me when I walked in."

"Oh. Right. Maybe that's why the unending stream of eager customers has slowed. It's Mugsy's fault."

"The place stinks."

"Well, you won't have to worry about that much longer. I'm turning in my notice," she said, and finally looked up at him. Her eyes were ringed with exaggerated black mascara and her full lips gleamed with ruby red lipstick. In spite of himself, Black felt a stirring, which quickly faded when he registered her words.

He hesitated, wary of some ruse. "Yeah, right. Sure you are."

"No, I'm serious. I'm moving."

Black walked like an automaton to his office and hung his jacket on the door before returning to make coffee. "Wait. You really mean it? You're moving? Where to?"

"To Germany. Berlin. In three weeks."

Black almost dropped the pot as he fiddled with the filters. "Berlin? Why? That's like a whole other country. And they don't speak English there."

"Glad you've heard of it. Your command of geography is always impressive. They speak German. Hence the name of the country. Germany. I kind of put that together already. It's on the internet."

"You haven't answered the why part," Black said, dumping an extra dollop of coffee into the reservoir and sliding it into place. "Do we have any bottled water?"

"I usually just scoop it out of the toilet when you have me make coffee. Which is poison, you know. I'm pretty sure just smelling it shortens my life."

"Which would be funny coming from someone sitting in Mugsy's methane den, if laughing didn't make me gag. But seriously, Roxie. Why Berlin?"

"It's Eric. His cousin lives there, and suggested he open a tattoo parlor. Business has only been so-so lately at his place up on the strip, so he agreed."

"Wait. So Eric can't make his business work in the tattoo capital of the world, and the solution is to go to Berlin and try his hand at it there? And you're going to follow him?"

"There's apparently a big demand for skin art in Germany. All the rage."

Black tried to frame a civil response but couldn't, so he went out into the hall and filled the pot from one of the bathroom sinks to buy himself time. For all their sparring, Roxie ran his business, and he wasn't sure he'd be able to replace her. She was a pain in the butt, but damn good at what she did, and...and the truth was, it wouldn't feel like Black Investigations without Roxie's sarcastic, deadpan delivery to greet him every morning.

When he returned to the suite, he decided to be casual about her revelation, play it cool. Eric was a malingering lowlife and probably wouldn't be able to scrape up the money to move, so this was likely all drama that would come to nothing.

He poured water into the coffee machine, switched it on, and waited patiently by it as it burped and sputtered.

"What's that on your pants? You have some kind of...accident?" Roxie asked.

Black remembered the coffee in the car. Damn. He'd spaced. Should have stopped at his apartment.

"I spilled something on them."

Roxie went in for the kill. "I know as men enter their golden years, they lose control of their bodily functions. Kind of like old dogs. They say the knees are the first to go, but I'm not so sure about that."

"That's something to look forward to, I suppose. But in this case, I had a little accident with some 7-11 coffee."

"Don't worry. It's nothing to be embarrassed about. I mean, it totally is, but I'm trying to be supportive so you don't feel bad about the natural effects of aging."

"That's very kind of you. Charity begins at home."

Her eyes twinkled with glee. "Are you going to get those adult diapers? I've seen them at the store. I can pick you up a bag..."

"I don't need diapers."

She smiled sweetly. "You do if you're going to poop your drawers."

"Can we get back to you moving to Germany?"

"Oh, yeah. Well, anyway, we're going to leave in three weeks, so you'll need to find someone else willing to work impossible hours for nearly nothing."

"You don't even work seven hours a day. And I pay you well."

"You pay me well if I was living in a mudhole in Bangladesh, Mr. Slum Dog."

Black refused to rise to the bait. "How sure are you about this?" he asked, his voice even. "It seems sudden."

"Oh, I'm sure. We agreed on it over the weekend. Eric's already arranging for someone to take over the shop here on a sub-lease."

"Wow. Well, what are *you* going to do in Berlin? What about the band? Your career?"

"There's a huge rock scene there. And these days, being in L.A. doesn't get you much. It's not like it was back in the Stone Age. Labels look internationally for talent, and they invented this thing called the internet a while ago, so it makes it pretty easy. I figure I'll move, find a band, and build it from there. Hell, it's not like Capital's knocking my door down, anyway. Can't be any worse in Germany."

"Yes, it can. It rains a lot. And snows. And all they eat is sausage, lard, and pig sphincter. And…you'll be leaving Mugsy to fend for himself," Black said, playing his hole card last.

"Oh, no. I already told Eric Mugsy's going with us. There's no way I'd leave my little fur baby behind."

"Little isn't the first word that comes to mind," Black said, eyeing Mugsy's sleeping form. "Unless you think an economy car's little."

"He's losing weight. I've got him on special food."

"Is that what that stink is?"

She glared at him. "Don't worry. He won't be here to sully your empire much longer."

"I'm just afraid the smell's going to trigger the fire alarm."

"Why do you have to bag on him? He loves you."

"Uh huh."

"Is it your incontinence that's hardening your heart against him?"

"I'm not incontinent."

"Right. And you didn't sleep in your suit, either. Weren't you wearing that yesterday?"

"I was on a stakeout."

"With a bottle of Jack for company? Little drinky drink after a fight at home, perhaps? And now you're taking it out on a helpless cat?"

"I haven't had a drink in two days."

She rolled her eyes theatrically. "I'm afraid you're not at a meeting, but I'll congratulate you anyway. One day at a time, and all that."

Black smiled good-naturedly. "Roxie. I'm not an alcoholic, and I'm not incontinent."

"They say you have to lose the denial to move forward."

Black considered continuing the circular banter but opted for coffee instead. He carried the pot into his office, wanting to reduce his interactions with Roxie until he could formulate a coherent response to her announcement. Eric was a first-class slimeball, but women sometimes fell for those, he knew, and Roxie had apparently decided that whatever Eric's faults, he was *her* slimeball. Black had no doubt Eric would screw her over, but he couldn't just blurt that out like a jealous lover. He needed hard facts, and right now he was so tired he couldn't think.

The phone rang, and it took Roxie three rings to break away from whatever she was doing online to answer it. Black poured himself a brimming cup of steaming brew and was dumping in enough sugar to drive him into a diabetic coma when his line buzzed and Roxie's voice called from her station.

"It's Bobby. Line one."

Black took a deep breath and lifted the headset to his ear.

"Yo. Bobby. The Bobster. Bob-a-licious. How's it hanging?" Black asked with fake good cheer.

"Um, good. Listen, I've got a potential client here with me, and you're on speakerphone."

Black's stomach did a flip, and he muttered an inaudible curse and switched gears. "Right. Well then. With whom am I speaking?"

"My client, Daniel Novick. He's got a deal in progress, but he's got some misgivings and is looking for some investigative talent. We were wondering what your schedule looked like?"

A higher pitched voice came on the line. "Hi, Mr. Black. Daniel here. I was hoping we could get together at some point today or tomorrow. Bobby has nothing but good things to say about you."

"That's good to hear. Let me look at my book," Black said, rubbing his face. He couldn't meet a client looking like he'd slept on a park bench. And he was too groggy to be coherent, much less impressive. So it would have to be tomorrow. "I'm afraid I'm booked today, but I could make it *mañana* in the morning. Do you want me to come to your office, or should we meet at Bobby's?"

"Either way's fine with me," Bobby chimed in.

"Would it be too much of an imposition to ask you to come to mine?" Daniel asked.

"Not at all. What's the address?" Black asked. Daniel gave him the information – an exclusive area of Beverly Hills just off Rodeo Drive.

"Can you make it at, say, eleven? I've got meetings before then," Daniel said.

"Of course. That would be perfect. Eleven tomorrow, at your office. Is there a business name?"

"Yes. It's DNA. We're one of the largest modeling agencies in the country. We have offices here, New York, and Miami. Maybe you've heard of us?"

"Mmm, no, I'm afraid not. But I'm not really in that business, so…"

"Well, no matter. I'll look forward to meeting you. I'm hoping you can help me with my issue."

"I'll certainly try."

Bobby's voice boomed in the background. "See you then. I'll call you back in a few."

"Okay."

Black disconnected, his head suddenly splitting, and jotted down the name and address before he forgot it. He took a gulp of coffee and burned his tongue, prompting another round of soft swearing. Aside from this possible new business, it had been a terrible day so far, and it had barely begun. He debated crawling under his desk, curling up in a ball, and going to sleep, but nixed the idea. Bobby would be calling any time. Maybe he'd go home after he talked to him. Catch a little shut-eye and try to recover. He couldn't keep going at his current pace – Stan's shirking ex-employee would have to take a back seat for a little while.

He took another cautious sip and grimaced as the tip of his tongue tingled. Whoever Bobby referred was usually a high roller, so the gig would be worth at least two hundred fifty per hour, plus expenses. He hoped that Daniel had a really complex problem that would take some serious time to unravel. Selfish, but there it was. Especially with Roxie's status in question, money might make things easier. If the impossible happened and she really did leave, he'd be running ads, interviewing, and maybe even paying more to get a qualified replacement.

Not that Roxie could be replaced. For all her difficult ways, she was a crack researcher, and kept his affairs straight. His bookkeeping actually made sense now; when he had a case her research was always fast and efficient, and other than Mugsy turning the office into a kitty litter box, he couldn't really complain.

Plus, in spite of her constant harassment, he had a weak spot for her. Actually liked her, if he was honest with himself. If she really left…he knew he'd miss her, even though he'd never admit that to anyone.

He checked his emails and killed time, and twenty minutes later Bobby was on the line again.

"So fill me in. What's Daniel's deal?" Black asked.

"He's a bigwig in the fashion industry. Does a ton of business. Mainly out of New York – he's only here occasionally to check up on the local office. He's buying another agency in town, and he's got problems with the transaction."

"Problems? What kinds of problems?"

Bobby sighed. "He thinks someone's targeting his talent."

"Targeting? What does that mean?"

"It means someone's killing the models."

Chapter 2

Black felt better the next morning after a long night's sleep and his first shave and shower in forever. He'd awoken to Sylvia's kisses, and after a languorous lovemaking session he'd selected one of his black suits and a teal tie that would have been at home on Sinatra, and prepared himself for an eventful – and hopefully profitable – day.

Once showered and dressed, he poured a bowl of cereal and sat at the postage-stamp-sized kitchen table, spoon in hand, munching on sugary puffs as he stared blankly out his grimy window. Sylvia shuffled in, still groggy, wearing one of his T-shirts and nothing else, and poured herself some orange juice. She'd been spending most nights at his place over the last month, which he didn't mind a bit, but had resisted bringing any clothes over – some kind of a girl thing, Black supposed.

"You look very handsome. Dignified," she said, eyeing him from the refrigerator.

"If I can fool you, I can fool anyone."

"You should wear that tomorrow night." Sylvia was an artist, and had a big show coming up the following evening that she'd been excited about for weeks. "I'll be the envy of everyone there."

"I'm more than a boy toy. Not much more, but still."

"That's what you think. I just keep you around for sex."

"Not that I have a problem with that. Just saying."

"Seriously. You'll be the star of the show."

"Except that I know nothing about art."

"Even better. Neanderthal sells big these days."

He finished his cereal and carried it to the sink. "You going to hang out here today?" he asked.

"No, I've got errands to run and some last minute stuff for the exhibition. I'm getting more nervous as it gets closer. Pulling my hair out."

"You could have fooled me. You'll do great." He glanced at his watch. "I've gotta go. See you tonight?"

"I'll call. I don't know yet. I might not be good company. I probably won't be able to sleep."

"Okay. Just touch base later. I've gotta run."

Sylvia's arms circled his waist. She stood on her tiptoes and kissed him. He gave her a long embrace, and when they parted he felt, as he often did, that he was a truly lucky man.

Which changed when he remembered that he had a therapy session with his quack, Dr. Kelso. He made another resolution to stop pouring money he didn't have down a black hole in the form of appointments every other week with the charlatan, but as usual chickened out once he was on the couch staring at the painting he was convinced the twisted doctor had placed there to torment him.

Black tried his hardest to ignore the thinly-veiled depiction of warring phalluses, but it was no good. Their cavorting, thrusting into a hellish sky rendered by the artist, was simply too much. He turned and looked at Kelso, his rubbery lips like two worms ringed by unruly strands of coarse graying beard, his thick horn-rimmed glasses a deliberate affectation, Black was sure, intended to lend him a scholarly air that was entirely undeserved based on what he'd seen of the good doctor's performance to date. Kelso seemed ready to fall asleep at any moment, as was often the case during their time together, and after asking a few perfunctory questions about Black's mood, could have easily been dozing between vaguely interested moans and monosyllabic grunts. Until Black touched on the topic of Roxie, which always seemed to perk the old pervert right up.

"Yeah, it was just odd. One day everything's fine, and the next she's giving her notice."

Kelso sat forward. "Yes. I see. And how does that make you feel?"

Black frowned. "Annoyed, to start with. Because now I need to find a new assistant."

"To start with. Hmm. And by annoyed, don't you really mean angry?" Kelso asked.

"No. More annoyed. And a little rejected."

"Because she's made a choice. To leave. And you take that personally, yes?"

"Of course I do. She's leaving *me*, isn't she?"

"Well, she's leaving Los Angeles. Perhaps everything doesn't hinge on you?"

Black waved him off. "This Eric – her boyfriend? He's a complete dirtbag. Cheated on her, treats her like garbage, lies all the time. He's one of those guys who's always got a sneer on his face, you know? Like everyone but him is an idiot."

"It's safe to say you don't like him?"

"Very perceptive. The thing is, he'll wind up hurting her. It's just a matter of time." Black sighed, the forest of stabby phalluses in the painting blurring as his eyes watered from his allergies. "I just can't believe she'd fall for his line of BS over and over."

"Are you still having sexual thoughts about her?" Kelso asked. Black didn't like his tone, but didn't call him on it.

"No," he lied.

"None at all?"

"Not that I recall," Black answered in his most lawyerly way.

"Remember that, for our time together to be effective, you have to tell the truth."

"Right. Well, okay…maybe a few times. But that's only natural."

"Because she's attractive."

"Well, yes. I mean, no, she's a freak. But she has a quality about her."

Kelso nodded. "Yes. A freak. And you mentioned before that she dresses provocatively."

"Sometimes. Although she thinks I'm a trainwreck. She actually accused me of soiling my trousers yesterday."

"Soiling?" Kelso repeated, savoring the word like a rare wine.

"Pooping my pants."

"I see. So you and your assistant were talking about…defecation? Your defecation?"

"No. I mean, she was giving me shi…she was teasing me about a coffee stain on my pants. Which turned into a discussion about my age. It was actually kind of funny."

"Your sexy young assistant teasing you about your pants and your age. Funny. I see."

"No, you don't. We have a different kind of working relationship. We tease each other. Or she teases me, most of the time."

"So she's a tease, is she?" Kelso now seemed extremely interested. More so than Black could remember.

"She teases. Yes."

18

"The young woman who dresses provocatively teases you."

"You make it sound sexual. It isn't."

"If you say so. Tell me, does she ever touch you when she's...teasing you? Perhaps rub up against you? Touch your arm or your hand?"

"Touch me? No. Of course not. It's nothing like that. She does it verbally."

Kelso seemed disappointed, but soldiered ahead. "Let me ask you a question, and I want you to be completely honest. Remember how important that is. Being honest."

Black closed his eyes. "If this is to help me. Right. Got it."

"Do you have fantasies about her?"

"Besides wishing she'd do her work, you mean?"

"Sexual fantasies."

"No. I'm not dreaming about banging my assistant."

"Or dominating her?"

"No."

Kelso eyed him skeptically. "You mentioned the boyfriend. You seem animated when you discuss him. You resent him, yes?"

"Because he's a lying scumbag."

"And because he treats her poorly...at least, in your estimation."

"Exactly."

"And you feel a protective impulse toward her."

"I suppose." Black found that if he squinted and then blinked fast, he could make the penises seem to dance. Sort of a hula. Or maybe a kind of polka circle, a penile line-dance.

"But you don't feel that she recognizes his negative qualities like you do?" Kelso pressed.

"No. She's blind to his faults. Or it's like pregnancy. She immediately forgets the pain and only remembers the positives."

"You think of your sexy young assistant in the context of pregnancy? Interesting."

A chime sounded. Black sighed with relief. Kelso sat back and studied his note pad, which Black would have bet contained nothing but obscene doodles. "You know what the bell means," Kelso said.

"Yup. I'm a hundred bucks poorer."

Kelso ignored the barb. "Same time in two weeks? Unless you'd like to come in next week to discuss Roxie some more. It seems like that situation's reaching a crisis point for you."

Black smiled humorlessly. "Actually, no. For some reason I feel better about that. I have a clearer idea of how I'm going to handle the problem. No need to beat a dead horse."

Kelso eyed him distrustfully. "A clearer idea? I trust there's nothing…you want to confide in me?"

"Nope. I know what the bell means."

He left Kelso sitting, looking uncomfortable, and with a final glance at the painting, walked out of the office, stopping at the reception desk to hand over his money. When he descended the stairs to the street he was whistling, and realized that he did indeed felt better. Whether Kelso knew it or not, talking to him had given him insight on how to deal with his Roxie issue. Of course Kelso would probably have disapproved of what he intended to do. Then again, Kelso had disturbing erotic paintings in his office, regardless of the innocent air he affected when asked about them.

No, to stop Roxie from going to Berlin, affirmations, analysis, and positive thinking wouldn't be much good. What would do the trick would be allowing her scumbag boyfriend to hang himself, with Black helping him to do so. Which, even though he was taking on a new client and had his hands full with Ernest, he'd make time for.

Although for a fleeting moment he wondered whether there was any way to get Eric to take Mugsy and leave Roxie behind, but then dismissed the thought.

No point expecting miracles.

Chapter 3

Black cut across town and entered the rarefied environs of Beverly Hills. Scores of the wealthy clad in the latest fashions ambled down the Rodeo Drive sidewalks, taking in the overpriced goods in prohibitively expensive shop windows. Black circled around looking for a parking place, wondering to himself about a society where buying crap you didn't need was considered a legitimate way to spend the day. He was early, so after he found a space, he decided to try a cup of eight-dollar coffee at a café with an unpronounceable Italian name and serving staff that would have been at home in a Lady Gaga video.

He ordered a cappuccino and checked his messages while the black-clad waitress sashayed to get his drink with the insouciant lack of urgency that typified the service the wealthy received in L.A. Stan had sent an email requesting an update. Ever since Stan had gotten an iPad from Black for his birthday, he'd transformed from a Luddite to an online fanatic. Black rarely spoke with him on the phone anymore, Stan's fascination with the colored screen rivaling a three-year-old's for the latest Pixar heart-tugger.

Black tapped out a quick ambiguous response and pressed send just as his drink arrived. The waitress' face resembled photographs Black had seen of deep water ocean fish: sallow skin, eyes bugging out as though her internal pressure was too great for her flesh to contain. She gave him a disinterested, dead glance and went back to her position by the espresso machine, practicing her silent Italian dismissiveness, her talents wasted on the likes of him.

He took his time, savoring every quarter's worth of coffee as he watched a parade of exotic cars drift by piloted by the powerful or their mates, each a glass and steel cocoon of privilege that strove to distance and elevate the lucky occupants from their fellow man. A trio of stunning women walked by speaking what sounded to him like Russian, and he wondered silently how the world had changed so much since he'd arrived in town. Black's bursts of self-awareness and introspection were few and far between, but occasionally he'd be overcome by the sense that he'd been left out of some important dialogue everyone else had participated in, missed the memo that explained how life actually worked.

Kelso had that effect on him, he decided, and resolved for the umpteenth time to end the sessions at the next appointment. His rage was under control, his impulses moderated, and lying on the couch blathering about whether or not he wanted to jump Roxie's bones wasn't doing him any good, as far as he could tell.

Black finished his cup and slid cash beneath the saucer before walking to the back of the café and using the restroom. He looked reasonably presentable, he decided as he studied his reflection in the mirror, and began the loop of silent positive affirmations he'd been working with since he'd started his Kelso ordeal. He *was* a winner. He was master of his own destiny. He *did* rule everything he could see. The fruit of success was dangling from the tree of plenty awaiting him to effortlessly claim it for his own.

Of course, that would have resonated with more conviction if he wasn't living from paycheck to paycheck in a fleabag apartment with moldy carpet and questionable plumbing, but no matter. Today was his day, and he was going to seize the moment.

Daniel's building was a copper-tinted glass monolith. His company occupied the entire sixth floor, and when Black stepped from the elevator his newfound confidence evaporated. Two female receptionists who should have had their own television show looked up at him, headsets locked in place with military precision, and waited as he approached.

"Yes?" the blonde asked, a single arched eyebrow making him question his existence.

"I'm here to see Daniel."

"I see. Your name?"

"Black."

"Black. That's it?"

Black tried a grin. "That should be enough."

She exchanged a glance with her companion and tapped something out of sight below the counter before murmuring unintelligibly for a few moments. When she looked back up at him she'd thawed a few degrees. But still no smile.

"Gunther will be out in a moment to show you back. Pellegrino?"

Black was stumped. "I don't know who designed my suit."

She didn't blink. "Would you like some water? Juice?"

"Oh. No. I'm good."

A tall man with a shaved head and pecan-colored skin emerged from a doorway behind the reception area and offered his hand.

"Mr. Black. I'm Gunther. Please. Right this way. Daniel's waiting for you." Gunther motioned for Black to follow him into the depths of the building. They passed offices with edgy young men and women with trendy clothes and expensive haircuts, all wearing headsets and engaged in phone conversations. When they reached the corner office, Gunther held the door open for him. Bobby was sitting on a black leather Scandinavian sofa under a huge, expensive-looking oil painting, all chaotic swatches of black on an arctic background, which looked like a Rorschach ink blot. His orange booth-augmented tan was highlighted by his white polo shirt and golf pants, his hair plugs lacquered back in a passable Godfather impression.

"Black. Good to see you. This is my client, Daniel Novick. Daniel, meet Black. The best in the business," Bobby said, not getting up.

A whippet-thin man with an equally deep tan and thick blond hair rose from behind a minimalist glass desk and approached. Black took in his five-hundred-dollar shirt and slim-cut tan trousers and noted that his shoes probably cost more than a month's rent for his office.

"Mr. Black. Nice to meet you. Please. Sit. We were just getting started," Daniel said, shaking Black's hand.

"Thanks." Black lowered himself into one of the chairs in front of the desk.

"I'm so glad you could make it. Where do I start?" Daniel asked, sounding slightly out of breath as he returned to his seat.

"I'll do the setup," Bobby volunteered as he eyed Black. "Daniel's firm is a major modeling agency, and he's acquiring another big player here in L.A., which is owned by a character named Thomas Demille. It's the largest in town, and a force to be reckoned with. They've agreed in principle to go forward, negotiated a price, and are in the diligence stage. But Daniel has some concerns. The largest is that several of Demille's models have met with ugly...accidents...since the deal became public knowledge, and there's been an exodus from the firm."

"Well, exodus is a strong word. But the talent's definitely on edge, and I don't blame them. We've lost a handful of faces to competitors, which diminishes the value of Demille's agency to us. Nothing critical yet, but I don't like the direction it's going," Daniel explained.

"Back up. What kind of ugly accidents?" Black asked.

"One of the biggest talents in Demille's roster committed suicide while at a shoot in New York. Only there are serious questions as to whether it was a suicide at all."

"What do the police say?"

"They're ruling it suicide, but I don't get the impression they're motivated to dig very deeply into it."

"Why do you think it wasn't suicide?"

Daniel leaned forward. "I had some models in that shoot as well, and they said that Daria — that's the girl who died — was upbeat and happy throughout the three days on location. She was dancing and having a great time at the wrap party, and then she disappeared, and the next thing anyone knew, she'd thrown herself off the building. It made no sense to anyone..."

"Did the cops do a toxicology report?"

"Yes. She had alcohol in her system, and a prescription pain medicine," Daniel said.

"Which one?"

"Dilaudid."

"That'll knock a horse out with the right dosage, mixed with booze."

"Be that as it may, she didn't overdose."

"Right. You said she street-dived?"

Daniel grimaced. "Yes."

"Okay. So what else? You mentioned several incidents?"

"About a month ago, another rising star was doing a beach shoot in Santa Monica, and the makeup base they applied was spiked with acid."

"Ouch. How could that happen?"

"Obviously, it was deliberate. The police investigated, but there was no final determination of any suspect. Someone laced the makeup with acid, but who remains a mystery. It was a big shoot, a lot of models, dozens of crew, security..."

"How's the model?"

"It's a tragedy. The damage was done before they could flush it all off. She's had some reconstructive surgery, but her career's over."

Black thought for a moment. "I can look into that. You said it happened here?"

"Yes. It was in all the papers."

"I must have missed it. If you can email me the details, I'll put out feelers."

Bobby cleared his throat. "Black's got ins with the police," he said, as though announcing Black's uncle was the Pope.

"I see. Very well, I'll shoot you something later," Daniel agreed.

Black studied Daniel's refined features. "What do you want me to do?"

"I want you to do some digging on the Demille agency, and see if you can find out who's behind the attacks."

"We don't know that the suicide was an attack."

"Fair point. But the timing's suspicious."

"Okay. What kind of background can you get me on the agency?"

"I'll have one of my people send you everything we have. History, the players, accounts, the works."

"That's a start." Black glanced at Bobby. "My rate's two-fifty an hour, plus expenses. Ten grand retainer. I'll give you progress reports when I have something to talk about."

"Very well. Gunther will cut you a check."

Black sat back. "Do you have any pet theories as to who could be behind this?"

"I've spent sleepless nights racking my brain. I just don't know."

"There were no disgruntled employees of Demille's? No angry partner who was ousted? No lawsuit that finished badly?"

"No. Thomas Demille started the firm and has managed it since its inception. No partners. Although…there was a high-profile incident with one of the models, just after Daria's suicide. It caused quite a stir. Scandalous, really. One of the agency's top names was caught on camera…misbehaving. They had to let him go. It was a big deal."

"Yeah? What happened?"

"Their marquis male model, Zane Bradley, got arrested by two African-American police officers at a traffic stop here in Los Angeles. For DUI. Anyway, Zane did a Mel Gibson and crossed a lot of lines. He was tossing the N word around like confetti. Really ugly. Unfortunately for him, somebody leaked the dash cam footage. It went viral, and the outcry was huge. Demille fired him, and he's been blacklisted from the industry. Nobody wants to use him. I don't blame them. Who wants their product or firm associated with racism?"

"That could be an incentive to be vengeful," Bobby agreed.

Black wasn't so sure. "But this Zane guy more or less brought it on himself, right? So it wasn't just Demille picking on him. It was the whole industry condemning his actions. And you said that happened after New York, so if that wasn't suicide, the timing's wrong for him to be the perp. Unless it actually was suicide, in which case only the acid attack's an issue."

"True. It could be unrelated to Zane. But he's one of the people I'd take a hard look at," Daniel said.

"Fair enough. Can you also send me whatever you have on him?"

"Sure."

"Okay. Anything else? You mentioned losing talent to competitors. Anyone in particular?"

"Well, there's a new agency, a start-up, that's gotten surprising traction. It's being run by an ex-Demille model, Gabriel Costa. Costa Brava is the outfit."

"Another Demille alumni? Is the world that small?" Black asked.

"On this coast it is. Demille has been the biggest agency in L.A. for years. Most of the business is concentrated in New York, but he's carved out a profitable niche here, and anyone who's anyone in West Coast modeling over the last ten years was probably in his circle."

"All right. Costa Brava. It would help if you added that to the list you send me."

"Will do. I'll also include anything else I think might be relevant," Daniel confirmed.

"That would be a good start. You said that the information about the buyout's public?"

"Yes. Everyone knows we're in the consummation stages with Demille. Obviously, my concern is that we'll lose more of his roster. Part of what we're buying is his talent, and the deal gets worse for me with every model whose contract expires and decides to go elsewhere."

"Would that normally happen with a buyout like this?"

"No. Ordinarily this would be viewed as a strong positive for his faces. They'll be part of DNA, which opens them up to a lot more work on the East Coast, and a shot at the big time. L.A. certainly has a presence these days, but New York is still the Mecca for American modeling. So I wouldn't normally expect much, if any, attrition. That was what my offer was based on. If we lose half a dozen of his biggest names, I'm overpaying and I don't like to overpay…or look like a fool."

Black nodded. "I think I get it. Is it all right if I contact you with any questions that come up?"

Daniel slid a card across the desk. "Absolutely. I'm supposed to fly back east tonight, but I might stay through tomorrow. That cell number works anywhere. Just call if you have anything come up. And I'll do the same."

Black pocketed the card and handed Daniel one of his own. "Great. Then all I need is the check and I'll hit the ground running."

Daniel punched an intercom button and issued instructions to Gunther. When he was done, he sat back and offered a practiced smile. "I'll find out what Demille's got scheduled and get in touch. You should try to meet with him as soon as possible. He's very concerned about all of this as well, as you can imagine."

"Can't I just go to his office? Let him know I'm working for you, and I'll do the rest."

"If only it were so easy. No, he likes to be at his bigger shoots, so he's usually traveling. I seem to recall him saying something about a beach shoot somewhere exotic. I'll check. I trust you don't have a problem flying to meet him…?"

"As long as you're paying, I'll do whatever's necessary," Black said, visions of palm trees in Fiji or Maui springing to mind.

"Fair enough. I'll call as soon as I know his plans. Mr. Black, I want to thank you for agreeing to take this on. Bobby says you're the best. I need this tied up quickly. I hope you can do so. If you can, you'll have no shortage of recommendations from my end. I know a lot of people," Daniel said, the implication clear.

Black stood. "Whatever's going on, I'll get to the bottom of it. That's my job."

"Perfect. If you'll have a seat out in the lobby, Gunther will bring a check in a few minutes. Now if you'll excuse us, Bobby and I have some other matters to discuss…"

Black took the hint. "Sure. See you around, Bobby. I'll call."

Bobby rose from his position on the couch and joined Black, pumping his hand like a car salesman as they walked to the door. "Good deal, buddy. Let's talk soon."

Black spent five minutes in the lobby skimming through trade publications that revolved around pouty headshots and occasionally peering at the receptionists, who could have been carved from blocks of ice. Gunther appeared just as Black was getting restless and presented him with a check with the sincerity of an ambassador signing a treaty.

His cell phone warbled in the elevator on the way to the street, but when he answered it, all he got was static and popping. Once out on the street, he pressed the redial button and waited as the line rang.

"Stan Colt."

"Stan. It's Black. You called?"

"Yeah. It was a lousy connection."

"What's up?"

"My blood pressure and cholesterol. Thanks for asking."

"Appreciate the update. But I was thinking more about why you called?"

"I want to get together. What are you doing for lunch? I wanna talk about our favorite dirtbag."

"Nothing. Usual spot?"

"Chez Carl. Half an hour?"

"I should be able to make it. I'm over in Beverly Hills."

"You win the lottery? Stalking a celeb?"

"Nah. Client meeting."

"Nice. So thirty minutes?"

"My arteries are already hardening at the thought."

Chapter 4

When Black arrived at the fast food restaurant the parking lot was full, and he had to circle around twice before a car pulled out so he could shoehorn the Eldorado into the spot. Stan was already seated at his usual booth, munching on a double burger with enough calories to sustain a small village. Black ordered a chicken sandwich, his concession to health since Sylvia had been pushing him to follow a more sensible diet, but went large on the fries and the soda so he wouldn't be shaking from hunger by late afternoon. He carried the plastic tray to Stan's table and sat down.

"Hey, big man. What's the haps?" he asked, noting the rivulet of grease trickling down Stan's chin without comment.

"Just another day in paradise. Had a double come in this morning – some kid high on 'lean' decided that his mother had scolded him one too many times, so he took a machete to her and then blew his own head off." Stan worked homicide, and he routinely saw the worst humanity could perpetrate. Which apparently didn't hamper his appetite – he was attacking his burger like a great white.

"Went sling blade on her, huh?"

"Yeah, the whole apartment looked like one of those performance art paintings, you know? Where everyone gets naked, pours paint on themselves and then rolls around on a big canvas? I'm talking blood everywhere," Stan said, chewing with gusto.

"What's 'lean,' by the way? Some new drug?"

"Been around for a while. Popular in the south, but it's showing up in California more and more. Made out of cough syrup, candy, and watermelon soda. Nasty shit. It can kill you, and it can also cause delusions, paranoia, hallucinations, violent behavior…basically a poor man's PCP."

"What'll the kids think of next? What ever happened to stealing five bucks out of Dad's wallet and buying some rotgut bourbon?"

"You just described my typical Friday night."

Black smiled. "Well, I spent my morning with the rich and famous. Got a live one." He gave Stan the rundown on his newest client, and asked him to run Zane Bradley through the computers to see what came up.

Stan phoned it in, and then returned to savaging his lunch. He washed down a huge wad of partially chewed beef, cheese, and bacon with some full tilt soda and regarded Black with a sad expression. "Wow. Look at you. So now you're going to be hanging out with supermodels? I so should have quit the force and become a PI. I hate you."

"Yeah, if you enjoy living hand to mouth and not sleeping for weeks at a time, this is the perfect gig. Not to mention learning to get really good at peeing in a Gatorade bottle during stakeouts."

"At least my subjects don't require that. They're usually not moving by the time I get to them." Stan scowled at Black's sandwich. "What the hell is that?"

"Chicken. I'm watching my weight."

"Why? You look like a triathlete."

"Hardly. More like three athletes strapped together, so I'm cutting back on the red meat."

"Okay, maybe a chunky triathlete. Does this have something to do with Miss Sweden?"

"Switzerland. Sylvia's Swiss. Like the chocolate."

"Is that where porno movies come from? I get confused."

"I don't think so. Anyway, I'm just trying to lose a few."

"Well, I found the ones you lost," Stan said. "The last time I went to the doctor, he wanted to shoot video to prove to his colleagues I was still alive. I think he's writing a book about me."

"At least you've got that going for you," Black said, and took a bite out of his poultry sandwich, which suddenly looked a lot smaller to him. He eyed the remains of Stan's burger with barely concealed envy.

"What have you found out about our buddy Ernest? Is he going out dancing at night? Pole vaulting? Parkour?"

"Nah. So far, dead end. He's not working a night job, either. I spent two nights outside his house, and he never left except to go to the store."

Stan nodded. "Damn. So much for that theory. Have you seen anything suspicious?"

"Nope. I mean, he's walking around, but that's about it. And he had the collar on when he went to the store just after dawn, so it could be genuine."

"Not a chance. The guy's a fecal speck. You saw his job history. This is his con. Gets a gig for a little while, hurts himself, cashes in and gets enough to live off for a year or so, then does it again. Beats the crap out of working."

"I'm not disagreeing. I'm just saying I haven't caught him doing anything sketchy yet." Black took another bite and shoveled a handful of greasy fries into his mouth. "You could always set fire to his house and film him when he comes running out."

"Don't think it hasn't occurred to me."

"Long story short, this ain't gonna be easy. If he isn't really hurt, he's being careful to keep up the act."

"Then what can we do? If we pay this dirtbag off, we have to shut down the business."

"I don't know. But we're smart guys. We'll think of something."

"I do like the fire idea."

"I know. Certain simplicity to it. Too bad it's illegal."

"Frigging cops ruin everything."

"They take the fun out of living, don't they?"

"Tell me about it. Used to be a guy could solve his problems in a civilized manner with a baseball bat and a pair of gardening shears. Now? It's all about attorneys. And I'm the bad guy."

"If you firebomb his house, it could be spun that way."

"Bastards."

Black was plowing through the rest of his fries when Stan's cell rang. Stan fumbled with fingers slick from grease and pulled the phone from his jacket pocket. After a brief conversation salted liberally with curses, he hung up.

"Sorry, man. Gotta run. Body turned up in Griffith Park, and I got the ticket. Never a dull day in murder central," he said, squeezing his impressive girth from the booth as he spoke.

"Not a problem. Don't sweat Ernest. If he's faking it, I'll nail him." Black took a final wedge of fries and stuffed them into his mouth, swallowed after chewing three times, and then stood. "Do me a favor. Stay away from Ernest, would you? Tempting as it is, I don't want to have to bail you out for putting him in a body cast."

"Was it that obvious I was thinking about having a heart to heart with him?"

"I know you too well, buddy. That's all I'll say. Leave him to me once I'm back."

"That's why I'm paying you the big bucks, dawg – or at least I should be. Now I have to go try to figure out why one bum would stab another over a shopping cart full of crap and then pass out drunk ten feet from the body. What a wonderful country we live in, huh?"

"Land of opportunity. Oh, and don't forget about Zane."

Stan wiped his hands on his jacket and then snapped his fingers. "Right. Come out to my car. I'll check my email on my iPad. Depending on how busy they are, the desk can sometimes get a simple trace like that done within a few minutes."

Black followed Stan to his unmarked sedan and waited while he tapped at his new toy.

"Eureka. We got a hit. Here's his home and work."

Black jotted the addresses down on the back of one of his business cards. "Thanks. Pretty cool technology. I was expecting it to take all day."

"It can, but there aren't a lot of guys with that name in L.A. So you got lucky."

"Nothing wrong with that."

"Let me know if you come up with anything on Ernest," Stan said as he started his car. The big engine roared to life and Stan slammed his door closed. Black nodded and gave him a mock salute.

"You got it, Detective. You'll be the first to know."

Chapter 5

Zane worked at a shop in the garment district that specialized in high-end furs. Black stopped at the drive-through window of his bank and deposited Daniel's check, and twenty minutes later parked a block from the fur merchant. The chicken sandwich burned in his stomach as he strolled down the grimy sidewalk past a group of runaway street kids passing around a joint, unconcerned by the uniformed LAPD cop standing obliviously on the corner watching the world go by.

Black's eyes roved over the shop signs until he found the one for Bardashian Fine Furs, mounted over a gleaming black marble façade with blue-tinted display windows. He approached the store and stopped in front of it, taking his time as he admired the mannequins draped in expensive-looking fur coats before entering the shop. A security guard sat reading a magazine in one corner as an impossibly handsome young man helped a teenage girl into a coat while an older woman stood inspecting the fit.

"I don't know, Mom. It just doesn't feel right. It's...too heavy," the girl whined.

"Lita, it's gorgeous. Seriously. Of course it's heavy. You'll need something substantial for Paris. It's cold there."

The man brushed imaginary lint from her shoulder and straightened the collar. "It does look fabulous on you. I mean, really. Makes a statement. If you want to stage a grand entrance at the *Place de l'Opéra*, this will do the trick, even in Paris." The young man's words were carefully pronounced, cultured with a worldliness older than his years.

The older woman nodded. "You hear that? I'm with Zane. You look like a million, dear. And the color's perfect for you," she said, eyeing Zane with a predatory smile that never reached her eyes.

"Fine. I just hope none of my friends ever see me in it. They'd never let me live it down. Fur's so...gross. Nobody in the U.S. wears it anymore," the girl complained. To Black's ear her nasal voice grated like nails on a chalkboard.

"Well, I predict it will make a comeback. Besides which, you're going to be in France, not Melrose. They're far more sophisticated over there," Zane declared with a theatrical hand wave.

"We'll take the coat, Zane. Put it on our account. Can you keep it in cold storage until her trip next week? I'll send one of the staff by to pick it up before she goes."

"Of course, Mrs. Avedikian. It's a wonderful choice. I'll put it with the rest of your furs."

Zane helped the girl out of the fur and she adjusted her polo shirt, relieved to have the coat off. The woman joined Zane at the counter and signed for the purchase, and then mother and daughter left in a cloud of expensive perfume, leaving Black alone with Zane and the sleepy guard.

"Yes, sir. May I help you?" Zane asked.

"Zane Bradley. My name's Black. I'd like to ask you a few questions, if you have a moment."

Zane studied Black and glanced away. "I don't know. I'm awfully busy just now."

"I can see that. It won't take long."

"Are you a reporter? I don't talk to reporters."

"No. Nothing like that."

The young man's gaze roved over Black's retro-cut suit and settled on his face. "You aren't a cop. I can see that from the outfit."

"No, not a cop. I'm a private investigator."

Zane's eyes narrowed. "What's this about?"

"I'm looking into some regrettable incidents related to an agency you used to work for. The Demille agency?"

"Regrettable incidents?" Zane echoed suspiciously.

"Yes. Apparently it's gotten dangerous being one of their models. Do you know anything about that?"

"No. I don't talk to anyone in that world now. Ever since…" his voice trailed off.

"I know about the…difficulty."

"Very diplomatic of you. That little episode should be a public service announcement – a cautionary tale against too much gin and coke. If I could turn back time…" Zane said softly.

"Yes, well, we all make mistakes, right?"

"Easy for you to say. Most mistakes don't go viral and result in the end of a fabulous career. Literally overnight. Mistake's a pretty tame word for it."

"What happened?"

"It's all been covered. I flipped out. I was drunk and high and hadn't slept for three days, partying with some friends in town for a concert they were playing. I got pulled over, and I went off on the cops. Not much more to tell. My modeling career got shit canned from the witch hunt. And now I'm selling overpriced pelts to snot-nosed brats in my dad's store instead of jetting to Milan. End of story," Zane spat, bitterness in every word. "What's funny is I'm not even a racist. I mean, I've had I don't know how many black boyfriends. It was totally unlike me. Needless to say, I'm not drinking or using anymore. My career in ruins sobered me up quick."

"It must have made you angry when Demille fired you."

"Oh, quite the opposite. When I saw the footage on the web I knew he wouldn't have a choice. I'm not stupid. I looked like some kind of psycho. I know the business well enough to know I'd just killed my deal. I don't blame Tom for what he did. I would have done the same thing. I mean, even my close friends didn't want to know me after that. And then when some of the talent gave Tom an ultimatum…Hailey, one of his hottest faces, and Trish, her mom" – Zane pronounced Trish's name like a curse – "threatened to leave the agency if I stayed…In the end, he didn't have much choice." Zane ran manicured fingers through his thick hair. "Which is just as well. Everyone in the life uses and abuses. I'd have a lot harder time staying straight if I was still hanging out with my old crew."

Black grunted noncommittally. "Can you think of anyone who would want to hurt Demille's models? Someone with a grudge? Or maybe a crazy?"

"Hurt them? Why would anyone want to hurt them? They're just bodies to hang clothes on. Mood setting for the garment manufacturers. I can't imagine anyone wanting to hurt them."

"Did you hear the news about the model who had half her face burned off with acid? One of Demille's people?"

"I saw it on TV. Poor thing. It must have been horrible."

Black's cell phone rang. His eyebrows raised when he saw the caller ID, and he gave Zane an apologetic look.

"Excuse me for a second."

"Sure. No problem. I need to go hang this thing up, anyway," Zane said, and carried the teenager's new mink coat into the back with a look of annoyance.

"Black."

"Mr. Black. It's Daniel. We just hired you?"

"Yes, Daniel. What can I do for you?"

"I just spoke with Demille's assistant. He's out of town on a shoot today and tomorrow, but it's not that far from Los Angeles, so if you hurry, you can get a flight this afternoon."

"This afternoon? A flight? To where?"

"Cabo San Lucas. In Mexico. It's a beach shoot. A large one for a new swimsuit company that's pulling out all the stops. Gunther checked, and there's a flight out of LAX at three-fifty. It'll put you in at a little past seven local time – they're an hour ahead of us."

"That'll be tight, but I can probably make it. Did Gunther already book a ticket?"

"Not yet. If you want to try to catch it, I'll have him do so. Say the word."

"How important is it that I meet with him ASAP?"

"Every hour we don't know what's going on is another hour something disastrous can happen. Since you're on the payroll now, I think it would be a good idea if you were there. A lot of our people are at that shoot. I want you at any of the big events between now and when we consummate the merger – you have a professional eye. Watch for anything suspicious. If you can prevent a tragedy, it'll be well worth the effort."

Black sighed. "All right. I'll do my best. Can you get me full access once I'm down there?"

"Of course. I'll tell Demille's assistant you're on your way. You'll have whatever you ask for."

"Fair enough. I'll head to the airport now."

Black hung up as Zane returned.

"Zane, thank you for your time. Unless you can think of anything relevant, I don't have any more questions just now," Black said.

"No problem. I really don't have any hard feelings. It was a great run while it lasted. But it's over, so it's time to move on. Besides, I would have been too old in another three or four years anyway, so maybe it was all for the best."

36

"I'll touch base if anything else comes to mind."

"You know where to find me. Every day except Sunday."

Black hurried down the street. He'd have just enough time to stop at his place, grab his passport and a change of clothes, and shoot to the airport. It would be tight, but if the traffic gods favored him, he could make it.

Once on the road, he dialed Sylvia and explained what had happened. When he finished, she didn't sound thrilled.

"That's exciting. But are you sure you'll be able to make it back in time for my event tomorrow night?" she asked.

"Absolutely. I'll spend this evening and tomorrow morning nosing around, and catch an afternoon flight back. I'll be at the gallery no later than seven."

"That'll be perfect. It starts at six. Safe travels. Don't drink the water."

"Thanks. I'll stick to tequila and beer."

"That's my boy."

At his apartment he stuffed a short-sleeved shirt and a pair of shorts into his bag along with his passport. He stripped off his suit and traded it for a silk cocktail shirt and a pair of linen pants. The entire exercise took four minutes, and he was on the freeway heading west in record time.

The security line at the airport was annoying but short. His ticket was waiting for him when he arrived at the airline counter, and he was pleasantly surprised to find himself booked in business class. He settled into the wide, comfortable seat and gratefully accepted a bourbon and soda to calm his nerves for takeoff. Within minutes the plane was accelerating down the runway and pulling up into the afternoon sky, banking over Santa Monica Bay before heading south. Black's eyelids grew heavy as he watched the earth drop away, and he was snoring by the time the plane hit cruising altitude somewhere over Ensenada, the endless blue of the Pacific Ocean stretching to the horizon.

Chapter 6

The jet shuddered on approach before lurching drunkenly, updrafts of hot air rising from the brown scrub of the desert batting it around like a leaf in an autumn wind. To the west, the Sierra de La Laguna Mountains jutted into the sky, cotton puffs of clouds hovering over the peaks. Black blinked as the pilot's voice over the public address system roused him from his slumber, and a smiling stewardess warned him to raise his seat back lest the plane crash from his thoughtless lack of compliance with airline rules.

He peered out his window at the turquoise water of the Sea of Cortez glittering in the late afternoon sun. A thin brown strip of mainland Mexico was barely visible in the distance, a mirage of land on the far side of an inland ocean. The plane bounced as an ominous grinding emanated from the wings, and then its wheels smoked on the tarmac and the passengers applauded, their vacations in Baja about to begin.

Black had noticed that the crowd had been singularly jovial in the departure lounge, the men sporting loud Hawaiian shirts, shorts, and flip-flops, the women in lightweight resort wear. Even in November the weather would be warm, since the thousand miles between Los Angeles and Cabo placed the popular vacation destination squarely in the tropical sun belt.

When Black stepped out of the plane, the heat struck him in the face. The hot wind gusted with the force of a hair dryer across the baking concrete, from where scores of private jets shimmered at the far end of the runway.

The customs and immigration line moved mercifully fast. He was waved through with hardly a glance, his passport stamped by an official more interested in continuing his running conversation with his colleague than giving Black the third degree. When he stepped into the arrivals area, a swarm of drivers holding tour company signs thronged near the exit. Off to the right, a squat man with mocha skin in a pith helmet and a white shirt and trousers clutched a cardboard square with "Black" scrawled on it in felt pen. Black introduced himself, and the driver, who informed him in accented English that his name was Juan Ramon, led him outside to where a silver Chevrolet Suburban waited in a full lot.

"So, Señor Black. I take you to the hotel, *sí*?"

"Sure. But do you know where the photo shoot is happening?"

"Of course. On the beach in front of the hotel. It's been closed off all day. Police cars at the gates. It's a really big deal."

"Is the hotel in town?"

"No. It's on the highway that runs between San Jose del Cabo, which is where we are right now, and Cabo San Lucas."

"How far outside of Cabo is it?"

"Maybe fifteen kilometers. Very exclusive. Very nice. Beautiful."

Juan Ramon had a lead foot and cheerfully ignored the speed limit signs on the toll road from the airport, preferring to barrel along at double anything sane. Once through the tollbooth he also demonstrated a remarkable lack of interest in stop signs, as well as any claim to the right of way that other vehicles might have had. Black cringed at five near misses to which Juan Ramon seemed oblivious, taking each as a test of his manhood. Fortunately for them both, his nerves were forged from steel, and they arrived at the hotel within twenty minutes of departing the airport.

Black checked in, dropped his bag in his oceanfront suite, and made his way down to the beach, where a crowd of modeling shoot personnel scurried over the sand. Sunset was now only moments away, and tiki torches blazed as the photographer worked to get the perfect shot. A stunning young woman with legs that ran to her chin stood with her hip cocked precociously. The tiny fabric strips of her salmon-colored bikini could have been painted on. She tossed her hair to one side, a smoldering look in her eyes, and Black felt his breath catch in his throat as he watched her performance. Shutters clicked feverishly as the sky shifted through purples and reds and oranges.

A security guard stopped him, but relented when it became obvious that Black didn't speak a word of Spanish and probably wasn't a party crasher. House music thumped from large speakers as he neared the shoot, and he could barely hear the photographer's instructions to the model over the seductive groove. Three young men with perfectly sculpted physiques and heavy makeup sat in robes nearby, and glanced at Black with disinterest. A tall woman in a white straw fedora approached Black carrying a clipboard.

She stopped in front of him, a Mont Blanc pen gripped in her free hand like a weapon.

"Who're you?" she asked, her tone all business.

"Name's Black. Daniel Novick from DNA sent me."

She looked puzzled and consulted her pad. "One second. Nobody told me anything about this."

"Take your time."

She thumbed a two-way radio on and murmured into it, and then they both waited, watching the shoot as the sun sank into the sea, its blinding glare fading into a red ember on the horizon. Her radio crackled and a male voice barked unintelligibly, but she seemed to understand, because her posture relaxed and her tone softened.

"Sorry about that, Mr. Black. It was an oversight. My name's Jeanie. I'm head of logistics for the shoot."

"Nice to meet you, Jeanie. Looks like I got here too late, huh?"

She gave him a long, appraising look. "Depends on why you're here. Shoot's over, but the party's about to start." She turned and walked back down the beach to where the crew had begun breaking down equipment and rolling up cables. The swimsuit model had moved to a nearby older woman, who handed her a terrycloth robe while an assistant jogged toward her with sandals and a towel. The music abruptly stopped, leaving the beach silent except for the low hum of voices and the periodic crashing of waves.

Black meandered to a table where a group of well-groomed men was gathered, sipping drinks out of polystyrene cups, talking in subdued tones. They ignored him, and he was preparing to introduce himself when Jeanie returned, looking harried.

"I have to apologize. I shouldn't have just left you to fend for yourself like that. If you'll follow me, I'll show you where the wrap dinner will be held after cocktails. We've got quite a spread laid out. You're in luck. Hope you're hungry and thirsty."

"I'm parched. Are those lights off in the distance Cabo?"

"What? Oh, yes. Have you ever been down here before?"

"No. It's my first time."

"Ah, a virgin. Well, the best advice I can give you is watch the margaritas. The natives respect tequila, and as you'll find out quickly, it's for a good reason."

"That's it? Respect tequila? That's all you have for me?"

"What more do you need to know?"

Black shrugged. "If I knew what I needed to know, I'd kind of already know it, right?"

"Come on. Let me show you around. We've got the entire pool area for the next hour, and the beach restaurant for the night." Jeanie led him up the sand to the hotel. Black followed her, noting that her shorts showcased her long tan legs admirably.

"Sounds nice," he said. "Where's Thomas Demille?"

"Tom? You were standing right next to him."

"Was I? And who were the other two?"

"The tall, younger one? That's Gabriel Costa. He's got a bunch of models in the shoot, too."

"Costa? They seemed pretty friendly for competitors."

"Costa used to model for Tom. They have a history. My sense is their competition's friendly."

"Huh. And the other guy?"

"Richard Engle. He's the VP of Marketing for the swimsuit company. He's here representing their interests."

"Not a bad gig."

"I imagine there are worse ones."

They climbed up a wide row of white stone stairs to where a mariachi band was strumming slightly out-of-tune guitars while a singer in full regalia crooned a haunting lament into the night. More torches flamed around the perimeter, lending a festive air to the proceedings. A bartender with a bright orange shirt and gleaming black hair grinned from his position behind the bar, flanked by tequila bottles and waiting glasses.

"Looks like quite a shindig," Black said, taking in the area. Four women in bright traditional garb, dazzling white smiles on their faces, carried trays of appetizers to the arriving guests. Off to the side, an older woman made corn tortillas by hand, forming them before using a roller and tossing the disks onto a portable grill.

"The modeling crowd knows how to let their hair down. Have you ever been to a wrap party before?" Jeanie asked.

"Not that I remember."

"Good answer."

A lithe woman with a dancer's body whose sequined dress clung to her like a second skin moved across the oversized flagstone decking to the bar, where she had a short discussion with the bartender. He nodded and selected a bottle of Stolichnaya Vodka from the display behind him, poured three inches of the clear fluid into a tumbler, dropped in two ice cubes, and slid it to her. Black watched as she lifted the glass to her lips and drained half of it in a single gulp, and then closed her eyes and smiled to herself. His attention was pulled away by Demille and his entourage mounting the steps, trailed by at least a dozen incredibly beautiful women and handsome men.

"Looks like the models are in the house," Black commented, but Jeanie had already moved away to tend to other duties. He returned his attention to the woman at the bar, only to find her standing five feet away, studying him with a frank gaze. He could see that she was older than she'd looked at first glance, perhaps mid-thirties, and in incredible physical shape. Her eyes glinted in the torchlight as she took two steps toward him.

"Well, hello there. I don't think we've met," she said, and Black immediately placed her accent as Russian.

"No. I'm a new arrival. I flew in for the party."

"Interesting. I'm Tasha Pushkin. And you are...?"

"Black."

"Just Black? Like your singer Prince, before he became just a symbol?"

"Kind of like that. But without the jumpsuit or the hair."

"Ah. You must be the investigator who DNA sent. Of course. Demille's assistant told me to expect you. And told me that I was to ensure you got whatever you wanted," she said, her eyes never straying from his.

"That's very...hospitable of you."

An uncomfortable silence stretched between them as Black wondered whether Tasha was coming on to him. She gestured to the *palapa* bar.

"Well, come on, mysterious Mr. Black. Let me buy you a drink, and then I'll show you around and introduce you to everyone who matters."

"Perfect. What's your poison?"

"I normally stick to vodka, but since we're in Mexico, I'm thinking I should make an exception. That young man was telling me that he makes the world's best margarita. I don't know whether to believe him, but he's certainly got a convincing way about him."

"How could you turn down an offer like that?"

"My thinking exactly." Tasha finished her vodka and set the glass on a nearby table, then slipped her arm through Black's and led him to the bar. She rattled off instructions in Spanish, and the man practically genuflected.

He selected two bottles of *Añejo* tequila and poured an inch of each into the waiting glasses, and then poured another inch of Controy and a quarter inch of Grand Marnier.

"I'm not sure I want to watch this. That seems like enough booze to bury me," Black said.

Tasha studied his profile. "Oh, I think you might be able to handle it. You look like you have…experience. I like that in a man."

Black watched another inch of Controy go into the glasses and turned to Tasha. "So what do you do with this group?"

She cocked an eyebrow and smirked. "The question is, what don't I do?" She dug in her sequined purse and extracted a cigarette and a lighter. "You want one?"

"Not right now, thanks."

She lit the cigarette and dropped the lighter back into her purse. "I'm an agent with Demille. I started as a model and worked my way down when I got put out to pasture."

"Oh, so you're going to be part of DNA. That's got to be exciting."

"Be still my beating heart."

Black was preparing to ask her why she seemed so unenthusiastic when the bartender set the two glasses in front of them, a crush of ice cubes floating in an amber sea. Tasha slid a five-dollar tip to the man and raised her glass in a toast. "To new friends, Mr. Black."

Black lifted his and tasted it. His eyes widened and welled with moisture. "Good Christ. What is that? Diesel fuel?"

She took a sip and smiled. "Mmmm. That's really good. The man definitely knows his margaritas."

"What happened to the ingredients that aren't alcohol?"

"I tasted a little lime."

"And maybe some heroin."

"I think there might be some orange juice, too. Not much." She took another taste. "It's better the second time around."

Black gave it another try and realized she was right. What had been a raw burn now was a smooth warmth as it glided down his throat, and he almost instantly felt relaxation seep into his muscles. "Wow. He does know how to make a drink, I'll give him that."

Tasha was looking across the pool area. "Tom looks bored. Come on. I'll introduce you."

"Lead the way."

They crossed to where Demille was sitting with the VP of Marketing at a table, and Tasha sat next to him and whispered in his ear. Demille straightened and offered Black a neutral expression.

"Mr. Black. Pleasure to meet you. Daniel sent you?"

"Nice to meet you, too. Yes, he asked me to look in on the shoot and familiarize myself with everyone."

"This is Richard. He's footing the bill for all this."

Richard shook Black's hand with the professional aplomb of a career politician.

"Quite a spread. You should try one of the bartender's special margaritas. They're pretty spectacular," Black said.

"I did. Last night. I was afraid I'd need to go to the hospital this morning after three of them."

"The first words of advice I received when I got here were, 'respect tequila.' Seems like that's a theme."

"So, Mr. Black, what exactly does Daniel have in mind? Why are you here?" Demille asked.

"I'm helping look out for his interests. After the acid incident and the suicide, he's nervous."

Demille gave Richard an insincere smile and stood. "Would you excuse us for a second?"

Richard nodded. "Sure. I need to make a call anyway. Nice meeting you, Mr. Black."

When he'd left, Demille turned back to Black and glowered as he took his seat. "What the hell do you think you're doing? That's the client. Your suspicions about our dirty laundry shouldn't ever be discussed in front of the client."

Tasha stood. "Time to find the little girl's room."

Black waited until she'd gone before answering evenly. "Mr. Demille, don't take this the wrong way, but I don't work for you. I'm not one of your models. I work for, and report to, Daniel. You asked me what I was doing here. I told you. If you don't want certain things discussed in front of others, don't ask."

Black could see the color rise in Demille's face, but to his credit, the modeling mogul swallowed his anger and assumed a relaxed tone. "Daria's regrettable decision to end it all is hardly connected to the acid assault…"

"How can you be so sure?"

"Because, Mr. Black, the NYPD determined that it was a suicide. Didn't you get the memo?"

"I understand what the cops put in their report. But Daniel's not comfortable with the talent loss you're seeing, and he wants to stop the bleeding. I'm his insurance policy."

Demille shrugged. "It's his ball game, so I suppose he can do whatever he wants. That said, I think you're wasting your time."

"Maybe so. But it's Daniel's call. So here I am."

"Fine. What do you need from me?"

"Nothing, really. He wants me to familiarize myself with your organization. And spend some time picking your brain."

"You mean interrogating me."

"Not exactly. But I'll need an hour with you."

"It's not going to happen tonight after cocktails and dinner. Tomorrow's the soonest I could fit you in. Late morning, before I fly out of here, work for you?"

"Sure. I'm easy."

Tasha returned, crossing the deck with the fluid stride of a cat. She sat down and took a long pull on her margarita. "That's much better. What a beautiful night. Look at all the stars. We never see stars in L.A. Too much pollution and ambient light."

Demille's drink arrived, and he gave it an approving taste and held it up in a toast. "Another day, another wrap. Tonight we party like it's 2099."

Tasha nodded. "It did go rather well, didn't it?" She glanced at Black. "There are never any guarantees, especially on a big shoot like this in a foreign country with multiple agencies involved. I don't have to tell you the complications that can arise."

Demille stood. "I see some people I need to talk to. I'll leave you in Tasha's capable hands, Mr. Black. If we don't speak again, let's get together at ten tomorrow morning, shall we?"

"Perfect."

Demille strode to where the young bikini model was standing. The older woman hovered around her protectively, and greeted them with refined good humor.

"Who's that with the model?"

"Oh, that's Trish. The model's name is Hailey. One of our biggest stars. Trish is her mother. Kind of a nightmare stage mom, if you want the truth. But Hailey's fifteen, so you get one, you get the other. A necessary evil."

"Fifteen! Wow. That seems awfully young to be doing this kind of shoot…"

"Why, Mr. Black. How charmingly old-fashioned. But young women are among the biggest consumers of swimwear, so it makes perfect sense that the models reflect that sensibility. Hailey's very popular not just because of her age but because of her look. She's very much in demand for all styles of shoots, not just swimwear. She's got a unique presence on camera. What they call star quality."

"She does seem to radiate something."

"So does Trish, but unfortunately, it's more annoying than anything else. But we do what we must to make the shoot go smoothly." Tasha took another gulp of her margarita, half done with it already, though Black's was barely touched.

"And who are they?" Black gestured at two raven-haired beauties who'd just arrived, attired in short shorts and halter tops, acres of flawless tanned skin on display.

"Ah. Lana and Sarah. Twins. They do a lot of swimsuit stuff together – it's gimmicky, but some clients like it. They feel that it stops the customer on the page and has them do a double take, pun intended. Solid earners, good portfolio, but they're not New York quality. Which isn't to say they don't have lucrative careers. Rather, the type of work they do is different from the highest end of the range. Hailey, on the other hand, has a very New York look. Years ahead of her age. And it shows in her billings."

"I don't see anything wrong with the twins. They're gorgeous."

"Yes, Mr. Black, but all of our models are beautiful. That goes with the territory. It's that special something that separates the rank and file from the stars, though. Whatever that quality is, they don't have it."

"But Hailey does."

"Yes. More importantly, it comes through the camera and shows on the page. Look at any of the biggest names in the business, and they all have a radiance that the average model doesn't. That's what we look for as agents. And that's what clients will pay almost anything for. Thank God."

Another female model arrived in a skirt so short it would have been illegal in most states. "Wow. Now she's got that quality," Black blurted.

"Yes. Good eye. That's Clarissa. She specializes in what I call low-rent Kate Moss. A waif quality, but very popular."

"She can't be much older than Hailey."

"Clarissa just turned nineteen. She's in her peak earning years, and we're happy to have her. She's one of our top producers. Really making a name for herself. Dumb as a bag of rocks, but very sweet."

The mariachis switched to an up-tempo number amid whoops and whistles from the guests, most of whom had the bartender's specialty in their hands. Black was struck by the number of models who were smoking, feeling the tug of his old vice returning with each swallow of tequila.

It seemed like he'd just gotten there when Demille silenced the band and announced that dinner was ready. Tasha polished off her second margarita as Black finished his first, and she clutched his arm for support as they moved with the crowd to the restaurant, which was situated beneath a three-story-tall *palapa* that fronted onto the beach. A jazz group was already warmed up when they took their seats at a long table with colorful Mexican tablecloths draped across it, easily twenty chairs on either side. Tasha signaled for another drink for them both as Black watched the phosphorescent surf pound the outcropping of rocks below. More stunning specimens of physical perfection joined them and inebriated introductions were made, nobody questioning who Black was or why he was there, the celebratory mood of the evening making all cats gray in the dark.

Tasha kept up a running commentary of snark as appetizers arrived and continued through the entrée, whispering about this model's sexual peccadilloes and that one's eating disorder. After his second margarita Black's head was spinning, but he felt like he'd learned more from Tasha than he could have in a week on his own. From what he could gather, the modeling game was fiercely cutthroat, filled with envy, bitterness, and recriminations, the stakes high and the careers short. He watched as the talent pushed their food around their plates, pretending to eat while avoiding most of the meal, and wondered at a business where anorexia could be the norm rather than an affliction.

"What's your story?" Black asked Tasha as the waiter cleared the table in preparation for dessert.

"Oh, nothing too special. I was discovered by Tom on a trip to Russia. He took me under his wing, I had a wonderful twelve-year run of it, and then the calls came less and less, until it became obvious to everyone that I needed another line of work. Thankfully, he gave me a shot as an agent, and that's what I've been doing for the last six years."

"Do you like it?"

"It pays the bills. Mostly it's dealing with prima donnas with oversized egos and brains the size of walnuts, but I'm used to that. And what about you, Mr. Black? How did you wind up as a private eye?"

"I tried everything else and failed at it. This was the only thing left," he replied, surprised at his own honesty.

"I have a hard time believing that. You seem very…seasoned. Worldly. I'm sure you have a story."

"Everyone's got one, don't they? Some just aren't very interesting. What's important is that I'm here, now, enjoying a margarita at my very first wrap party. What happens from here?" Black asked.

"Oh, everyone will hit the hotel disco later, drink too much, stay up way too late, misbehave. It's always the same."

"Sounds like a young man's game."

"It can be. Depends on the man. I'm guessing you could go the distance," Tasha said, her words beginning to slur as she touched his arm again, her hand lingering longer each time.

Black couldn't understand why she was coming on to him, but decided it didn't matter – he was a big boy and didn't have to swing at every pitch thrown his way. He begged off on having a final margarita, switching to beer, but Tasha seemed unrepentant and instructed the waiter to put some booze in hers this time. Dessert came and went, and Black suspected he was the only one who had actually gotten any into his mouth.

As predicted, the crew drifted off once the dinner was over, and soon it was just Tasha, Demille, Gabriel, Richard and a few others left at the table, everyone else gone in search of more stimulating fare.

Tasha leaned into him and whispered in his ear like a lover sharing a secret. "Mr. Black. May I impose upon you to escort a lady to the disco?"

Black was tired and half drunk, but couldn't see any graceful way of extracting himself from the situation. They rose unsteadily and moved slowly to the entrance, where they could hear the booming of a dance beat from the far side of the pool area. Tasha stopped halfway across, lit another cigarette, and offered Black one again. This time, in spite of his best intentions, he took it, and soon was watching the surf, smoking, as he'd sworn to never do again. The sober part of him was disgusted at his weakness, and he stubbed it out halfway through, ignoring how good it tasted to him.

"What's wrong?"

"Nothing. I quit smoking about six months ago. This is my first since then."

"Don't worry. It's not the end of the world. It doesn't mean you'll start back up. Besides, you know what they say."

"No. What?"

She gave him a long look. "What happens in Cabo, stays in Cabo."

The nightclub was already full with models and crew. The obnoxiously loud music and the mindless droning beat vibrated his fillings as they took a seat at a table near the dance floor. More drinks were ordered and consumed, and before long an hour had gone by and Black was dizzy and tired. He left Tasha dancing with two of the female models and found his unsteady way back to his room. The hotel seemed far bigger after dark with its empty corridors. He barely got his clothes off before he collapsed onto the bed, breathing heavily, exhausted and drunk, and was asleep in a minute, the dull hum of the air conditioning his gentle lullaby.

Chapter 7

A shriek split the silence and Black bolted upright, his heart jackhammering as he struggled to remember where he was. The room was dark, a tribute to the quality of the blackout curtains. He glanced around for the source of the noise. The phone screamed again like a startled seagull, and Black fumbled for the cursed instrument as pain throbbed in his frontal lobes. He got the handset to his ear and cleared his throat.

"Hello?" he croaked, his voice dry and harsh.

"Mr. Black. It's Tasha. Did you hear what happened?"

Black's splitting headache made it hard to think. "What? What happened?"

"It's…Clarissa. She was found dead early this morning by room service."

Black struggled to process what he was hearing. "Clarissa? Dead? Of what?" His words sounded hoarse to his ear, and his regret at his tequila intake doubled.

"Looks like an overdose. But the police aren't talking. They're all over the place. Were you awake?"

"No. What time is it?"

"Nine."

"Damn. I need to get moving. Where are you?"

"I'm at the beach restaurant having breakfast. Everyone's freaked out. It's all they're talking about."

"I can understand why. Let me get into the shower. I'll join you for a cup of coffee before I talk to Demille."

"I'll be waiting."

Tasha sounded like she'd drunk nothing but spring water the night before, whereas Black was as rough as he could remember. He groped around for the wall switch and winced when the room flooded with light. After a few deep breaths to steel himself, he stood, and his head swam. A wave of nausea hit and his mouth filled with saliva. He barely made it to the bathroom before he threw up, the toilet rank with partially digested margarita and beer.

A hot shower rinsed away the worst of the fumes seeping from his pores, although it did nothing for the anvil chorus pounding in his head. Black stepped out of the stall and stared with dismay at his reflection in the partially fogged mirror. His face seemed to be hanging off his skull like a mastiff's, his eyes bleary, his color jaundiced. He coughed, half expecting to see blood. His lungs felt tight from the cigarette, and his headache intensified as he took stock. It wasn't good.

He pulled a comb through his wet hair and debated shaving, but decided not to risk his face to a razor. His hands trembled as he buttoned his shirt, and a momentary blood sugar dip left him weak. Jeanie's words came back to haunt him, each of the five syllables like the pounding of a coffin nail.

"Respect tequila."

Black stepped out of his room to find himself facing a throng of blue uniforms – stern police with automatic rifles hung from straps around their necks and bulletproof vests, dressed for a terrorist compound assault. His anxiety intensified as he brushed by them, their stern gazes weighing on him like a parent's disapproving scowl. The bright sunlight was blinding, and it took all of his concentration to fish his Ray Bans out of his pocket and shield his eyes from the worst of it.

Tasha was waiting for him at a table near the water. She looked fresh as a schoolgirl, and her skin exuded vitality and good health. Black collapsed into a chair opposite her and tried not to vomit again.

"Good morning, Mr. Black. You look…well rested."

"I must not have slept very well last night. I don't feel well."

"Yes, well, perhaps you caught the tequila flu. There's a lot of that going around Cabo, I hear."

"How late did you stay up?"

"Oh, not too late. I went into town with Demille and the girls around midnight. I only stayed until…about 2:45. Apparently some of them shut the place down."

"You were up till 2:45 in the morning?"

"Well, when you're only in Cabo for a short time it seems a shame not to see the sights."

"Was Clarissa with you?"

"She was part of the group. I took off before she did, though. Poor thing…"

Nausea rose in Black's throat as he got a whiff of a lobster omelet at another table. He fought it to a standstill, but the color drained from his face. "Do you see a waiter? I need some coffee."

Tasha waved their server over and fired off a snare roll of Spanish. The man nodded and gave Black a knowing smile, then disappeared.

"I took the liberty of ordering you a Mexican Coffee. I don't think you're going to make it otherwise."

"Mexican Coffee? Should I ask what's in it?"

"Better not to. But it should fix your head, at least a little."

"Do I look that bad?"

"Not to me. But if you're going to go toe to toe with Demille in" – Tasha checked the time – "fifteen minutes, best if you're not having a seizure."

"What happened with Clarissa?"

"The police are being tight-lipped. They're interrogating everyone she was out with last night, which was half the models and most of the crew. So they obviously don't think it was a simple overdose."

"Heroin?"

"Of course. Mother's milk to some of these girls. Occupational hazard. They have a ton of money, lots of free time, and they don't want to eat. Who knew that junk was bad for you?"

"Actually, heroin is less harmful, as a substance, than alcohol. Just saying."

"I can believe that. Oh, good. Your coffee's here. This should help."

The waiter set down a tall cup with whipped cream floating on top and caramelized sugar crusted around the rim. Black took a sip and set it down, exhaling loudly.

"Whoa. What is that, eighty proof?"

"Just drink it. You'll feel better in no time."

Black did as instructed, and after chugging it, felt the worst of the symptoms recede. "It's a miracle."

"Brandy, Kahlúa, tequila, and coffee. Mother's milk. Better than a Bloody Mary."

"What else do you know about Clarissa?"

"Just what I overheard from the staff. She'd ordered room service at 3:15, after getting in from the club, and it took almost an hour to arrive. They knocked on her door, but there was no answer, so they unlocked it to leave the food inside…and she was lying on the bed, her skin blue. They called the ambulance, but she was already dead by the time it got here."

"Did you know she was a junkie?"

"I suspected. But in this business, you take a don't ask, don't tell approach. You don't want to get involved in the personal lives of the talent. You want them to show up, look good, and stay out of trouble. As long as they do, you win. When they don't…well, it depends on who it is."

"She didn't look like she was on the needle."

"Maybe she wasn't using that much. Who knows? And what does it really matter? She probably scored some of the local stuff, it turned out to be purer than what she was used to, and she got the dose wrong. Happens all the time."

The waiter arrived with a cup of regular coffee, and Black drank it greedily, beginning to feel, if not alive, at least less dead. He glanced at his watch and swore.

"Shit. I need to go. I have my meeting with Demille."

"Where?"

Black racked his brain. "I…I don't know."

Tasha gave him a long stare. "I'll call him and ask."

"Would you? That would be awesome."

"Just remember, Mr. Black, you'll owe me one."

"After the coffee, I'll owe you two."

"I might hold you to that," she purred, holding her cell phone to her ear. "Darling. Yes, I heard. Terrible. I agree. Listen, I have that charming Mr. Black here, and he wanted to know where you agreed to meet." She listened attentively, then shrugged. "Okay. I'll tell him."

She hung up and took a long sip of her coffee, then set the cup back down. "He's in the lobby checking out. Said there was a change of plans. He's got to go back to L.A. first thing, so he can't spend a lot of time with you today. But he'll be in town all week, and wants to reschedule."

"Damn it. I need to go. Now."

"I'll be waiting right here."

Black hurried to the lobby, where Demille was finishing with the reception desk and folding a receipt. Demille saw him and moved to one of the small tables near the entrance. "Come, Mr. Black. I'm so sorry, but with Clarissa's death, I have some fires that need to be put out back home. My car should be here any minute, but I'll make it up to you. Let's get together tomorrow, if that's all right."

"It's really not all right, Mr. Demille."

"Please. Tom."

"It's not all right, Tom. I need to ask you some questions, and they won't wait."

Demille appraised Black, and his gaze drifted to the two federal policemen standing just outside the entry doors. "I'm afraid they'll have to. I've already spent half my morning answering questions for the police, and that ate my available time. I have a business to run, Mr. Black, so as much as you want me to stop everything for an hour, I can't. Tomorrow's the best I can do."

Black didn't like the man's attitude, but he couldn't wrestle him to the floor and force him to submit to an interrogation, so he opted for a gentler approach. "I suppose one day won't make a difference. You must be in shock about the model who died. I mean, what is that, two dead in a little over a month? It seems like it's bad for your health to work for your agency, doesn't it? Not that you could have done anything about it...but still."

"That's one of the fires I'm fighting right now. I have big clients who are trying to pull out of their shoots. It's like a panic. I can't let that happen. So I'm doing damage control."

"How well did you know Clarissa?"

"As well as any of them, I suppose. We weren't especially close, if that's what you were asking."

"Why did the police want to talk to you?"

"I was part of the group she was out with. We went to Squid Roe, in town, and she left at three. I stayed a while longer. That's the last I saw of her."

"How much longer?"

Demille glared at Black. "Maybe forty-five minutes."

"So you returned to the hotel by...4:00?"

"That would be about right. Maybe a hair earlier."

"Do you have any idea what she ordered?"

"What?"

"Clarissa. I heard she was found by room service."

"How would I know? Food, I'm guessing."

"It was just a question."

A white Cadillac Escalade pulled to a stop in front of the entrance and the driver got out. After a brief discussion with the bell captain, he approached Demille.

"There's my ride. Give my assistant a call tomorrow and we'll get together. Tasha has the number," Demille said dismissively.

"Count on it."

Annoyed by Demille's demeanor, Black retrieved his cell phone and called Daniel, who answered on the second ring. Black broke the news about Clarissa and filled Daniel in on what little he knew.

"Good lord. Not Clarissa. She was one of Demille's top faces. Damn it, Black. The value of this transaction for me just took a big plunge."

"I'm sorry to hear that. And I wish we had more to go on."

"I'll reach out to Demille and let him know that he's not to blow you off, no matter what the circumstances, again."

"I'd appreciate that. So far I feel like I'm getting the cold shoulder. He didn't have time to talk to me yesterday, and then today, after one of his stars dies, he's running for a plane. You'd have thought he would have wanted to stick around and know what happened."

"Message received. Do you have anything else for me?"

"I wish I did. Hate to be the bearer of bad news, but there it is."

"Let me make some calls."

Black returned to Tasha, who now had three companions – the twins and a ruggedly handsome Latin man in his early twenties. Everyone looked shocked and drawn, and Black wondered how much of that was due to the news and how much from alcohol poisoning. Tasha introduced Black again and the three moved to a table next to the ocean. Black noticed that Tasha had ordered herself a Mexican Coffee, and decided that if one had blunted the worst of his ordeal, perhaps a second one could actually make him feel human.

"Demille couldn't get out of here fast enough," Black said softly, so only Tasha could hear.

"Sometimes he gets like that. He doesn't do bad news well."

"Do you know who Clarissa was out with, in addition to Demille?"

"Sure. The twins were there. The photographer, Miguel. And Gabriel."

"Gabriel Costa? He and Demille were partying together?"

"Why not? Once the working day's over…"

"Have you seen him this morning? I'd like to have a chat with him."

"Oh, he left early. Alphonso there is one of Costa's models, and saw him leaving just as he was getting in this morning. Around 6:00."

Black glanced at the young man. "He was making it back to the hotel at 6:00?"

"He probably found a new friend. It happens."

"So Costa was gone before the cops could talk to him?"

"I presume so. I don't know what time they showed up in force. Probably after that. It's not like they get paid more to show up earlier."

Black's drink showed up and he drained a third of it as he stared into the distance. The azure Sea of Cortez practically glowed in the sunlight, flat calm, no wind to stir it.

"I want to see the room," he said. Tasha pointed to her lip and nodded at him with raised eyebrows. He wiped at his mouth and came away with a smear of whipped cream.

She smiled. "That might be a problem. This is in the hands of the *Federales* now. I doubt they'll be that impressed with a PI from the U.S. wanting access to the crime scene."

"I was hoping you could use some of your seductive feminine charm to help me out."

"What's in it for me?"

"A margarita?"

"You're going to have to do better than that. Although plying me with alcohol is never a bad idea."

He'd grown accustomed to her flirtatious style, and ignored the obvious invitation. "Two margaritas. Final offer."

"You drive a hard bargain, Mr. Black."

"You better believe it."

Chapter 8

Black contacted the airline with the help of the front desk and changed his one o'clock flight to four-thirty so he would have enough time to snoop around. Once his travel was taken care of, he and Tasha went upstairs and located the head detective, who stood outside of the room talking to one of the forensics technicians – a comely young woman with a warm smile and sparkling eyes.

Tasha made her pitch as Black stood by like a wooden Indian, and even though he couldn't speak Spanish, he was able to read the inspector's body language well enough to understand that Tasha had her work cut out for her. The discussion went on for a good five minutes, and when Tasha motioned for Black to accompany him back downstairs, he didn't have a good feeling.

"He started out with absolutely not. So I stretched the truth a little. I said you were a well-known investigator from the United States, and that you would go over his head to his superiors if you weren't granted access to the site. That didn't work, so then I switched gears. We discussed how difficult it was to make it on what they paid even senior officers, and agreed that any generosity was always appreciated. We agreed that being granted access to the room after they're done would be worth two hundred dollars. That seemed reasonable. I told him we'd be down by the pool waiting for someone to get us."

"Tasha, you're a miracle worker."

"Next best thing – an agent. All I do is negotiate and bullshit. It's in the job description."

"Whatever you are, I owe you big."

Tasha nodded in agreement. "Yes, you do. He said it would take a while. I asked him why, and he said he didn't like some of the things he'd found. I have no idea what, because he wouldn't tell me. But it sounds like he may have his doubts about it being a simple overdose."

"But he didn't have any idea how long it would be?"

"Nope. Why don't we put on swimsuits and get some sun? And you can have breakfast. Coffee isn't going to satisfy you for very long."

Black hesitated. "I didn't bring a swimsuit."

Tasha looked at him disbelievingly. "Who comes to Cabo and doesn't bring a swimsuit?"

"I was only planning on being here long enough to interview some of the key players and get a feel for who knows what."

"How's that going?"

"Not so great," Black admitted.

"Fine. You go have breakfast, and then you can join me once you're done. Because I'm going to enjoy Cabo."

"Don't you have to check out?"

"No. I'm staying till tomorrow. One of the perks of being a lowly agent is my schedule's not as hectic as the boss's. I figured since the company paid my way here, I might as well get in a day or two of vacation before heading back to L.A."

"All right. I'll catch you soon. Now that you mention it, I'm starving."

"Mexican Coffees will do that to you. Try the eggs and chorizo. It'll put hair on your chest." She looked over her sunglasses at him. "Not that you need it."

Tasha left and Black's gaze followed her as she made her way to the stairs. He shook his head, thought about Sylvia, and felt a wave of revulsion at having broken his vow and smoked a cigarette. Regret wouldn't solve anything, he knew, so instead of beating himself up, he decided to take Tasha's suggestion and try to eat something.

Service in the oceanfront restaurant was slow, but given Black's wounded state he was fine with that. He watched two Mexicans make their way down the beach with milk crates and set them down on the sand just above the surf. The older of the two men unrolled a hand line, baited it, and threw it into the water. Within fifteen seconds he had a bite, and he battled a sizeable rooster fish through the waves and onto the wet sand. Over the next hour, the two caught another eight fish, and after loading their catch into a stained burlap sack they trudged away, their day's work over, dinner for the family and then some in their bag.

The food helped, and after paying his tab he circled back by the pool, where Tasha was holding court with one of the models – a tall, lean man with skin the color of coal who appeared to have no more than three percent body fat and obviously spent serious hours at the gym. Black sat down on one of the sun chairs next to her, noting that she too looked like a workout maniac.

"There you are. Feeling restored?" she asked.

"Much better, thanks. So far you haven't steered me wrong."

"Mr. Black, this is Sima. He works with Gabriel's firm, but he only just started with them. He used to be with us."

Black reached across Tasha, noting that she smelled like coconut and vanilla, and shook hands.

"Why did you change agencies, if you don't mind my asking?" Black probed.

"With Demille's girls dropping like flies…after the acid attack, I figured it was bad juju. Someone's got it in for him, and I didn't want to be the first male they added to the roster, you know?" Sima looked at Tasha. "Girl, you know I love you all, but I don't need a facial peel that bad. I have my condo to pay off. I can't afford any accidents."

Black shook his head. "That was just one incident, though. Couldn't it have been as simple as someone who had a grudge against that model? The others have been natural causes."

Sima greeted that idea with an eye roll. "Sure. All I know is that Demille's models are dropping faster than Detroit real estate, and now that I'm not with him, I'm sleeping easier." Sima winked at Black. "When I get any sleep at all."

"What's your theory? If you had to guess?" Black asked.

"Me? What do I know? I'm just face candy, right, Tash?"

She nodded and smiled. "Dark chocolate and full of love."

"You do know how to sweet talk, don't you?"

"So no ideas?" Black pushed.

"Well, just between us girls, I think Demille stepped on the wrong toes or dumped the wrong boyfriend. And I think that shit's gone crazy, and wants to take down his company."

"Can you think of anyone specific?" Black asked.

"Who do I look like – Perez Hilton? I don't track the man that closely. But I do know he's got that love-'em-and-leave-'em look. That's certainly his reputation around town. You never heard that here, though. Mmm mmm. No suh."

"But that theory would require this jilted lover to be following him around to his shoots, right? Was Demille at the one in New York, Tasha?"

"You know, now that you mention it, I think he was," Tasha said.

"Has anyone seen someone who would fit that bill here in Mexico?"

Sima pouted as he thought. "It could be one of the crew, too. Or a model. Although I highly doubt that a model would be behind this. Everyone I know's a lover, not a fighter, baby."

Black checked his watch. "Crap. I need to get my stuff and check out. I'll be right back."

"You can put your bag in my room if you want, Mr. Black," Tasha said. Sima swatted at her.

"Oooh, girl, listen to you. I have to remember that line." Sima gave Black a come-hither gaze. "Yes, Mr. Black, you can put your junk in my trunk anytime."

Black decided to make himself scarce. Sima's giggling and the musical tinkling of Tasha's laugh followed him from across the pool. He inspected himself in the room mirror and decided on another quick shower. After standing under the hot stream for ten minutes, he felt better than he had all day. Checking out took forever because everyone else had also waited until the last minute, and by the time he made it back to Tasha, it was one o'clock.

"Where'd your friend go?" Black asked.

"He opted for a *siesta*."

"He's not going back today?"

"Almost nobody is. Like I said, when the company pays for you to come to Cabo, you're crazy if you don't make the most of it."

Black felt stupid sitting clothed by the pool while everyone else was clad in as little as possible, but Tasha made him feel at home – and an icy cold Pacifico beer brought by the wait staff didn't hurt, either. By two o'clock he was getting sunburned, and it occurred to him that if he was going to get a peek at the room, it would have to be soon.

Tasha joined him, and after she slipped some cash to the inspector, he was waved in with the admonition that he only had five minutes.

Clarissa's body had been removed earlier, though her things still lay where she'd left them, right down to the room service tray. Black glanced at it: a bottle of unopened champagne, two glasses, and an order of chocolate cake – not exactly model food, he thought, and an awful lot of booze for that early in the morning. Especially if you were planning on shooting up and spending the next few hours in an opium haze.

The syringe was a typical disposable available over the counter in Mexico, and the heroin looked to be the local brown variety. He peered at the small bag and nodded to himself. He was no expert on different grades of the drug, but it looked brown enough to him.

Tasha translated for him, and the inspector reluctantly answered a few questions about the corpse. Yes, she'd had track marks on her arms and legs, although relatively few, so she had probably only recently graduated from smoking or snorting the drug to injecting it. Yes, that appeared to be domestic Mexican heroin. And yes, it was relatively easy to find someone who sold it in the clubs; getting heroin, cocaine, or anything else you wanted was pretty straightforward.

After further prodding and considerable flirting by Tasha, the inspector dropped a bombshell – they were treating this as a suspicious death because by all appearances, Clarissa had died not from the overdose but from suffocation. Their working theory was that she'd been smothered with a pillow and then turned onto her stomach, the syringe still in her arm.

"Then it's a murder?" Black asked, after she'd translated it.

"That's how they're treating it. But he did say there was always a possibility that forensics got it wrong, and that her lungs stopped working as a result of the overdose. He's being cagey, but judging by the way they've been questioning everyone, including the hotel staff, he must think she was murdered."

"But they let Demille and Costa leave the country…"

Tasha said something to the inspector, who shrugged and offered a few sentences.

"There was no reason to hold them. And he says that in this country, they lack the resources to do in-depth investigations and keep suspects for days or weeks, like they do on your American television programs. He says he's a big fan of CSI, by the way."

"That's good to know. So you're getting the feeling that this will never be solved?"

"Based on his demeanor, barring someone coming forward as a witness, that's the impression I got."

Black asked Tasha to thank the inspector, which she did with much smiling and flashing of skin. With nothing further to do in the room, they walked together to the lobby. "I hate to impose on you, but I need to ask you for one more thing," he said.

Her eyes locked on his and held them. "Depends on what it is, Mr. Black."

He was again struck by her flirtatious persistence – he didn't think he'd done anything to encourage her, but she didn't seem to need him to. "I'd like a list of everyone at this event. As well as at the New York assignment where Daria died, and the beach shoot where the acid attack took place."

"That shouldn't be a problem. But I don't have the non-Demille personnel who were there. In other words, crew members and other agency-repped talent won't be on it."

"That's okay. At least it's a starting point. Although…were you at both of those shoots?"

"Of course. Tom has me go to all the big multi-agency events."

"Could you jot down any names that you remember? Like…Gabriel, for instance?"

"I don't think he was in New York, but I do recall he was at the beach. Okay, I'll compile that for you once I'm back in town."

Black slowed. "Tasha, I want to thank you for all the help. That will go a long ways toward me figuring out at least the beginnings of what I'm dealing with." He checked the time. "Damn. I have to get to the airport. I really appreciate everything you've done."

She slipped her business card into his shirt pocket and smiled. "Remember, you owe me, Mr. Black. By the way, what's your first name?"

"Jim. But everyone calls me Black."

"Yes. I think that's more fitting. I like you better as Black." She leaned into him and gave him a kiss on the cheek, and he smelled coconut and vanilla. "Have a good flight. I'll be back in L.A. tomorrow. You should give me a call."

Black handed her one of his cards. "If any light bulbs go on, those are my numbers. My cell's always on."

"That's good to know," Tasha said, managing to make it sound lascivious.

The taxi to the airport took twice as long as the Suburban had on the way to the hotel, and when he got there he was sweating through his shirt – the car's air conditioning was in desperate need of a Freon charge, though the driver seemed oblivious to it.

Black checked in and called Sylvia from the departure lounge. "Hi, sweetheart. I'm still on the ground. I had to take a later flight."

Sylvia sounded harried, which he could well believe on the day of a show. "What time will you be in?"

"The flight should be on the ground by six-thirty. So allowing some time for immigration, I should be there by…eight."

"That'll work. See you tonight." He heard discussion in the background, and then she returned. "I've got to go. Have a good flight."

The next call went to Daniel.

"The Mexican police are treating the overdose like it could be a homicide."

"Could be? Or is?" Daniel demanded.

"They aren't sure yet. But there are suspicious circumstances." Black filled him in on his discussion with the inspector. "One telling thing, though. Could mean nothing, but there were two glasses with the champagne bottle."

"Did the inspector think that was odd? Whenever I order champagne, they always bring at least two glasses."

Black rolled his eyes. Of course they did. He should have known that from all the times he'd never ordered champagne – or anything else – from room service.

"No, but he did say that investigations down there weren't as sophisticated as in the U.S., so not to expect too much."

"That sounds like it could go either way, then. I mean, there's no evidence that she was killed…" Daniel mused, thinking out loud.

"No, but they think it's fishy, and they're going to continue to dig."

"Did you get the feeling that they were particularly competent?"

"That wouldn't be the exact word I'd use."

"That's what I was afraid of. Okay, thanks for filling me in. Keep me informed."

Black ended the call. His head pounded as the last of the alcohol faded from his system, but he decided to tough it out and drink only water to give himself a chance to recover. He wandered the departure area and quickly grew tired of the shops. After purchasing a T-shirt for Sylvia he sat with the rest of the passengers, staring at his navel. Time crawled by and he found himself nodding off. When he came to, he looked up at the podium and saw the flight was delayed. He spoke to the attendant who told him she had no idea what the problem was, but would let everyone know just as soon as she had more information. One hour dragged into two, and Black was getting really worried when the attendant came onto the public address system and informed everyone that the flight had been cancelled.

He must have groaned out loud, because the woman next to him gave him a look like he'd been fondling himself outside the ladies room. Grabbing his bag, he raced the rest of the disgruntled travelers to the ticket counter, where a line was forming – a long one. After half an hour of waiting, a fatigued Mexican woman informed him that there were no more flights to Los Angeles that evening, and that the flights to San Diego, Phoenix, and San Francisco were all full. Black called Sylvia, but she didn't pick up.

With a dawning sense of panic, he went through his alternatives, and settled for a flight leaving for Mexico City in half an hour, and then standby on a flight to L.A. from there. A lousy option, but one that would get him in by 10:30 or so. With any luck, he'd make it before the gallery closed – not a great solution, but better than missing Sylvia's showing entirely.

The ride to Mexico City was packed. A baby in the seat behind him howled the entire way, and Black wondered what he'd done to offend a God who'd singled him out for torture. Once on the ground he raced to make his connection, and found himself facing a wall of tired travelers with the dull stare of pound dogs for whom time had ceased to have any meaning.

His was the last name called before they closed off the standby list, and he'd never been so pleased to sit next to a poorly ventilated lavatory in his life. The flight was a rough one, with substantial weather as they moved north, which slowed the plane by fifteen minutes. Black was an unhealthy shade of green when the plane pulled to a stop on the tarmac at LAX, and his heart skipped when he realized that they weren't going to dock at a gate – they'd be trooping onto two nearby buses, which would ferry them to the terminal.

That little adventure added an additional delay, as did the two 747s of bewildered tourists that arrived at the same time, packing the customs lines. A stern agent eyeballed Black like he was smuggling a volleyball of cocaine in his sphincter, but after a few questions stamped his empty passport and waved him through.

Sylvia wasn't answering her phone, and when Black reached his car it was already pushing 11:00. He slid behind the wheel and twisted the key, only to be welcomed home with a dull click...and then nothing. A quick glance at the dashboard confirmed the sinking feeling in the pit of his stomach – he'd been in such a hurry when he'd pulled into the perennially gloomy parking structure, he'd left his lights on, and now his battery was dead. He sat in the darkness, wondering if crying or putting his fist through the windshield would do any good, and then resigned himself to his fate.

Ten minutes later a heavyset German man gave him a jump, and he broke every land speed record to get to the gallery. When he pulled to the curb in front, the windows were dark. His watch read midnight.

Sylvia's line went to voice mail, and he knew as he drove home that he'd let her down, whether deliberately or not. This had been the most important event in her recent life, and he'd opted for a trip to Mexico instead of being there to support her. Never mind that it was for a job, or that he'd done everything humanly possible to keep his promise to her. He knew that what would be remembered was that he hadn't been there, which sent the clear message that she couldn't rely on him when she needed him the most, excuses be damned. He left a long, apologetic message for her, and when he disconnected, he felt like complete crap.

The streets from the gallery to his apartment had never seemed more hostile, and it was only with a Herculean effort that he resisted the urge to stop at the market and buy a bottle of mean streak and a pack of cigarettes with which to dull the ache between his eyes. Instead, he went home, cracked a beer and chugged it, called Sylvia a final time, and fell onto the mattress, exhausted, his day finally at an end, having accomplished nothing but ruining his relationship and stressing his liver.

Chapter 9

Black was just stepping out of the shower the next morning when his cell rang. He ran, dripping wet, and answered it, out of breath from the unexpected exertion.

"Yo, big dog. So how was Mehheeeco?" Stan's voice boomed.

"Great. I spent most of yesterday flying to hell and back, missed Sylvia's big gallery show, and had a model murdered three doors down from my room. How'd your day go?"

"Wow. Compared to yours, not so bad. Only one body – a dope deal gone wrong, and a traffic cam caught the killer red-handed. Slam dunk, another loser goes to the joint for life, and the streets are safe for women and children again."

"I'd call that a win."

"Yeah, but the depressing part is that the only reason we have so many easy solves is that the criminals are complete idiots. I wish I could say it was because we're so bitchin' smart, but it ain't so."

"Hey, if it wasn't for morons, you'd be out of a job. Look at it that way. Job security."

"Always the glass half full. That's why I call you. That, and because I was hoping you'd had time to figure out how we're going to nail Ernest."

"I wish. I literally haven't had a free second. But I will. I promise."

"Clock's ticking, my man. And I'm not getting any richer or thinner." Stan paused. "Wait. Did you say a model died down the hall from you?"

"Yeah." Black gave him the short version as he padded back into the bathroom in search of a towel, leaving sopping footprints on his faded beige carpet.

"Bad luck for you, huh? First day on the job."

"The cop thinks it's murder, but he was playing his cards close to the chest. You got any pull with the police south of the border?"

"No, but some of the guys in the department speak perfect Spanish. You want me to see what I can find out from the locals down there?"

"You're a hero, you know that?"

"Save it till I see what I get from them. Hey, hang on a second." Black heard muffled voices in the background. When Stan came back on the line, his tone had changed from relaxed to harried. "Call me when you come up with something on Ernest, okay? I gotta go."

"*Ciao*, baby. Don't forget to check with the Baja *Federales*."

"Got it."

Black tossed the phone onto the bed and returned to his morning routine. He was pulling on his suit trousers when he heard his front door close. He hopped over to the bedroom doorway and saw Sylvia, hands on hips and her face tense.

"Sweetheart. Did you get any of my messages?"

"I'm trying not to be angry with you for missing my biggest event of the year, Black."

"How's that going?"

"So far, not so good."

"I called a half dozen times. It was a nightmare getting back here…"

"That's your story, anyway."

Black leaned against the wall and slid his free leg into his pants. "It's the truth. I had to fly to Mexico City, and there were delays, and bad weather, and—"

"Tell me again why you had to leave the country the day before the show, and not any other day?"

"My new client had a photo shoot in Mexico, and ordered me there. I didn't have any choice."

"There's always a choice. Like, 'I'm sorry, I can't do that, but I can start full-time in two days.' See? Not hard. It's just a question of priorities."

"In retrospect, I should have done that. One of the models was murdered down the hall from me, so my presence didn't do any good."

Sylvia's expression changed. "A model was murdered?"

Black sighed, and told her the whole story, leaving out Tasha's flirtation, his boozy evening, and the cigarette.

"How did the murderer get into her room?" Sylvia asked.

"Unknown. Maybe she was expecting him. She ordered champagne from room service in the wee hours of the morning. That's not something I would expect a junkie to order for a nightcap."

"No, more like a romantic rendezvous."

"Which means she could have given one of her room keys to her date," Black mused.

"Or she could have left the door open for him, and gone to get her fix before he got there. But she misjudged the strength of the local stuff…could that have knocked her out?"

"Absolutely. Addicts nod off all the time."

"Maybe she was thinking she was doing just a little maintenance bump, and wound up with an overdose?"

"Could be. Only remember, they think she was smothered."

"So the murderer came into the room, found her unconscious, and decided to kill her?"

"That's a possibility. Another is that she wasn't smothered, and suffocated as a result of the overdose. They were unclear on which, but they're treating it as a murder."

Sylvia frowned, thinking. "Do they tape the room service calls?"

"Good question. I doubt it. Why?"

"How do you know she's the one who called them? Couldn't that be a, what do you call it in English…a red herring?"

"But why?"

"To make it look like she was expecting someone and throw the blame onto whoever it was who was seeing her?"

Black appraised her with new respect. "You have a devious mind."

"Just tossing it out there."

"How did the show go? Did you sell any paintings?"

"It was good. Lots of people, a few press interviews. And yes, I sold four paintings. Big ones, so the rent's paid for the foreseeable future."

"That's awesome! Congratulations."

"It would have been more awesome if you'd been there."

"Sylvia, I know. I really did try everything to make it. You can check with the airline…"

"I did. Last night. I verified the flight was cancelled."

"Then why bust my chops?"

"Don't look at me like that. You deserve it. You picked work over me. A girl doesn't easily forget that."

Black went to her and hugged her, but she pulled away when he tried to kiss her. "Don't push your luck. I'm still working on the forgiveness part."

"Maybe a nice dinner tonight? Wine? Violins?"

"I'm still angry."

"I'll make a reservation somewhere way too expensive. We'll pretend we're celebrities."

"You're not going to get off that lightly, Black. Besides, I'm busy tonight. I have to go settle up on the purchases, and I already agreed to go to dinner with Stella after." Stella owned the new gallery Sylvia had moved to three months before. "But maybe tomorrow. Assuming I've cooled off."

"I'll do anything to make it up to you, Sylvia, really. I know I blew it, even if it wasn't my fault."

"Yes, you did. But you're moving in the right direction with the apologies."

"That's my evil plan. Oh, and I got you a T-shirt!"

"Don't think that giving me extravagant gifts is going to get you out of the doghouse."

"It's a really nice shirt."

Sylvia smiled for the first time. "I'll be the judge of that."

When Black made it into the office, Roxie stared at her monitor, muttering to herself, her brow beetled. Mugsy was contentedly sleeping, his head resting on the toe of one of her combat boots. She was dressed in a sleeveless blouse, her tattoos on full display, and a pair of black leggings that left little to the imagination. As usual, she didn't look up when he entered.

"Good morning, Sunshine. What are you up to? Praying? You planning on converting?" Black asked.

"Studying."

"You? I don't even want to ask."

"Then don't."

"Okay, what are you studying?"

"Funny, that sounded exactly like what I imagined you asking would sound like."

"Come on, Roxie. Give."

"German. I'm studying *Deutsch*."

"Ah, right. How about Mugsy? Is he brushing up on his language skills, too?"

"I've been researching how to import him. It's a hassle, but mostly paperwork."

"They'll probably want to charge you for an extra seat for the fat bastard. It could get expensive. Might break the bank. I think you should rethink going. Be a shame to run out of money before you even started."

"Thanks for the support, Mr. Negativo."

"If they charge by weight, you're totally screwed."

"Ha ha. Inside I'm laughing." Roxie returned to the screen, the conversation done.

"Any calls? Clients stop by to offer me huge cases?"

Roxie brightened. "Now that you mention it...no."

"Don't you want to know how my trip went?"

She frowned and issued an exasperated sigh. "Sure. How did your trip go, boss?"

"I hung out with famous models. One of whom was murdered while I was sleeping."

Roxie raised an eyebrow. "Not with her, I presume."

"Good guess. Even in Cabo they frown at killing your partner. Although they understand it..."

"Seriously though. How did she die?"

Black did an info dump, and Roxie actually listened attentively. "What do you think? Is it Demille? Costa?" she asked when he was finished.

"I don't know. Costa couldn't get out of there fast enough, but that could be a coincidence – the shoot was over, so why waste a whole day? Demille? He was trying to avoid me, and he also was in a hurry to get to the airport. But the truth is that it could also have been Tasha, who was out with them and conveniently left just before Clarissa did. Or any of the crew who weren't accounted for at that hour."

"Tasha. The agent who was showing you the ropes? You think she was...dating Clarissa?"

"Not really. I'm just saying that she was there, she left just before Clarissa did, so...I don't know what I'm saying, really."

"At least you finally realize it. That's an important first step."

"I meant about Tasha."

"Oh. So much for progress."

"Do me a favor. Pull up everything you can on Gabriel Costa, Thomas Demille, Tasha – or Natasha – Pushkin. Like the Russian president," Black said.

"I'm pretty sure you're thinking of Putin. Vladimir Putin. Not Pushkin, although there are similarities."

"What kind of name is that, anyway?"

"I can think of presidents with weirder names."

"Ouch. Point awarded to the woman with the blue hair. Anyway, see what you can dig up. I want to understand their histories, any intersections…"

"Like what cross streets they live near?"

"Don't lose that sense of humor while you're freezing to death, starving in the German snow."

"Mugsy will keep me warm."

"True, given the amount of gas he generates. You could probably sell the excess and have a thriving business there."

"Oh, there's the phone."

"You realize I'm standing right here, and can hear that there's nobody calling, right?"

"Are we done?"

Black shook his head. "Hate to tear you away from your new appreciation of Germanic languages. But I could use that sooner rather than later."

"Yes, Master. I'll get right on it after I take this call."

"Phone's still not ringing."

The phone rang.

Roxie answered it, listened for a moment, and said, "Sorry. Wrong number," and hung up.

"You called using your cell. I can see it in your other hand, Roxie."

"I wanted to make sure the line was working. Can I get back to what I was doing now? Or do you have vacation pictures you want to show me?"

"The Germans will have to wait. Get me the info on them all, please. Today would be nice."

"Sure thing, Bwana."

Black figured that was the best he was going to get out of her, and elected for a strategic retreat to his office. She would have it done within the hour, he knew, and as he closed the door, his thoughts turned to how to keep her from moving to Germany with Eric. The surefire way would be doing the one thing he hated the most – staking Eric out and waiting for him to screw up, which Black had no doubt he would do. He'd met Eric a number of times and disliked him on sight. He was a swaggering thug with an insulting smirk who clearly thought he was better than everyone else. He'd cheated on Roxie once – once that she'd caught him at. Black had no doubt that he'd done it more often. It was like DUIs. Nobody got caught the first time they drove drunk. It was far more likely they'd get nabbed on the hundredth time. Same applied for Eric.

Which made Black's life easy.

He checked his emails, fiddled around online, and then placed a call to Demille's office, where he was told that the great man was out but would return his call whenever he got back. Black pressed the receptionist, but she was as unhelpful as Roxie and gave him nothing but the stock response that she'd leave a message and ask him to call. Black was annoyed by what he perceived as Demille dodging him again, but decided to make the best of it and spend his day dealing with the Eric problem. The sooner he could put a bullet in Roxie leaving, the better.

Black poked his head out of his office. "I asked Tasha for a list of Demille models who were at the New York, beach, and Mexico shoots. We can cross-reference them and get a start on who the common players were. She also said she'd jot down anyone from other agencies she saw."

"Let me guess. I'm in charge of figuring that out?"

"Nobody's better than you at that sort of thing, Roxie."

"Right. Basic pattern recognition that a trained chimp could do."

"I don't have time to train a chimp."

"I think it's the sweet-talking that I'm going to miss the most."

Black checked the time. "I'm going to be on a stakeout the rest of the day. Patch any calls through. And send the info to my email when you get it."

"Hang on. I have a bunch of stuff already. I'm printing it. Give me two minutes."

He collected his jacket and hat from his desk and returned to Roxie's station. Mugsy stood, looking like a furry beer keg, walked stiffly to Black, and rubbed against his legs – a maneuver guaranteed to coat his suit with hair that always proved nearly impossible to completely clean off. Apparently satisfied with his performance, Mugsy leapt up onto the couch, curled up in his favorite spot, and was dozing before Black had a chance to complain.

Roxie glanced at Mugsy and smiled. "He loves you. I hope he'll be able to adjust to a new place."

Black forced his facial muscles into what he hoped was more grin than grimace. "I wasn't going to say anything, but I'm going to miss the little rascal no end. It won't be the same without him. Especially once I get the walls repainted and the furniture burned."

"Maybe I should leave him here…"

"No," Black blurted, and immediately softened his tone. "No, I mean, you're his life. It wouldn't be fair to Mugsy."

"That's what I thought," she said, leveling a skeptical glare at him.

"But—"

"Here's your homework." Roxie handed him a thick folder. "I think Mugsy's thinner from that new food. I really do."

Black considered ten responses, none of them nice, and decided to cut his losses. He glanced at Mugsy with as sweet a look as he could manage without triggering his gag reflex and nodded.

"That's exactly what I was thinking, too."

Chapter 10

Sunset Boulevard always depressed Black, but never more than during the day, when its shabby buildings and peeling paint were exposed under the sun's unrelenting blaze, its nighttime allure revealed to be nothing but a mirage come morning, a figment of the collective youth imagination fueled by alcohol, drugs, and dreams. Eric's tattoo parlor was shoehorned between a shop that catered to those looking for bondage and discipline leather goods and a T-shirt shop advertising three shirts for ten dollars.

Black rolled to a stop on a side street and walked with his laptop under his arm to a Bohemian café across the boulevard from the tattoo parlor, where he resigned himself to spending a few hours while he watched for anything suspicious. Eric didn't know Black's car by sight, but he was afraid that Roxie might have described it to him, and it would stick out on Sunset with so few other vehicles parked around it.

Part of him wished he could do what he'd advised Stan not to do to Ernest – break the punk's legs or send a couple of violent friends around for a chat. But word would get back to Roxie, and that would be the end of his relationship with her. So he had to take a less frontal approach, much as he would have preferred the shortest distance between two points. In Black's experience scumbags only understood one thing: superior force. As with all liars, cheats, and miscreants, predators in the concrete jungle respected more powerful or dangerous animals. He hadn't invented the rules, but he understood them.

Since a baseball bat was out of the question, he had to wait for Eric to hang himself. With him planning to leave town, Black's bet was that he'd be pulling out all the stops to tag whatever honeys came his way while he still could. The likelihood was he'd be doing his act during the day while Roxie was safely at work, leaving him a finite window of opportunity.

Black ordered a cup of drip coffee and settled in with his laptop in front of him, closed, and his file on the spare chair beside him. The waitress brought his drink and he began reading, starting with Gabriel, as that was the dossier at the top of the pile. First came the photos: Gabriel thoughtful. Gabriel brooding. Gabriel smiling. Gabriel, his hair tousled, looking off into the distance. A good-looking man in a Ricky Martin kind of way.

Next were the details on his new enterprise, Costa Brava. Formed six months earlier. Already making waves on the West Coast, representing a host of names, including several Demille alumni. An office in Santa Monica. Plans for a New York office next year. Not bad for a man who'd spent most of his adult life looking dangerous for the camera while wearing underwear. A smattering of press clippings and screen shots from the company's website rounded out the file.

Finally, slim details on his personal life. Single. Thirty-four. Born in Brazil to wealthy parents, moved to Los Angeles when he was seven, trained in ballet until he was seventeen, when he was discovered and began posing for cash. Joined Demille's roster six years ago at the peak of his career and stayed with Demille until retiring from modeling a year ago.

The information on Thomas Demille was encyclopedic, covering his fifteen years as owner of the top agency on the West Coast, from his humble beginnings as a trunk-of-his-car agent to his current position at the summit of success. Forty-eight years old, former model with three big New York houses, moved to Los Angeles after an unremarkable career to help start a Hollywood office for his employer. Left that agency a year after moving, in an acrimonious parting of the ways, and within five years had all but put them out of business with his new venture.

Black paged through a sheaf of press clippings featuring Demille at movie premieres, restaurant openings, and award shows, always in the company of a new starlet or model. Handsome, tall, lean, aging well, athletic, and regal, with a strong jaw line and steely gaze.

None of that jibed with Sima's description of him as a fixture on the Los Angeles gay circuit; then again, after twenty years in La La Land, Black had seen everything, so he didn't jump to conclusions, and certainly didn't judge anyone by his press coverage. If he'd had a dollar for every film or television star who was married or in a high-profile relationship with a female celebrity, and whom he knew from being on the inside secretly enjoyed a firmer hand on the tiller, so to speak, he could have been comfortably retired. The entertainment industry was oddly hypocritical, and when careers depended on perceptions, you kept your private preferences out of the limelight.

One photo caught his eye and stopped him – Demille, Clarissa, and Gabriel at a charity for breast cancer, Clarissa's face flawless, Demille's exuding the glow only power and money could supply, Gabriel's smiling, the life of the party. Gabriel had his arm around Clarissa and they looked comfortable together. Perhaps just Tinseltown posing; or maybe something…more?

The final pages were Tasha, and underscored how short her career had been. Tasha barely out of her teens working runways in Milan, jumping in the air for Ralph Lauren, riding a bicycle for Skechers. As she'd aged, more serious work, evening wear and jewelry. She'd been stunning in her youth, and he was reminded of how she would still stop traffic in most restaurants as much with her preternaturally intense cobalt blue eyes as her stunning figure.

A single page summary of her stint as one of Demille's agents, a listing of the talent she managed, a bio that told him nothing he didn't already know, and that was it.

He finished his coffee and looked out the window at the shop. Inside, he could see Eric's distinctive white-trash profile talking to a prospective customer – male, unfortunately. Black quickly lost interest and turned his computer on, after ordering another coffee and getting the WiFi access code. He was browsing Demille's obviously expensive website, thinking about how crap his own looked, when his phone rang.

"Black."

His mother's distinctive voice echoed from the earpiece. "Hello, honey. Did I get you at a bad time?"

Black briefly considered answering in the affirmative. "No, not at all. I have a few minutes. But Mom? Are you on your headset? Because there's an echo."

A loud crackling forced him to hold the phone away from his ear.

"Is that better?" she asked.

He listened intently. "Mom? Say something."

"Like what?"

"Anything. So I can see if I can hear you better."

"Oh, I hate it when you put pressure on me like this."

"Okay, that's better."

"What is?"

"The echo."

"Oh. Fine, then. How are you, Artemus?"

He cringed at her use of his first name, which he hated and never used, and debated correcting her, but decided it wasn't a battle he felt like fighting today. "Tip top. Never better. And you?"

"Oh, as well as can be expected. You know."

"What does that mean? Is something wrong with you? With Dad?"

"No, nothing we know of. Why? Do I sound strange to you?"

Black tried to remember a time when his crazy mother hadn't sounded off to him, but bit his tongue. "No, you sound great. What's going on in your life?"

"Nothing much. I'm painting some. That's been fun. And your father's taken up model boat building. That keeps him occupied."

"Great."

"I was just having tea with some of my friends, and they were saying they hadn't heard any stories about you in a while, and that got me to thinking that we haven't seen you in all kinds of forever. Not since your birthday."

"That wasn't that long ago."

"Six months."

"Like I said. Seems like only yesterday."

"So anyway, I called your office and talked to that Roxie, and she told me she was moving to Munich! How exciting is that?"

"It would be even more exciting if she wasn't moving to Berlin, I suppose."

"Oh, right. Munich, Berlin, it's all kind of over there, right? A long way away."

"Yes. She's planning to move in a few weeks."

"Isn't that something? She's so brave. I would never leave Berkeley, you know? Imagine going to a foreign country, with different customs and language and all."

"Roxie is a free spirit, all right."

"We're thinking we should fly down there and have a big night out with you and Roxie before she takes off."

Black slowly counted to three, as Dr. Kelso had advised him to do when he was becoming annoyed. One one-thousand, two one-thousand...

"That's nice of you. But I'm on a big case right now, and I might not be around."

"Nonsense. You're always around."

"Not lately. I was just in Mexico. I may have to fly to New York next," Black lied. "It's been crazy."

"Mexico! Oh, sweetie, I'm glad I didn't know. All I see on the news is how dangerous it is there with the drugs and the shootings and everything. I wouldn't have been able to sleep…"

Black considered Stan's reporting of an average night on the homicide beat in L.A. or the San Francisco East Bay, where his parents lived, and contrasted it to the pool party he'd attended at a four-hundred-dollar per night beach hotel.

"Well, I managed to make it out of there without any bullet wounds. I count myself lucky. Although a girl was killed only a few feet from my room," he threw in, unable to resist.

"Oh, my God. But you're okay? That could have been you."

No, Mom, not unless I was a supermodel with a heroin jones. "Like I said, I'm fine. Never better. All in a day's work. Really. How's Dad?"

"Please. Chakra. He's fine. Puttering around, going a little stir crazy since we sold the candle business."

"Probably for the best. Who needs the headaches?"

"I know. Not me. Although I've been playing with another idea. Some of the girls love it, so I might pursue it, at least on a small scale."

Black was almost afraid to ask. "Another idea?"

"Sure. You know, all the kids these days, with their clothes and hair, the sixties and seventies nostalgia…"

"Uh, that's just Berkeley, I'm pretty sure."

"No, I went with my friend Ruby to San Francisco yesterday, and you should see it. The Haight is almost exactly like it was in the Summer of Love!"

"Uh…right. That's because it's in suspended animation. It's been like that for forty years."

"Well, anyway, I got to thinking, and you know how fixated I can get."

The customer left the tattoo parlor, and Black watched him strolling down the street. Black took a sip of coffee and tried to figure out how best to terminate the call.

"What's your idea? I'm sort of running out of time here. My phone's beeping. Battery's dying."

"I don't hear anything."

"It's only on my end."

"Oh. What will they think of next?"

"The question is, what have you thought of?"

"Then I'll let you go, honey. Call me back when you have more time."

"I will. But what's your idea?"

"We love you. Take care of yourself." He heard her calling out in a controlled scream. "Chakra! Artemus was in New Mexico and his girlfriend was killed!"

"No, Mom. I was in Mexico, and some other woman was killed."

"What? I didn't get that."

"Never mind. Bye, Mom."

The call left him feeling dead inside, as most conversations with his mother usually did. Something about his parents' complete lack of self-awareness coupled with their insane financial success could stoke the flames of anger in him like few other things. They acted like the world was a playground, where they could pursue any idiotic daydreams they cooked up and turn them into viable projects. And what was the most frustrating for him was that, more often than not, they'd been successful at it – always as a result of luck versus acumen.

He contrasted that to his own reality, where he was clawing for business every day, wading into a swamp filled with hungry crocodiles, and shook his head. Life wasn't fair.

The day stretched on, and he discovered that the café served a pretty good turkey and Swiss croissant, which accounted for it getting crowded at lunch. But nobody had any problem with him sitting and tapping away on his computer as long as he kept ordering every hour or so, which he continued to do until he was floating in a sea of coffee. The caffeine gave him a jittery feeling, and he made a mental note to switch to decaf for the rest of the day, or he'd be bouncing off the walls that night, unable to sleep.

His rumination was cut off by an attractive blonde wearing tight jeans and a colorful top walking toward the tattoo parlor. Eric was outside, taping a poster in the window. She stopped near him, the shop apparently her destination. Black's pulse quickened. From where he sat she looked like the sort Eric would be putting the moves on – young, hot, curvy, and judging by her walk, not the least bit shy. The tattoos on her arms reminded him of Roxie, but that was where the similarities ended.

Watching their body language, it was obvious both that Eric knew her and that he was flirting, as was she. He finished with the poster and stood, hands in his front pants pockets, his black tank top displaying his full sleeve tattoos, a flat brim Dodgers baseball hat cocked at a rakish angle, grinning at whatever the girl was saying. She was flipping her hair with her hand, shifting from foot to foot, occasionally reaching out to touch his arm. He pointed to the poster, and Black could see him laugh.

A young man approached from down the street, and all three entered the shop. Black squinted to better make out what was going on inside, and after a few minutes, realized that the woman was operating the tattoo gun while Eric watched her performance. Black didn't know that Eric had someone working with him, but then again, he didn't know much besides that he didn't like the guy.

An hour later the customer left, a gauze square on his arm, and a few minutes afterward Eric and the young lady exited. They stood on the sidewalk for a few moments, and then she leaned in to Eric and kissed him on the cheek before turning and strolling slowly back from wherever she'd come.

Black felt a prickle of excitement. While the kiss could have been a chaste goodbye, something about how she'd lingered and how his hands had found her waist said it might be more than that. The problem was that one goodbye *mwah* wasn't proof of anything. He needed more.

Eric returned to the shop and spent the remainder of the afternoon inside. Only one more customer, a heavyset biker type, stopped by. If that was any indication of his typical traffic, Black could understand why he was jumping at the chance to start anew somewhere more promising. Los Angeles probably had more tattoo parlors than any other city in the U.S., so competition was fierce. And a couple or three customers a day would barely pay the rent, if that.

Daylight was fading and he was getting ready to pack it in when his phone rang. He glanced at the screen but didn't recognize the number.

"Black."

"Mr. Black. Nice to hear your voice again."

Black thought for a second. "Tasha?"

"I like that I made enough of an impression so you remembered my name."

"Of course. What can I do for you?"

"I want to meet."

"When, and why?"

"I've been thinking about what's been going on. I have a theory, or at least some facts you might want to know if you're going to get to the bottom of things."

"Facts?"

"Right. Inside dirt."

"Okay, Tasha. I'm on a stakeout, but I can meet you tomorrow."

"No. I want to meet now. I might run out of courage by tomorrow."

"Why do you need to be courageous to tell me your theory?"

"You'll know when you hear it."

Black checked his watch. "Where are you?"

"I'm at a little Russian restaurant near Beverly Hills. It's called St. Petersburg. Do you know it?"

"Nope. What's the address?"

She rattled off the information, and as Black scribbled it down, he could hear Russian music in the background.

"It could be a while with rush hour."

"I'm not going anywhere. But don't take too long. I might chicken out."

"Something tells me you haven't chickened out of anything in a long time, Tasha."

"You don't know me that well. Just hurry. I was going to have dinner. You can buy it for me, and I'll confess everything, Mr. Black. You'll have your way with me. There won't be any secrets left."

Black hesitated for a split second, and then nodded to himself. "With an offer like that, how can I refuse? I'll be there as soon as I can."

Chapter 11

Traffic was a snarl, stop and go in many places, and Black was restless from all the coffee as he inched toward Beverly Hills. He punched the stereo on and tapped the steering wheel with his fingers. The driving dual guitar assault of The Four Horsemen's *Rockin' is Ma' Business* cheered him as it always did. The early November weather was balmy and dry, a residual effect of the Santa Ana winds, so he dropped the top, trying to enjoy sitting in an unending line of cars.

The restaurant was between Century City and Beverly Hills, tucked away on a smaller street. Black circled the block twice hoping to find a parking place, but wound up leaving his keys with the valet, resigned to having to fork over five bucks at the end of the meal in addition to buying dinner – which, judging by the red velvet of the walls and the upscale look of the patrons, wouldn't be cheap. Thankfully, this would be a legitimate business expense, so it was coming out of Daniel's ample pockets, not Black's.

Tasha sat at a quiet booth near the back of the restaurant, a tumbler of vodka in front of her on the white tablecloth along with an untouched silver bowl with three bread rolls. Her face lit up when she saw him, and he felt like she was undressing him with her eyes.

"Why, Mr. Black. I'd just about given up on you," she said, rising as he neared. Her obviously expensive peach dress was perfectly tailored to her form. She leaned across the table to give him a courtesy peck on his cheek, and he smelled alcohol and expensive perfume.

"I said I'd come. I'm a man of my word."

"So you are. Another admirable trait among many. And what a wonderful outfit. Very...classy," she said, taking in his suit and hat.

"Thanks," he said, removing the fedora and taking the seat across from her.

"Have you ever been here before? The food is magnificent. Makes me homesick."

"No, this is another first for me. What are you drinking there?"

"Russian vodka, what else? You can't eat here without washing the meal down with vodka."

"I may stick to beer."

"Nonsense. You're now on Russian soil. When in Russia…"

Black eyed her drink with trepidation, but it was too late – she was ordering in Russian from the waiter who'd appeared next to her as if by magic. He listened with a dour expression on his thin, gray face, the overhead lights reflecting off his round steel-rimmed glasses, and then he nodded curtly and marched off to fetch their drinks.

"I'm not a huge vodka fan," Black said.

"That's because you've never had good Russian vodka with a Russian. Trust me, there are few experiences quite like it."

"What part of Russia are you from, Tasha?"

"Moscow. It's been many years since I left, but I still get homesick."

"You mentioned that you left when you were young?"

"Yes. And I've been back a number of times. But nothing's like it was. Anywhere, I suppose, but I see it there more than here. So different."

The waiter returned with two more tumblers of straight vodka. Tasha downed the last inch in her original drink like it was water and handed it to the waiter as he departed. She raised her new glass in a toast. "To better days, Mr. Black," she said, and took a large sip. Black did the same, and winced at the burn as liquid fire slid down his throat.

"That's…strong," he sputtered.

"Like the margaritas, the first taste is the worst. You'll get used to it. This is very good vodka, by the way. Beluga. One of my favorite unflavored vodkas."

"Are the flavored ones popular in Russia?"

"Oh, they're huge. You have no idea how many different types there are." She reached into her purse, removed a manila folder, and handed it to Black. "Before I forget, here's the list of everyone I can remember being at the three shoots."

"That's awesome. I appreciate it. I've been having a tough time getting my head around all this. It'll help a lot."

"So will more vodka, Mr. Black."

They both swallowed another gulp, and Black was surprised to find that the second dose indeed went down easier. Warmth blossomed in his stomach, and he decided that maybe a drink or two was just the thing he needed to counteract all the caffeine.

"Okay, Tasha, I'm here, as requested. You have something special you want to share with me?"

She batted her eyes and smiled seductively. "Very perceptive, Mr. Black. But let's order dinner. The kitchen can be slow when it's crowded."

"I don't have a menu."

"You don't need one. You have me."

"Ah. Then do your worst. Only I'll warn you – I don't eat any parts of an animal that McDees wouldn't serve."

"That leaves you open, but I'll be gentle with you."

She flagged the waiter down and he returned with an expression like he'd just cleaned out a septic tank. Tasha rattled off a string of requests, and he nodded before repeating the dishes back to her. He gave Black a look that bordered on insulting, then pushed his way through twin stainless steel doors to the kitchen.

"I don't think he likes me," Black commented.

"That's because he doesn't know you. How could anyone dislike you, Mr. Black? You're a perfect gentleman."

They made small talk until the first course arrived, which Black was disappointed to see was a cold soup that looked like something he normally would have put down the garbage disposal. Tasha ordered more vodka for them both, and seeing Black's puzzlement at his dish, offered an explanation.

"This is okroshka. It's a staple in Russia. I think you'll like it," Tasha said, holding up her spoon. "It's served cold, but it's quite good."

"Stupid question, but what's in it?"

"There are no stupid questions. It's mainly cucumbers, green onion, beef, and spices. Try it."

Black did as instructed, and did his best not to gag at the unfamiliar taste and texture. He finished his vodka just as the second glass was being set down before him, and took a cautious sip before nodding.

"It's…different."

"Yes. But do you like it?"

"I haven't decided yet."

"Don't worry. The next course will be pirozhki, which are pastries with a meat filling. More accessible for American palates, I think. You'll find that the vodka makes the soup more satisfying. Actually, it makes everything more satisfying."

"You're the expert," Black said, and took another gulp of Beluga, which he now found didn't have nearly the searing quality of the first glass.

Black waited until the pirozhki arrived before raising the subject of why Tasha had called.

"So what's this theory you wanted to tell me about?" he asked, his second glass of vodka drained.

"More a collection of facts that you'll find interesting. First is that Demille's agency is basically broke."

Black stared at her, dumfounded. "How can that be? He's the biggest on the coast."

"Simple. Tom lives large, and he's lousy with money. He's got a huge home in the hills, drives Italian sports cars, and likes to fly on private jets. If he makes five million, he spends six. He's always been irresponsible, but as he's gotten older, he's gotten worse. It's like he thinks he can turn back the clock if he behaves like a child. His parties alone cost as much as you or I would make in a year, if not more."

"I wonder why Daniel's accountants didn't tip to that?"

"Because he keeps enough in the company so that it can pay its expenses. And frankly, because its real asset isn't its cash – it's the talent roster and its reputation. But trust me, Tom doesn't want to sell. He's a control freak. If there was any other way for him to dig himself out of the hole he's in, he'd keep the company. Daniel must be handing him a big slug of cash with a hell of a profit share, because otherwise, why sell? For the up-front money, obviously."

"Interesting. I wouldn't have guessed that."

"Few would. He's an icon on the social scene, and donates lavishly to a variety of hip charities. But he's in trouble. Which explains why he's screwing all of his agents for a quick buck," she said bitterly.

"How so? Won't this be good for you? A bigger organization, more clients…"

"Right. An organization that already has an installed base of seasoned agents in New York. The rumor going around is that once the deal's done, half of us are going to be let go. It's a classic way of instantly juicing profits from an acquisition. Use your existing infrastructure to handle the workload – especially if it's underused right now."

"But you've been with Demille for a long time. Surely…"

"I'll be fine. But a lot of the more junior agents are getting nervous, as they should be. I don't trust Daniel. Not that I trust Tom, but at least I know what I'm dealing with – or I thought I did."

"What do you mean?"

"This announcement came out of the blue. No warning. He didn't discuss it with anyone. Which has also made the talent nervous. Models are a flighty bunch, and their agency is their meal ticket. If they think there's trouble in paradise, they'll go elsewhere. And a sale out of left field hints at trouble. Which is why he's already seeing some faces going to competitors."

"Like Costa."

"Right. And Elizabeth Warren's outfit. Mirror Image Associates. She's been actively recruiting from his models, too. Although you're correct that Gabriel's gotten most of them."

"Interesting. And yet Demille and Gabriel seemed to be on good terms."

"Oh, more than just good. They were an item for a while. But like all Tom's dalliances that didn't last long."

"Right. I remember Sima alluding to Demille being…liking the fellas."

"Tom likes anything that moves. Boys, girls, whatever. Depends on his mood. It feeds his ego. And like the spending, that's gotten more desperate as he's gotten older," she said, a touch of rancor in her tone.

"Wait. Did you and he…?"

"Oh, Mr. Black, you're so conventional. I love that about you. And your look of shock is priceless. To answer your question, yes, when I was very young, I fell under his spell for a while. But that was back when cell phones were the size of a brick. It's been strictly business for more than coming up on twenty years." She downed half her latest glass of vodka – number four or five – Black had lost count somewhere after the pirozhkis had arrived. "Not that I missed anything, I don't think. For him, it was the novelty more than anything back then. I was just eighteen, and he…well, he wasn't. It's not the first time that youth has been a powerful aphrodisiac, Mr. Black."

"I guess not. I'm sorry, I didn't mean to pry."

"Don't worry. It was ages ago. My skin is thick. And coming from a handsome, charming man, your interest is endearing."

The entrée arrived on cue, and looked to Black like the shish kabob you could get at any of the hundreds of Persian restaurants in town.

"This is shashlyk. That's chicken, this one is lamb, and this is beef. All very tender," Tasha said, her eyes now bright from the alcohol.

They munched on meat while Black mulled over Tasha's insights. He hardly noticed when yet another glass of vodka arrived, although he noted absently that his head was starting to spin. So Demille was a switch hitter. And a broke one. Who was losing models to his competitors, and needed this deal. At least on the surface. He cursed silently – something was tugging at the edges of his awareness, but he'd had too much to drink to focus.

His thoughts were interrupted by Tasha's bare foot touching his calf. He sat back and smiled, hoping to extricate himself without losing an apparent ally.

"Tasha, I like you, and honestly, I'm flattered, but–"

"But you're not interested," she said flatly, her smile turning mean as she said it.

"No, it's not that at all."

"Then you *are* interested?"

"I have a girlfriend."

"Ah. Lucky her. But she's not here, is she?"

"If I wasn't with her…"

"Right. I know. You'd be in my panties faster than a teenage boy." She swallowed her drink and stood unsteadily. "No hard feelings, Mr. Black, but I thought I sensed something from you that was a little more…promising."

She was starting to slur, which was only surprising because she'd held it together pretty well up until then.

"I'm sorry if I gave you the wrong impression…"

Tasha swayed slightly, taking his measure, and shook her head. "You have no idea what you're missing, Mr. Black. No idea at all."

"Tasha – I didn't mean it like that…" Black said, trying to do damage control.

She shook her head and stalked off, her high heels clicking against the marble restaurant floor, leaving him sitting alone, wondering how it had all gone wrong so quickly. He debated going after her, but what was the point? They were both drunk, and nothing good ever came from trying to clarify a misunderstanding when wasted.

The waiter arrived to clear the plates, and Black asked for the check before heading to the bathroom. When he stood he had a sudden bout of dizziness, and realized just how much alcohol he'd had. After an unsteady trek to relieve himself, he paid the bill, which was almost three hundred dollars, most of it vodka, and made his way to the entrance clutching his folder. The valet brought his car, and Black drove it two blocks before parking and calling a taxi on his cell phone. The last thing he needed was to add a DUI to his list of problems. Even drunk, he had enough sense to cab it home. He'd retrieve the Caddy in the morning. It would be safe in that neighborhood, he was sure.

The taxi ride took fifteen minutes, and he sent a text to Roxie as the cab eased to the curb. He wove his way to the stairs that led to his second-floor apartment, which demanded his full, unsteady attention. His fingers felt thick, like they were being operated by somebody else, and he fumbled for his keys. He groaned when he got his door open, and was in real trouble as he staggered to the bedroom, swaying like a sailor on the deck of a boat pitching in rough seas. It was all he could do to get out of his suit before he dropped onto the bed, assuring himself that he'd only rest for a minute before hanging up his clothes and brushing his teeth. He closed his eyes, the room spinning ominously, and was snoring almost instantly, vodka fumes drifting from his open mouth as his body battled to process the ocean of abuse to which he'd subjected it for the second time in a week.

Chapter 12

The morning started rough. It took Black a half hour to rinse the metallic taste from his mouth, and even as he dressed he suspected he was still sweating out about seventy proof. The only positive he could think of was that at least he hadn't smoked – so he'd avoided inhaling over a hundred additional toxins, and ducked the compounding effect on his body. Still, it was rocky going as he negotiated his apartment stairs, and only when he couldn't spot the Eldorado on the street did he remember he'd left it near the restaurant. He was momentarily seized with a bout of anxiety, and his brow beaded with sweat even though the morning was cool. He had a recurring nightmare from his band days in which he'd gone to a party after playing a club, drunk too much, and found himself on the street in front of the party house, unable to find his car.

Fortunately, that was only a dream. A taxi arrived a short time later in response to his call and whisked him back to the restaurant, where he was able to easily locate the Cadillac. He stopped at a franchise coffee shop for a large cup of wakeup, but didn't have the energy to go on the offense with the perennially superior service staff, who correctly interpreted his somber tone as a sign of weakness and exchanged smug smirks with one another as he shuffled to the cashier, a broken husk of a man, at least for the moment.

By the time he made it to the office he was half an hour late, but relatively energized by the caffeine. He did his best to put a bounce in his step as he climbed the stairs, which would have been more convincing if his liver hadn't pulsed in pain with each footfall.

When he swung his office door open he was treated to Mugsy rolling on the floor with a new kitty toy while Roxie gazed at her computer with the intensity of a programmer working on a string of code.

"*Gutenmorgen, Fraulein* Roxie!" Black exclaimed with a giddy edge of fake cheer. She looked up at him and returned her eyes to the screen.

"You look like you're having an allergic reaction," she said.

"Really?"

"Yeah. You're puffy. And your eyes are swollen. Did something bite you?"

He was tempted to say the Beluga bug had stung him, but elected discretion. "Maybe I'm retaining water. I've been all moody, too. Could be that time…"

She ignored his quip. "As long as you're okay. I was just concerned, is all."

He stopped and stared at her. "Roxie. Are you feeling okay? That almost sounded heartfelt. And this is the first time in months you haven't bagged on me over my clothes, or my hair, or something I said. I mean, don't get me wrong – I like it. But it worries me a little…"

"I figured since we only have another couple of weeks together I'd suck up to you in the hopes that you give me a severance bonus."

"Oh. Good strategy."

"Does that mean I'll get a big bonus?"

"Depends on what you mean by *get*, *big*, and *bonus*, I suppose. One could argue that the invaluable experience you've gained working with me will last you a lifetime, and there can be no greater bonus than that."

She stared at him with dead eyes. "I knew it was a bad idea. You smell like booze."

"I do?"

"And you look like a burn victim or something. Flushed. Oh, gross. You're sweating."

"I just walked up the stairs. It's a little warm in here."

"Uh huh."

"I see Mugsy's got a new toy."

"Yeah, I spent some of the nonexistent bonus money you're not going to give me on something to keep him occupied so he doesn't destroy anything more in the office."

"A good move."

"A waste of seven bucks, now that I know I'll be living off my experience and not some hard cash."

Black changed the subject. "How did the band take the news about you leaving?"

"They were bummed. But they'll get over it. It's not like we were getting rich playing in the clubs around here. L.A.'s full of singers. They'll live."

"How about Eric? He's got to be running pretty hard, tying up all the loose ends with the shop before he takes off."

"Yeah, he's been super busy. And he's got a trade show he's exhibiting at in a few days. He's got a small booth already paid for, so he's trying to pull that together, too."

"Why doesn't he skip it?"

"I guess he's hoping he can get some international contacts for the new shop. The only good thing is that he's got a new tattoo artist who's helping him out. From Berlin. A friend of his cousin's who wanted to spend some time over here."

"Oh, really," he said noncommittally.

"Yeah. She's the one who gave Eric the idea of partnering up with his cousin to open one in Germany."

"Huh. Have you met her?"

"No, she only comes in part time. But she's probably hella cool. I mean, the chick's an ink jock. Can't get much more badass than that."

"Right. Probably all dark and Goth. Germans are like that."

"How would you know, Mr. I-know-nothing-about-Berlin?"

"Hey, I said good morning in German."

"Little internet translator action there, I'm guessing."

"See? This is why we have tension in the office. I do something nice, and you twist it into something ugly."

Roxie swiveled back to the screen. "You should go blot your face. You look like someone sprayed you with water."

"I do not."

"What's that disorder where you sweat profusely for no reason?"

"I don't have a disorder."

"I forget what causes it. I think it's male menopause. The body starts breaking down…"

"I'm not going through male menopause. There's no such thing."

"Hyperhidrosis. That's what it's called. I saw it on the Discovery Channel. Kind of gross. And there's no real cure."

"Roxie…"

"The lady they were interviewing said it's like a curse…"

"Roxie, I don't have hyper…I don't have that." He held Tasha's folder aloft and placed it on her desk. "Here are the lists of the models at the three shoots. Can you work your magic on them, please?"

"Sure. Because you're so generous with me, and all."

Black walked to his office. "You look nice today," he said, using the old kill 'em with kindness feint to disarm her. Unfortunately, he was forgetting who he was dealing with.

"Are we back to the sexual harassment thing now that I'm leaving soon?"

Black stopped at his doorway. "I've never harassed you."

"That's your story. I'm going to start taping these exchanges. I feel icky just having them. Ew."

"Maybe you should tape how many hours you don't do work while at the office."

"Mr. Grumpy. A common side effect of hyperhidrosis. Tragic, really."

Black closed his door and hung up his jacket, and then mopped his brow with a tissue. Roxie was partially right – he wasn't feeling so good. He slid his desk drawer open, removed a bottle of aspirin, and washed down three with the tepid dregs of his coffee.

A half hour after he turned on his computer, Roxie's summary appeared in his inbox. She'd assembled her first set of matches on Tasha's list. Black scanned the list of names and nodded, and then called Hailey and Trish, who showed up as having an address in the San Fernando Valley. The voice that answered the phone sounded young, so he assumed he'd gotten Hailey.

"Ms. Stills, my name's Jim Black. I'm handling an investigation for Thomas Demille's agency, and I'd like to talk to you as soon as possible. This afternoon, in fact, if you're going to be around."

"I…I don't know. I need to ask my mother. But she's not here right now…"

"I'll swing by at three o'clock. It'll only take a few minutes. Will she be back by then?"

"I guess."

"Okay. I'll see you at three."

"What was your name again?" Hailey asked, her voice uncertain.

"Black. Of Black Investigations."

"Oh. Right."

Black hung up and opened the email Daniel had sent him, with all the contact information for Demille's models. He hadn't had time to go through the whole roster, but it was way overdue. He checked off the names that were on the list Roxie had compiled, and quickly saw that there weren't as many who had been at all three shoots as he'd feared. Hailey. Clarissa. James. Regina. Gabriel at the beach shoot and Mexico, but not New York. Three more names he didn't immediately recognize. Zane at the New York shoot, but not at either of the others. And, of course, Demille.

Which reminded him that Demille still hadn't returned his call. Annoyed, he dialed Demille's number again. The receptionist gave him the same stock response as the prior day, and Black dutifully left another message, hoping that his stern tone would put the fear of God into her, but doubting it from her bored assurance that it would be passed on.

Black looked on the list and found Demille's cell number, but when he called it, it went to voice mail. Black repeated his request that he call as soon as possible and left his number, hoping he'd kept the anger out of his voice. His next call was to Daniel.

"Demille's dodging me. He never called me back, and he's not answering his cell phone."

Daniel exhaled loudly. "I'm sorry, I should have told you. He has a sailboat, and he told me yesterday he was going to be taking it out to Catalina for the night. So it's not that he's ducking you. He's probably in an area where he doesn't have cell service."

"At least that's one mystery solved today. I'll work on being more patient. But I really do want to talk to him as soon as possible."

"I'll pass that along. I'm sure it's not deliberate. He has every reason to cooperate."

"You'd certainly think so."

By noon, after a trip to the corner donut shop and two cinnamon rolls down the hatch, Black was starting to feel human again. The vodka was kinder to him than the tequila had been, for which he was thankful, although even the thought of alcohol made him queasy.

He read the rest of the background information Roxie had assembled, and at 1:00 he announced that he was going to lunch and would be out the rest of the afternoon. Roxie didn't try to pretend interest, which Black found strangely reassuring. He found a diner that specialized in colon-clogging cuisine, ordered a double chocolate milkshake and the big boy special with extra grease. He could feel his arteries harden just from breathing the sad establishment's pervasive perfume of deep-fat-fried everything.

His meal arrived swimming in an oil slick, and he pushed his doubts out of his mind, trusting that when his subconscious had figured it out, it would let him know. He took a heaping forkful of mystery meat coated in congealed lard and chewed contentedly, washing it down with a gulp of milkshake, and reached for the salt, determined to add insult to injury. Maybe when he was done with his meal he'd call Sylvia and see if she'd forgiven him yet. With everything that he had going on, he'd almost forgotten that he was still in the doghouse, and he made a mental note to make amends, even though in his mind he'd done nothing wrong.

An old woman with raccoon mascara and makeup apparently applied with a paint roller shambled down the aisle toward the cash register, clutching her faux leopard skin coat around her like she was freezing, holding a muttered conversation with an invisible companion. Black watched her go by and wondered how people wound up in places like the diner – what her story was, whether she'd ever loved, or lost, or been well. Melancholy settled over him like a heavy blanket, and he followed her progress as she unfurled a small wad of dollar bills and counted each off like it was her life savings being exchanged for lunch – which perhaps it was. He felt a moment of kinship with her, a sad sense of sharing the same reality, if only for a second, and then she was gone, off to whatever purgatory she inhabited, leaving the diners to their mastication. Black gazed out the window at the stream of traffic, the only constant in the city, and wished for a cigarette and a margarita and the warm kiss of the tropical sun. In his mind he drove to the airport and boarded a plane for Mexico, this time never to return, his future uncertain but better than his present.

Instead, he flipped out his notepad and considered how he was going to catch Ernest and Eric in their lies while stopping whoever was killing the models. Perhaps not the same as escaping to Baja, but at least a way to pay the rent while he figured out what he wanted to be when he grew up.

Assuming he ever did.

Chapter 13

The drive over the hill and into the San Fernando Valley took longer than Black had anticipated. A semi-rig had blown a tire, which had shredded and struck the car behind it, causing it to lose control and ram the van next to it. By the time the whole mess had played out it was a six car pile-up, and all but one lane was blocked by the Highway Patrol as they tried to restore a semblance of order.

Hailey's neighborhood turned out to be one step above trailer trash. Her house was a modest rancher built in the sixties, all yellow stucco and cheap aluminum windows, the lawn moderately overgrown and a twenty-year-old Chevrolet truck in the driveway. Black swung the rusting iron front gate open and approached the porch, amazed that a budding supermodel lived in such a modest manner. He didn't know what he'd expected, but this wasn't it.

He rang the doorbell and waited. When the door opened, Hailey was framed in the sunlight, her long hair cinched in a loose ponytail, wearing gray sweat pants and an oversized flannel shirt. She regarded him for a long moment, silent, and then a loud female voice called out from behind her, in the depths of the house.

"Hailey. Show him to the living room."

She turned slightly, her eyes still on Black. "Yes, Mom."

Black waited for her to invite him in, but she still gave him the same dead stare. Something about it made his flesh crawl. She was breathtakingly gorgeous, of course, but her gaze seemed…vacant, or drugged. Not all there.

"Come in," she said, her voice flat, and Black did a double take as he stepped into the house. The entire foyer and hall were lined with headshots of Hailey from childhood through the present, creating the sense that he'd entered a shrine to her – the Church of Hailey. She shut the door behind him and brushed by, eyeing the photos as she led the way.

"It's a little weird. But you get used to it," she said in a low voice, the tone still…detached…and led him into the living room, where her mother, Trish, was sitting in a reclining chair. The television was tuned to a reality show, the sound barely audible.

Black removed his hat. "Hello, Mrs. Stills. Thanks for taking the time to see me."

"Mr. Black. Sure, no problem. Have a seat on the couch. Hailey, did you offer Mr. Black anything to drink?"

"No, Mom," Hailey answered, her tone that same odd timbre.

"Well, I'm sorry, Mr. Black. Hailey's just worn out from all the shoots, and trying to cram for her PSAT. Would you like something? Water? Soda? Beer?" Trish asked, her voice the polar opposite of Hailey's, with a nearly manic quality of excitement.

"Thanks. I'm good." Black handed Trish his business card and sat where directed on the worn Sears sofa. His eyes roved around the room, where there were at least a dozen more photos of Hailey in large frames, mostly magazine shots, including three recent covers. Hailey seemed luminescent in the photographs, appearing to leap off the page with presence – a stark difference to her subdued mood today.

"Hailey, leave us to this, would you? Mr. Black has some questions for me."

Black cleared his throat. "Actually, Mrs. Stills, I'd prefer if Hailey stayed. That will save me the time of having to ask her all the same questions afterward."

"Please. Call me Trish. Are you sure? She's awfully busy…"

"Which is why I don't intend to take up much of your day with this" – Black paused – "Trish."

Trish appeared confused for a moment, and he could see the wheels turning in her head. She leaned forward and smiled at him, her eyes on Hailey. "Honey, have a seat." She returned her attention to Black. "Now, am I correct that you're with DNA?" she asked, picking up his card and studying it.

Black nodded. "They've hired me to look into the recent incidents with Demille's firm, in anticipation of the merger."

"I see. Well, I suppose that's good. These poor girls work so hard. I'd have hoped that someone would start looking out for their interests."

"That's my job."

"Wait...you look very familiar. Were you...were you at the Cabo shoot?" Trish asked.

"As a matter of fact, I was."

"Wasn't that horrible about Clarissa? So sad. She had her whole life ahead of her."

"Yes, she did. Which really brings me to the reason I'm here. I'm trying to piece together how that night ended, by collecting statements from everyone who was there." Black's gaze strayed to Hailey, who was sitting silently, her legs folded beneath her on the far end of the couch. "You were at the dinner, right?" he asked Hailey.

"Oh, yes. Wasn't it wonderful? The food was heavenly," Trish said.

Black returned his focus to Trish. "What did you do after dinner?"

"After? We went into town. Neither Hailey nor I had ever been in Cabo before, and she wanted to see what all the fuss was about."

"About what time was that?"

"Oh, I don't know. Probably...11:00 or so? I don't really remember."

"Where did you go?"

"We had the driver drop us off at the mall, and we walked along the marina. Isn't that right, Hailey?"

Hailey nodded assent, her eyes on the television screen.

"Okay. And what time did you return to the hotel?"

"Boy, it had to be a couple of hours later. We wandered around town, and then Hailey wanted to see Cabo Wobo – she'd read about it on Facebook, I guess."

"Cabo Wabo," Hailey corrected softly.

"Yes, well, anyway, we stopped in there and looked around, and after a few minutes we called the driver and had him pick us up."

"What time do you think that was?"

"Maybe 1:00. No later. I remember we were both tired after a long day."

"And after you returned to the hotel, you went to your rooms?"

"Room, Mr. Black. Yes, we did. Like I said, we were exhausted by then. And we had a morning flight to catch. You know, I told the police all this..."

"The Mexican police?"

"Of course. They had a very nice man translate and take my statement."

"I see. Unfortunately, they haven't shared that with their U.S. counterparts yet. Sorry if these are all the same questions. Tell me, did you see anyone else you knew out that night?"

"Two of the photographer's staff were on the Marina, having drinks at one of the little bars there. The Nowhere Bar. I remember that because it was such an odd name. It was crowded, too, although I don't understand what the draw was. At least that other place had music and dancing."

"Never been, but I'll take your word for it. So you didn't see anyone else, is that correct?"

"Right. We tend to keep to ourselves, Mr. Black. Hailey's younger than the other girls, and she has a different…lifestyle. It's not staying out at all hours, drinking and doing God knows what else."

"No, of course not. Hailey, I'm sorry, I should know this. How old are you?" Black asked.

Hailey looked to her mom for approval. Trish nodded. "Go ahead. Tell him."

Hailey turned to Black, her piercing blue eyes fixing on him with quiet intensity. "I'm going to be sixteen in three more months."

Black smiled and nodded, but his stomach fluttered. The way she'd answered the question reminded him of adolescents who wanted to appear older than they were. Like a six-year-old assuring him that she was almost seven, any day. He wondered for a fleeting moment whether she was on some kind of powerful tranquilizer, or maybe illegal drugs, but her eyes were clear and her pupils normal-sized.

"That's an amazing career you've had for someone so…young. You're very lucky," Black said, for lack of anything better.

"Oh, yes. Hailey's going to be one of the top stars in this business one day. Her popularity's exploding. She's going to do big things, Mr. Black. I keep telling her that in a few years she'll be on the cover of every major magazine. While that seems like crazy talk right now, it could happen," Trish assured him with the devout conviction of the true believer.

"I have no doubt. How long have you been modeling, Hailey?" Black asked her.

She shrugged, a very childlike gesture, and while her expression was completely neutral, Black would have described her attitude as sullen. Maybe she'd had a fight with her mom before he'd come over? Or it was a bad time of the month? Black was the first to admit that he understood very little about women of any age, so he was having a hard time getting a handle on her.

"Hailey's been in the business since she was four. She grew up in it," Trish said.

"Wow. So already an eleven-year veteran."

"I know. The time flies, doesn't it?" Trish said, making a show of looking at her watch. "Speaking of which, is there anything else?"

"Just a few more questions. Let's go back to the New York shoot, where Daria...Daria's last job. Were you there?" Black asked, already knowing the answer.

"Of course. There hasn't been a major shoot this year Hailey hasn't been in," Trish responded defensively. "I told you. She's one of Demille's biggest stars now."

"Mom..." Hailey protested, her voice still quiet.

"It's true. It's not conceited to tell the truth, young lady."

"I certainly didn't take it the wrong way," Black said. "Then you were at that wrap dinner, too?"

"Absolutely. I can still remember it. They had one of the top restaurants in town cater it. And everybody who was anybody was there."

Black took them through a list of routine questions, switching to the beach shot after covering New York. Much of what he, or Stan, did was to question and probe, waiting for an inconsistency to appear or for the stories not to add up. Unfortunately, that was a time-consuming and thankless process, and usually required a larger cohort group than just one. He'd done a soft version of the questions with Tasha, but other than her statements, he really had nothing to go on, so part of what he was doing was collecting stories so he could spot the flaw when he compared them.

"This may seem a little out of left field, but can you think of anyone who might have it in for any of the models?" Black asked.

"No, not really...although I know Zane Bradley blames Hailey and me for killing his career."

"Ah, yes. I heard about that."

"I just felt we didn't want to be associated with a company that would condone that sort of behavior. It would be bad for Hailey's image."

"Interesting. Did he ever threaten you?"

"No, but I heard that he was badmouthing us before he was fired. Apparently he'd thought there was a chance he could stay with Demille, and believes we were the deciding factor."

"Did Zane have any problems with Daria or Clarissa?"

"Oh, quite the opposite. He and Clarissa were inseparable at one time. BFFs."

"What about the model who was injured in the acid incident?"

"I…I honestly don't know."

Black probed that line of reasoning a little more before switching gears. The question of the merger came up, and Trish, for the first time, became almost as introverted as her daughter.

"I know a fair number of Demille's models are considering going elsewhere after the merger. Why do you think that is?" Black asked.

"Honestly, Mr. Black, I can't speak for the rest of his talent. Demille's been nothing but good to us, but I can see how some might think that they could advance their careers with more personal attention than what he's going to be delivering once he's part of a big corporation," Trish explained.

"That's funny, because I would have thought that becoming part of a larger, more prestigious firm would be good for everyone."

"From the outside, maybe, but a model's often only as good as her relationship with the person repping her, and if Demille's not handling things personally anymore…well, that's a judgment call every model needs to make for herself. There's no right answer. Some will do really well with a bigger company behind them. Others might feel like they're working for a faceless entity with a lot more talent to push, and no real personal relationship or loyalty."

Black nodded. That made sense. Being a smaller fish in a bigger pond might work out poorly for some, and if the sense was that Demille was going to be missing in action a lot…if they were only as good as his agents were, it might not be all that great, judging by Tasha's alcohol-fueled nights. He wanted to ask her whether she'd had second thoughts, but decided that wasn't his place – it wasn't his problem, and knowing the answer wouldn't help him with the case.

As he wrapped up with his closing questions, he couldn't shake the feeling that there was something really wrong with Hailey. Maybe it was just her personality, but it was creepy. She was an absolute stunning beauty, no doubt, but talking to her was like talking to a rock with a face painted on it.

Trish, on the other hand, was every bit as annoying as Tasha had led him to expect, so no surprises there other than the house as an altar to Hailey's image. A part of him conceded that he hadn't had it so bad with his parents in comparison. Maybe parents who were completely spaced out weren't the worst possibility, if Hailey's demeanor was anything to go by.

He took his time making his way back to the car, mulling over Hailey's odd behavior. He was out of his depth with that, but thought maybe Tasha could offer some insight. Black fished his phone from his pocket and dialed her cell, but it went to voicemail. He hoped that their miscommunication the prior night hadn't soured her on helping him. But the truth was he hadn't done anything besides behave honorably, so she didn't have a lot of ground to stand on. If she didn't call back tonight, he'd reach her at the office tomorrow and go the official route rather than the personal. She still worked for Demille, after all, whose self-interest was best served by the merger going smoothly, and if he had to lean on that to get what he needed, he'd do so. He hated to play that card, but he wasn't being paid two hundred and fifty smackers an hour to not deliver results, and if Tasha couldn't get over that he wasn't interested, so be it.

Black lowered the convertible top and pointed the Cadillac at the freeway, feeling better as the wind blew through his hair, a long nap on the horizon before picking up Sylvia at eight.

At dinner, he told Sylvia about Hailey's odd state, in the hopes that she could offer some perspective.

"Maybe she's got some kind of personality disorder. Although, are you sure she wasn't high? Because that would be my first guess," Sylvia said.

"That's kind of what I thought, but I didn't get the stoned vibe from her. Then again, I have no idea what kids these days are taking, so what do I know? And for all the glamour, she's really just a fifteen-year-old girl, still adjusting to moving toward adulthood – and with a domineering mom from hell."

"That can't be easy. Especially if she's been performing since she was just a child. Sometimes I wonder what parents are thinking when they turn their kids into wish fulfillment tools for their own broken dreams. There should be laws against that sort of thing."

"Luckily that's not my problem. I just thought it was weird, and figured maybe you had some ideas I didn't."

"Sorry. Do you suspect her, though? A kid?"

"Not really, but my first rule is, you never know."

"That's a rule? Sounds more like a maxim."

"You're probably right. But the point is, I never assume anything, because I'm usually wrong, and I run the risk of coloring the data with my bias."

Sylvia reached across the table and took his hand. "I love it when you get all analytical on me."

"I was hoping we could stop by my place and you could watch me do algebra equations or something."

She raised her glass. "Keep pouring the red and miracles can happen, Black."

He smiled and toasted.

"Like I said, you never know."

Chapter 14

Black was whistling as he bounced down the apartment stairs in a lightweight herringbone suit paired with a black and white checker-patterned tie. A stiff breeze blew from the east, rustling the treetops as he neared his car and pushing dust clouds down the street. He sniffed at the air and confirmed his fears – the wind was unseasonably dry, which meant the possible resumption of the Santa Anas, and with them his allergies.

He stopped at the franchise coffee shop four blocks from his office and ordered a large drip for himself and a chai for Roxie, figuring that a little forethought might go a long way. The barista was new, barely up to the task, and Black decided not to spar with him, the young man's attitude lacking the requisite snide superiority that made Black's blood boil. He had no doubt that within a few days he'd be as dismissive and arrogant as a veteran, but Black would fight that battle when the situation warranted and not before.

He tried Tasha's cell as he waited in line for the cashier to ring him up, and it went to voice mail again. After leaving a message, he decided to give her an hour to get into the office and call him back, and if she didn't, he'd go on the offensive.

Next he called Demille, whose cell just rang and whose receptionist assured Black that he'd be in later and would certainly get all his messages – an empty promise he knew better than to take at face value. If Demille didn't call him back by noon, Black would show up unannounced and camp out in his lobby, with Daniel waiting on the other line. Let Demille explain to his new boss that he had better things to do than speak with his representative. A part of Black hoped he wouldn't get a call so that he could bring the hurt, but the adult portion of his brain wanted to question Demille with as little fanfare as possible. There was no evidence he was guilty of anything but blowing Black off, which might well have been because he simply found it annoying, or beneath his station, to have to talk to him. Be that as it may, today was the day he'd go to war with Demille unless he showed a serious attitude adjustment, and quick.

When he got to the office, Roxie was lying on the floor, her face inches from Mugsy's plump jowls, scolding him. Black watched her for a few moments before setting the chai on the coffee table.

"Should I get some popcorn and pull up a chair? This looks like it could be good."

"I could strangle him," Roxie fumed.

"Assuming you could find his neck. What did he do?"

"This," she said, standing and stomping over to her desk. She held up what looked like a sheaf of paperwork that had been put through a blender.

"Wow. Go, Mugsy, go. What is that?"

"My travel paperwork and immigration forms for Germany."

Black felt a surge of emotion he didn't recognize, and realized that it was pride in Mugsy's performance. He fought to keep his face a blank, sensing that even the slightest twitch would be correctly interpreted as unsupportive, and he didn't want to risk making Roxie any angrier than she already was. "Could be worse. It could be your chair. I know what that's like."

"Still. I mean, I was only gone for two minutes. What was he thinking?"

"I think he's just destructive. He doesn't think. He just eats, sleeps, and claws things to pieces." Black pretended surprise as he looked at the cup he'd placed on her desk. "Hey, look! What's that? Oh, nothing, just a tasty hot chai for Roxie. Courtesy of the best boss in the whole world."

She held up two fingers and pointed at her eyes, and then pointed at Mugsy. "I'm watching you, Mr. Mugs," she growled. Black stifled his natural urge to smile.

He continued as though he hadn't seen her warning to the bloated feline. "What's that? Chai, you say? 'Wow, boss, I love chai, and I especially love that you got it for me without being asked. How thoughtful. Really. I've completely misjudged you.'"

Roxie sat down hard and shook her head. "I guess it's not the end of the world. It'll just take more time to fill it all out again."

"Time which I'm confident you'll find somewhere in your busy workday."

She took a sip of the chai. "Thanks. Although it still doesn't make up for a big bonus."

"No, I suspect not. But it's not a bad way to start the day, especially when the porky wrecking ball's had his way with your visa application."

"I just don't understand him sometimes."

"Maybe he's trying to send you a message. I wonder what it could be? Oh, wait, I know. Maybe he doesn't want you to go to Germany?"

"I doubt that. It means shame on me for leaving important stuff where he can get to it when I'm not around."

"An equally plausible possibility, I'll grant you."

"So how did your interview go yesterday? Or do you think of them as interrogations?"

"Gentle questioning. Probing for the truth. As much art as science."

"Right. Did you learn anything?"

"Only that being a supermodel might kill brain cells."

"There's a newsflash."

Black told Roxie about Hailey. By the time he was done, Mugsy was snoring, the excitement of his morning too much.

"Sounds like she's whacked."

"That's the technical term?"

"Good as any. I mean, I don't have anything for you on that. I'd have to see it for myself, but if she's not on dope, maybe she should be."

"I know. I'm not sure it's relevant to the investigation anyway."

"Maybe not, but what if she's like that Bates character in Psycho? You know, pushed around the bend by controlling mom, so now she's got the butcher knife out?"

"Well, nobody's been stabbed…"

"Yet."

"I suppose it could be her behind this. But I doubt it. Call that a hunch."

"Yeah, because as I recall your hunches are so accurate."

"They've been described as laser-like."

"Maybe by the blind. I'd describe them as more flailing and off-base."

Black smiled. "Nice to see you back, Roxie. You had me worried with the whole scolding Mugsy thing. I don't think I've ever seen you do anything but tell him he's not fat. Which he is, by the way."

"No, he's not. He's just stocky."

"He's got his own gravitational field. Like a furry dwarf star."

"Did you need something?"

"No, I just thought I'd get in as much Roxie time as I could before you're gone for good."

She eyed him skeptically. "Why are you F-ing with me this morning?"

"Enjoy the chai," Black said, and stepped into his office before closing the door behind him, leaving Roxie bewildered, he was sure.

His coffee tasted all the richer for his interaction, and if she hadn't been there, he'd probably have kissed Mugsy's furry jowls for his fine work. He knew that celebrating Roxie's setback was childish, but he couldn't help it.

He tapped at his computer and went through his emails, and when an hour had gone by, called Tasha at the office. The receptionist was cautious, and Black figured she recognized his voice from the calls for Demille. She seemed surprised when he asked to speak with Tasha.

"I'm afraid she hasn't made it in yet."

"She's not answering her cell, either. I've been trying since yesterday. What time did she leave?"

"Leave?" The receptionist hesitated. "She didn't come in yesterday."

"She didn't? Is that unusual?"

"I don't discuss staff members' work schedules with strangers, sir," she said, which told Black that yes, it was most unusual.

"I'm pretty sure we won't be strangers much longer. If Demille doesn't return my call, I'll be camping out at your desk for the duration. That's a promise."

He hung up, tried Tasha's cell phone again, and got nothing but voice mail. Butterflies flitted in his stomach as he recalled how much she'd drunk. If she'd tried to drive, she might have gotten into an accident…

Black scanned the list of Demille's staff and found Tasha's name and home address. He jotted it down and walked out of his office. Roxie looked up at him from her screen, her customary disdain firmly in place.

"I'm going out. Tasha's not picking up."

"The Tasha who was being so helpful?"

"Exactly."

"You headed over to their office?"

"No, they haven't seen her. I'm thinking I'll stop by her place."

"I'll hold down the fort. If any clients show up with mail sacks full of money, I'll call you."

"I'd appreciate that. Try not to be too mad at Mugsy. He probably thought he could eat the paper."

"Oh, I'm already over that. It won't take too long to do it all over again now that I know what goes on the lines."

"That's the spirit."

The wind had kicked up and was blowing harder, the gusts moaning through the overhead power lines as he walked to his car, hand on his hat to keep it from sailing to Maui. Tasha's address was an easy twenty minutes from his office, and he told himself that he'd want someone to do the same thing he was about to do, in similar circumstances.

When he pulled up to the high-rise condo building, an ambulance and a police car were out front, and his heart sank. He found a space and killed the engine, dreading what he knew he would hear but forcing himself to the front entrance anyway. The doorman looked up at him when he entered, and he approached the reception counter with an officious air.

"I'm here about Tasha Pushkin."

The man's face fell. "The officers are upstairs with the techs."

Black nodded knowledgeably. "What happened?" he asked.

"We had a complaint. Water damage to the condo beneath hers. Apparently the overflow finally seeped through the floor early this morning. The owners called maintenance, and when they went in...she'd passed away a while before."

"All right. Which floor?"

"Seventh."

Black strode to the elevator. "Always a damned shame."

"She was a very sweet lady."

"I'm sure she'll be missed."

The elevator opened with a soft hiss and he stepped inside and stabbed the seven button. He was on thin ice, he knew, because impersonating a police officer was a felony, even if he hadn't explicitly claimed to be one. That area of law was a gray one, but under the circumstances, one he preferred not to test. He watched as the floor indicator blinked through its count and formulated a plan for approaching the cops. When the door slid open he stepped out, wearing a look of concern he didn't have to fake. At the end of the hall, one of the officers was talking to his partner, relaxed, enjoying the air conditioning while the techs went about their work.

"I just heard. Oh, my God. When did it happen?" Black exclaimed as he approached.

"Whoa, buddy. You can't go in there," the beefier of the pair warned, holding up a hand.

"Of course not. I just heard. It's…it's terrible. She was too young."

"And you are?"

"Oh, I'm sorry. One of the neighbors. She was always so sweet. How could this happen?"

"It's more common than you'd imagine. A slip in the shower, hit your head, bam, you're down. We see it all the time."

"At least she's at peace now," Black said. "It's just such a shame she was taken from us."

"Yeah, well, you have to move along. Just go home. There's nothing you or anyone can do for her now."

"I know you're right. I'm sorry. I'm just…I'm trying to process it all."

"Sorry, pal, but can you process somewhere else? Not to be rude or anything, but this is technically a crime scene…"

"Crime! Do you suspect foul play?"

"It's just a term. Now go home. We're done talking. Sorry for your loss, but you need to leave."

Black nodded, pretending to be speechless. On the way downstairs, he dialed Stan's cell number.

"Colt."

"Stan. Black. Got a favor."

"As long as it doesn't involve me getting out of my chair or lending you money, consider it done."

"I need you to get any info you can on a body at the following address." Black gave him Tasha's information.

"What's the deal on it?"

"Sounds like she slipped in the shower while drunk and hit her head. Probably bled to death. Can't have been pretty, if so, with warm water running on her for at least a day and a half…"

"Did a William Holden, huh? I'll see what I can find out."

"I'd appreciate it."

"What about our boy Ernest? You kind of went dark on me about him."

"Sorry, man. I've been snowed under with this latest assignment. But I haven't forgotten. I just need to clear the decks. I do think I've got a pretty decent idea for nailing him, though."

"Oh, yeah?"

"Yup. I actually got the idea from something on the web. An article I saw. But you'll probably have to shell out a few bucks to make it happen, and get some friendlies to play ball."

"What kind of money are we talking?"

"Less than a grand."

"And you think it will work?"

"If anything will." Black told him what he had in mind.

"Dude. That's genius. Really. And I know just the guys to help me out on this. They owe me a favor or two. It's perfect."

"Only if he's faking. Otherwise you'll be out a grand."

"Nah, no more than six hundred. I've got pull."

"I figured you might."

"When do you want to do this?"

"Figure after I get some of my other stuff settled. Let's talk in a few days, okay? Besides, for this to work, we need some pieces in place. I'll get you a list."

"If you weren't so ugly, I'd kiss you, my man."

"I'll consider myself lucky, then. Call me when you hear something on Tasha."

"Roger that, buddy."

Black hung up and descended the front steps, ignoring the doorman, which seemed in character for the role he'd assumed. When he reached his car he stopped, keys in hand, something tugging at the periphery of his awareness. Tasha made the third suspicious death from the agency in the space of six weeks. True, she wasn't a working model…but she was an integral part of the team, and had been one until only a few years ago. Was it possible that this was another killing, disguised as an accident? Or was that paranoia raising its ugly head?

The hot wind tugged at his suit and threatened to claim his hat as its prize. The arid gusts smelled of the peculiar combination of aromas he associated with the desert. He squinted, popped his door open and slid behind the wheel, thinking about how Tasha had gone from being a sexy, vital force of nature to a corpse, and a vision of himself, drunk out of his mind, sprang to mind. While his natural suspicion was alert for foul play, as accidents went it wasn't so far-fetched. All it took was one slip, one moment of carelessness, and game over. As the officer had said, it happened all the time.

He rolled away from the curb, lost in thought, a feeling that he'd cheated fate in his gut – like it could just as easily have been him going for his final ride in the coroner's van, the only variable an errant sliver of soap or a too-slick piece of marble. Black shivered in spite of the warm breeze and caught a glimpse of himself in the rear view mirror – his face had lost all its color, and a few telltale beads of sweat dotted his forehead below his hat. He drove especially carefully back to the office, more than aware of how precarious all of humanity's grip on life was, and how quickly it could all be over.

As it now was for Tasha.

Chapter 15

Roxie's voice called from her station as Black sat in his office, pushing paper from one end of his desk to the other.

"Line one. It's Gabriel Costa."

Black had called Gabriel the day prior, hoping to meet with him so he could grill him about his movements in Mexico. Now that he was on the line, Black realized that he hadn't really come up with a convincing reason for the man to accommodate him. Left with nothing but the truth, he decided to try the direct approach.

"Black."

"Mr. Black. Gabriel Costa returning your call." Costa's voice was silky smooth and refined. And something else. Worried?

"Yes, thank you, Mr. Costa. I appreciate it."

"How can I help you?"

"My firm is doing some diligence work on the Demille merger, and I was hoping you could take a few minutes to meet with me."

"What do I have to do with the Demille merger? We're competitors."

"Yes, but you worked with Demille for years, didn't you? First as a model, then as an agent?"

"Right…"

"I'm interviewing all of Demille's agents, present and former, for perspective."

"I don't see what you hope to learn…"

"I know, it all seems like a waste of time, but DNA's paying me quite a bit to do this, so I'm going through the motions. Come on, Mr. Costa. Help me out. I only need twenty minutes of your time. I promise."

Gabriel hesitated, and a heavy silence hung on the line. Black listened intently for any tells – a slight increase in breathing rate, a gasp, a tremor in Costa's voice.

"When did you have in mind? I have a very full schedule, Mr. Black."

"I understand. I'm available all afternoon. Whenever you have time, I can be at your office…"

"Today? Hmm. I don't have anything at 2:00. I can slip you in then, if you're here right on time."

"Thanks so much. I'll be there early. Again, I appreciate it."

"You have my address?"

"It's on your website."

"Oh, right. Okay then."

Black punched the line off and frowned. "Roxie. What's that stink?"

"What stink?"

"The odor like someone put dirty sweat socks in the microwave. That stink," he said, rising and moving to his door.

"Oh, you mean my lunch?" Roxie asked innocently as he stared her down. "It's from the deli down the street. Bratwurst and sauerkraut. They eat a lot of it in Germany."

"It smells like pickled ass."

"What is it with you and smells in the office lately?"

"You mean my complaining about that fat, flatulent eating machine? That's completely justified. Some days I come out of my office and I feel like I need a gas mask."

"Well, anyway, I answered your question. That odor is lunch."

"How can you eat that?"

"I'm getting the hang of it early. So I don't go into culture shock when I get there."

"That's admirable, Roxie, but you do know that rumor has it McDee's has discovered the good German people, right? As in, there are fast food places all over Berlin? I'm pretty sure I saw that on the web."

"I want to have an authentic experience."

"Which, assuming you mean eating stuff that smells like fermented garbage, you most certainly will. You just don't have to. More importantly, you especially don't have to in the office. It's unprofessional."

"But it would be okay if this was a sandwich?"

Black glanced at her, wary of a trick in the question. "I suppose…"

"But because it's German, it's unprofessional."

"No, Roxie, it's because it smells like an open grave in here. That's the unprofessional part."

"Why don't you go back into your office, and five minutes from now, it will be gone? Then we can all go back to getting along, okay?" Roxie suggested, her tone dangerously quiet. Black knew that tone.

"Fine. Only please don't bring your culinary experiments in anymore, all right? I know it's a long shot that anyone's going to show up, but if they did…"

"I got it, boss. But the longer you go on, the longer until I can eat lunch, which means the more this is going to stink up the office."

As always, Roxie's logic was unassailable.

When she was done, he returned to the front office carrying his hat and jacket. "I've got an appointment at 2:00 with Gabriel Costa. I'm going to grab a bite, see him, and then I'll probably be out the rest of the day. In case anyone calls."

She eyed him glumly and nodded. "That tasted pretty awful, by the way."

"I tried to warn you."

"I don't know how I'm going to survive if that's what the food's like. Seriously."

"You can always cut steaks off Mugsy. That should last you a good month, if you go for seconds."

"That's sick."

"I meant it figuratively." Mugsy, hearing his name, cracked one eye open and glared at Black. "Besides, I think all anyone does there is drink beer and smoke."

"You know I hate beer. And I don't smoke."

"Look on the bright side – you can always start."

"You want me to put your calls through to you? Assuming you get any? I mean, it's theoretically possible you could get one."

"That would be great, Roxie."

Lunch was a turkey sandwich – a small concession to the health consciousness Sylvia had been guilt-tripping him into recently – at the sandwich shop on the next block. He had a heaping mouthful when his phone warbled, and he groped for it in his pocket as he struggled to chew and swallow before the caller gave up.

"Black," he managed, the syllable sounding more like 'blech,' pronounced by a mush-mouth with a speech impediment.

"Black, this is Thomas Demille. You've left several messages for me?"

"Yes. We spoke in Mexico. Daniel wanted us to get together as soon as possible so I can get some background from you on the incidents that are plaguing this transaction."

"I remember. I have time today. At 2:00. Can you make it?"

Black cursed silently to himself. "I…I have an appointment at 2:00. Could we shoot for later?"

"I'm really snowed under. I'm afraid it's either 2:00 or it has to wait till the day after tomorrow."

"Why that long?"

"I've got an out-of-town engagement tomorrow. I'll be back the following day."

Black sighed. "Then it will have to wait. I can't cancel this, I'm afraid."

"Fair enough. Or you can just ask me your questions over the phone. I'm fine doing it that way."

Black wanted no part of that. He wanted to see Demille, read his body language, and watch for subtle signs of stress or dishonesty.

"No, let's just plan on doing it when you get back. It can wait."

"If you say so. I thought it was some kind of an emergency, from all the messages on my cell and at the office."

"Not an emergency. Just being the squeaky wheel."

"Well, then, let's take this up again in a few days. I'm available, but with an insane schedule. That's what I'm trying to convey."

Black was unconvinced when he disconnected, but decided to make the best of a bad situation by letting Daniel know that he was still being blown off, albeit in a less obvious way. When Daniel came on the line, he was obviously dealing with more than one thing at once – Black could hear people talking in the background.

"Hello."

"Black here. I just spoke with Demille and he can't see me for another couple of days. He said he'd be out of town tomorrow and is full up today," Black said, stretching the truth just a bit – in Demille's defense, he had been available at 2:00.

"I know. I just got his schedule in. He's got a big shoot in Vegas tomorrow morning, early. I was going to call you. I want you there."

"In Las Vegas? Why?"

"I can't go, and all my people are busy. Do the same as you did in Mexico – keep your eyes open, and watch for any threats to the models."

"Part of the problem is that the danger's never been overt. I didn't see anything in Cabo that would have led me to believe there would be a dead model the next morning. I'm not sure my time's well spent hanging out at a photo shoot."

Black heard rustling, like a hand being held over the speaker of a phone, and more talking, and then Daniel came back on the line. "Black, I don't have a lot of time. Gunther will send the details of the shoot. You're on the clock, and the merger is done in the next couple of weeks, so play along, will you? I'll feel better if I know you're there. And it'll enable you to watch Demille in action and have your chat with him."

"Fine. Shoot me the info and I'll see what flights look like."

"Will do. I'll have Gunther call Demille and tell him to make time for you tomorrow, one way or another, and also arrange for you to have complete access to the location. It's at one of the big casinos."

"Anything special I need to know about it?"

"Gunther will send everything we have on it."

The rest of the sandwich tasted like lead, each bite a struggle to get down. He'd made dinner plans with Sylvia, which he'd have to cancel. He considered calling her, but decided to wait until he had a firm agenda. Instead he called Roxie.

"Black Investigations," she answered, sounding as unenthusiastic as he'd ever heard.

"Roxie, it's me. I need you to look at flights to Vegas tonight. The later the better."

"You adding gambling to your list of vices?"

"No, it's for the Demille case."

"When do you want the return?"

"Just look at one-way."

"Wow. A one-way ticket to sin city. You aren't planning on doing a Nick Cage, are you? A little Leaving Las Vegas?"

"I think in the movie he drove, didn't he?"

"I don't know. I think that was made when I was, like, ten. My mom wouldn't let me watch that kind of thing."

"Just as well. It was pretty depressing."

"But if the shoe fits…"

"Send me an email with my options, okay?"

"Sure thing, Bwana."

The wind had picked up to a sustained twenty miles per hour by the time he walked back to his car, and his eyes were already beginning to burn from the dust and pollen. He checked the time and saw that he had forty-five minutes to get to Gabriel's.

Halfway to Santa Monica he checked his email on his phone and saw one message from Roxie. He opened it and his shoulders slumped as he read. All flights were sold out – there was a major electronics trade show in town for four days, so it would border on impossible to fly in. Which left driving – four hours, best case, and likely far more if others like himself decided to make it to Vegas the hard way.

Gabriel's building was a two-story art deco affair that would have been perfectly at home in South Beach, all jutting edges and graceful arcs rendered in lime and peach and pastels that positively screamed avant-garde. A row of meticulously groomed palm trees swayed in front, their fronds flapping like the wings of a giant bird in the stiff breeze as Black strode up the sidewalk toward a glass portico.

Gabriel's office was on the second floor, and when he entered the lobby he was struck by how small it was compared to the other agencies he'd been in – the entire suite could have easily fit in DNA's foyer. A reed-thin young man with an aggressively modern hair style and ferret-like darting eyes greeted him with a disapproving purse of the lips.

"Yes?" he asked, as though Black had disrupted something important in which he'd been immersed.

"I'm here to see Gabriel Costa."

"And you are…?"

"Black."

One cocked eyebrow signaled his curiosity. He spoke in a low voice into his headset, the fabric of his pale blue shirt shimmering in the bright overhead lights, and then sat back and fixed Black with a bored stare.

"Mr. Costa will be right with you. Please have a seat."

So far this wasn't starting out well, Black thought as he settled on a tan leather couch that was every bit as uncomfortable as it looked. Two minutes later Gabriel emerged from one of the office doors and approached, wearing a silk shirt with all the colors of the rainbow represented and a pair of distressed oversized jeans that would have been at home on a coal miner.

"Mr. Black? Right this way. You look familiar…"

"I think I saw you in Mexico. Cabo. At the dinner."

"Oh, right. You were at the Demille table."

"That's correct. Good memory."

Gabriel led him into a small conference room. He took a seat at the head of the table and folded his hands in front of him, an earnest expression on his handsome face. Black had to admit that Gabriel was a stunningly good-looking man – the kind that women swooned over and sculptors carved statues to commemorate – as different from Black as an alien species. Thick dark hair hung carelessly over tanned features that were perfectly symmetrical, and he exuded an aura of exotic mystery that must have made him a fortune in his modeling days.

"Well, here we are. What can I do for you?" he asked, his eyes belying the calm demeanor he was studiously projecting. They were anxious, Black thought.

"Thanks for seeing me. As I told you, I'm trying to get some background on Demille's agency for DNA, and as a part of my due diligence I'm speaking with everyone I can find – both current employees and alumni. I've found that former colleagues tend to be more willing to spill the dirt than current ones, which is why I'm here."

"Makes sense. I'm just not sure I have that much dirt to spread. But I'll do my best to keep it interesting," Gabriel responded with an easy grin – but again, his eyes were edgy, if only slightly. Maybe he just wasn't good at meeting people?

"How long were you with Demille's agency?"

"Oh, let's see. Eight years as talent, and one as an agent."

"Who were you with before that?"

"One of the big New York houses."

"Why leave them?"

"I relocated to the west coast and wanted something more specialized. Demille offered that local flavor I was after. It was a good fit."

"I'm glad to hear it. Then as your career wound down, you decided to give the agent game a shot?"

Gabriel nodded. "That's right. I sort of knew all the players by then, and it was a natural segue for me from modeling to artist representation."

"How did you do?"

"Pretty well. I like it a lot, which helps."

"But you left and started your own agency…what, about six months ago?"

"Has it been that long? Wow. Yes, that sounds right."

"And by all accounts you've been fabulously successful."

"Well, I'm not sure I'd describe it quite that way. I've been very fortunate so far. Clients are happy, and I've been able to attract some quality talent."

"I'll say. You've got three of Demille's former models, right?"

Gabriel shrugged. "Sure. I know everyone over there. It makes sense that I'd get some of them. Especially with the merger coming up."

"Of course. That has to have everyone a little nervous."

"Some, at least."

"How long has it been public knowledge?"

"Oh, at least ninety days."

Black smiled his *aw, shucks* grin. "When did you first hear about it?"

Gabriel's eyes darted to the side. "I…I don't know. Probably around then."

"But it worked out well for you in terms of recruiting, didn't it?"

"I'm not sure what you're getting at."

"Just that it hasn't hurt your artist roster, that's all. I don't mean anything by it. I don't really know much about this industry, so this is all educational for me."

Gabriel seemed to relax now that Black had assured him that he was basically an idiot. A transparent tactic, to be sure, but one that usually worked on those who wanted to believe that they held the upper hand. Black took him through a list of industry-related questions, which Gabriel answered without hesitation, and then steered the discussion to his real agenda.

"What a shame about those models, huh?" Black asked, shaking his head.

"Those models?"

"Oh, like that gorgeous creature in Mexico. What was her name? Clarissa?"

"Ah, yes. A real tragedy. She had a promising career. Really starting to make waves."

"Did you know her well?"

Gabriel hesitated for a split second, but it was enough of a tell for Black to register. "Sure. We'd done shoots together. But she wasn't my talent when I was at Demille's. I didn't rep her."

"Did anyone have any idea she was using? She didn't look like a junkie to me."

"It had been a while since I'd seen her. A lot can happen in a few months, you know?"

"Sure. It's all a whirlwind, I'll bet. Exotic locales, jetting away at a moment's notice, big money...What about the other one – Daria? Did you know her?"

Gabriel started to rub his thumb against the tip of his forefinger, unconsciously – a nervous habit he seemed unaware of. "She was another rising star. Another tragedy. Nobody saw that coming."

Black shifted gears abruptly. "Were you at the beach shoot where the girl got the acid peel?"

Gabriel blinked, surprised by the question. "What?"

"The model who had acid in her makeup. Were you there?"

"I...I don't remember. What does that have to do with anything?" Gabriel stammered, his polished veneer cracking slightly.

"I was just curious. Think. Were you?"

"I told you I don't remember." His tone was now hostile, but only slightly. More...frightened.

"Would it surprise you to know that I have a list of everyone who was at the shoot, and that you were? I'd have thought that would have been sort of like, where were you when the World Trade Center got hit, in your business...something you'd remember. Everyone else said it was a big deal."

"Now that you mention it, I might have been. But I think I left before anything happened. That's probably why I blanked on it. I wasn't around when the screaming started."

"I see. Kind of like Mexico, right? You left early that morning...before anyone else, didn't you?"

The speed of the finger rubbing increased. "I had a plane to catch. What are you getting at with this, Mr. Black?"

"Nothing. Sorry if it's a sensitive subject. I just thought it was worth noting that you were at both shoots. Tell me, were you in New York when Daria...decided to end it all?"

Gabriel pushed back from the table, clearly rattled, and stood. "Why don't you look at your list?"

Black was unfazed, still sitting. "I did. You weren't at the shoot. But that wasn't what I asked. I asked whether you were in New York, not at the shoot in New York."

"Mr. Black, I'm afraid I've taken all the time I can to help you with your questions. I hope it's proved enlightening. But I have other, pressing matters I need to get to, so if you'll excuse me…"

"Did you hear about Tasha?"

Rapid blinking. "Tasha?"

"Your old colleague at Demille's. Is Tasha that common a name in L.A.?"

"What about her?"

Gabriel's face was unreadable. Black wanted to nail him to the wall with some serious questions about where he'd been the night of her death, but instead stood, deciding not to press. He'd seen what he needed to see. Instead, he offered Gabriel his hand to shake. Gabriel reluctantly grasped it, and Black felt moisture – his hands were sweating. "Sorry about that last bit – I see conspiracies and connections everywhere. Professional hazard. I didn't mean to imply anything by it."

Gabriel regarded him distrustfully. "You come on pretty strong."

"Like I said, goes with my line of work. Mr. Costa, I appreciate the time. I know you didn't have to meet with me."

"No problem." He glanced at his watch. "But now, I really have to get going…can you find your own way out?"

"Sure. Thanks again."

Black walked slowly to the lobby, intrigued by Gabriel's discomfiture. He was obviously hiding something, and visibly nervous. That didn't mean he was the killer, but it certainly made Black more curious about his affairs. He took the stairs carefully, lost in thought, and when he reached the ground floor, he stopped just inside the doors and retrieved his phone. Roxie took four rings to answer.

"I just finished with Costa. Something's off with him. I don't know what, but he was as twitchy as a crackhead. Do me a favor – pull everything you can on his company, his holdings, his credit, everything."

"Can you be more specific?"

"If I could, I'd know what I was looking for, wouldn't I?" Black snapped.

"Ouch. Sounds like he got under your skin, boss."

Black took a deep breath. "Yeah, sorry. Just peel the onion on him, would you? Corporate filings, the whole bit. Something stinks in Santa Monica."

"That's just the beach. All the sewage washing up. And the used needles."

"I'll cross going for long walks there off my Match profile, then."

"Depends on what you're looking for. Some girls like the whole fecal clumps and syringes thing. Some guys, too."

"Thankfully I'm spoken for."

"If you say so. How soon do you need this?"

"Stat."

"Have you been watching *ER* reruns again?"

"No. *Scrubs.* Better songs."

"You really need to get out more."

"What's the deal with the Vegas flights? You're seriously telling me that there's nothing? How can that be?"

"Well, let's see. Last minute, biggest trade show of the year going on, reduced routes…I'd say you're screwed. Why not try one of the Indian casinos? You can probably put it all on red there, and I hear the drinks aren't too watered."

"I told you. I have to get there for a shoot."

"Right. Well, I'd start driving, because you aren't going to be flying."

"You don't think it's worth trying standby?"

"Oh, you mean where you wait at the airport for the five or six hours it would take you to drive there, worst case?"

"I just hate that road. Especially after dark."

"Then you better get moving. You've got about five hours before nightfall."

Black watched the page of a newspaper sail down the street like a ghost bound for the sea. The gap between the two doors whistled at him. He hung up and pushed through, making his way to his car, the wind tearing at his suit like an angry ex, his eyes stinging from windborne grit. He climbed into the Cadillac and sat for a moment, staring at his reflection with watery eyes, and resolved to make the best of a lousy situation – at least he could bill for his travel time. Viewed that way, five or six hours of driving came out to fifteen hundred bucks each way – not a bad return on his investment.

He drove to his apartment to grab his overnight bag and called Sylvia on the way, apologizing profusely for having to cancel their dinner plans, which she'd been looking forward to – he'd gotten them at one of the hot new restaurants on the Hollywood border she'd been bugging him about, and had to book them two days in advance.

"They just called out of the blue and told you to go to Las Vegas?" she asked.

"Yup. No notice. No warning. But I don't have a choice. They really want me there."

"And you can't fly out late tonight or first thing in the morning?"

He explained the flight situation. She didn't seem impressed.

"How long are you going to be gone?"

"I should be back tomorrow night. Or the next day, at the latest. Depends on how long the shoot goes. And of course, there's travel time. I lose half a day each way…"

Sylvia was understanding, but Black sensed she wasn't happy. He'd gone from being relatively dependable to leaving her on a moment's notice, and she probably couldn't help but wonder whether his enthusiasm for the assignments didn't have something to do with being around some of the most beautiful women in the world. Over their last dinner that had come up – she'd had numerous questions about the Cabo shoot, most of which centered on the models: what they were like, what they wore on their off hours. He supposed that if she had suddenly started working with endless phalanxes of super-hot men and cancelling their plans together at every turn, he would have had second thoughts about it, too. Although for once in his life, he was pure of heart and mind, having not even been tempted by Tasha, who'd made it about as clear as possible that she was up for anything.

None of which put him in a very good mood. He peered at his gas gauge and made a mental note to fill up before hitting the freeway east, and then had a depressing thought. He called Roxie back.

"What. Already miss my unique charm?" she asked, deadpan.

"Can you look for hotels for tonight? It just dawned on me that they could be sold out, too."

"I wasn't going to bum you out, but I already did. You're hosed."

"Nothing?"

"Even the crappy ones. And I do mean crappy."

"So what am I supposed to do? Did you look at Henderson?"

"Yup. Nada. Nothing. Zilch."

Black groaned inwardly. Or so he thought.

"You're groaning again," she said.

"Oh. I thought I was using my inside voice."

"Nope. Long groan."

"Noted."

"What's your plan?"

"I guess I'll drive there and look around in person. There has to be someplace with a vacancy."

"Good luck. Sounds like you're going to be sitting up at the blackjack table all night. Wanna bet ten bucks you start smoking again?"

"Thanks for all the positive vibes, Roxie."

"I live to pump you up, boss. Call me anytime. Except tonight. I've got a show. I'm leaving early for sound check."

"Won't that cut into your doing a bunch of personal errands on company time?"

"Nah. Sounds like I'll have all day tomorrow to do them while you're hung over in Vegas."

"I think you've got a really twisted idea of what I'm going to be doing there."

"Ten says you smoke again."

"I'm not going to bet you on something like that."

"Figures."

"Will you at least do the background work on Costa?"

"I'm already on it. You'll have it when I have something."

"Any idea how long it will take?"

"Two hours, twenty-seven minutes, eighteen seconds."

Black groaned again.

"You're groaning again."

"I know. This time I meant to."

"Uh huh."

"So you don't know how long it will take?"

"Good guess. Think of this as a chance to work on your Zen-like patience."

"I don't have much Zen at the moment."

"I got that. Have a nice night, boss. Remember that not all the ladies in the bars there are nice girls."

"Thanks. I'll remember that."

"In fact, not all the girls are even girls."

"Even better."

Chapter 16

An endless procession of tail lights, strings of glowing red fireflies in the night, crept over the final pass before Nevada. As Black had feared, the trip had taken forever. The road was clogged with vehicles, and the occasional accident or breakdown caused bottlenecks that slowed traffic in either direction for miles. He glanced at his fuel, which was reading only a few scant notches above empty, and resolved to pull over at the state line – as bizarre a place as ever existed with its garish neon glow lighting the sky from afar and its tawdry carnival atmosphere.

He had his window down. The cool high desert air felt good after hours battling the hot Santa Anas as he made his way east, the winds in some areas so powerful that tractor trailers had chosen to pull off the road and wait them out rather than risk being blown out of control. The radio had said that in the mountain passes gusts were topping ninety miles per hour, carrying the effective wallop of a category two hurricane minus the rain.

Now, at 9:20, he was only an hour out of Vegas, with any luck at all. He pulled off at Primm, with its freakish roller coaster blinking at the moon, a faux castle on one side of the freeway, an Old West-themed monolith on the other, and was struck by the incredibly bad taste on display. Primm seemed to want to up the ante on cheesy, raise the bar on gauche, and it did so unapologetically, with all of the dignity of an aging streetwalker in too-tight fluorescent yellow leopard-patterned spandex hot pants, and about as much class.

He coasted to a stop at one of the open gas pumps and shut off his engine. His back stiff from sitting for hours, it was a relief to step out to pre-pay for fuel. On the next island over, a low-rider muscle car rumbled with a group of tough youths with shaved heads leaning against the fenders, scowling at the patrons as though daring them to fight. Angry rap music shouted from oversized speakers, vibrating the entire car with pulsing bass beats like distant bombs detonating. Black did his best to ignore them, and breathed a sigh of relief when they pulled away, their California plates the tip-off that they'd come from East L.A. or thereabouts to raise some serious hell on the strip that evening.

Ninety dollars later, he eased back onto the highway, wondering at the density of cars even at that hour, and pointed his hood east at where Las Vegas lit the horizon, easily visible from space, a flare fueled by vice that was a bright tribute to man's ingenuity and avarice.

As he pulled over the final hill and began his descent into town, a garishly lit billboard with a stadium-sized display flashed a familiar figure wiggling across a stage, dancers surrounding her. A name he knew like his own blinked at him like a taunt: Nina, his ex-wife, would be appearing at one of the largest venues in town for a limited set of engagements. If it was possible to feel any more dislike for the city, he managed, and choked down a bitter taste as his tires rumbled over the pavement.

Once on the strip, he sought out the hotel where the shoot would take place the following morning at 6:00, and wasn't surprised when the front desk told him the establishment was regrettably full. He asked for some tips on nearby hotels that might have vacancies and disliked the smirk the clerk gave his associate before turning back to Black and politely declining to offer any guidance.

Three hours later, after a tepid buffet dinner and an hour of driving around to increasingly distant and seedy establishments, it was obvious to Black that he'd badly misjudged the lodging supply equation. From what he could tell, he'd either have to drive back to Primm or Pahrump and hope there were rooms available, or sleep in his car – a prospect with exactly zero appeal to him as the temperature dropped, not to mention the likelihood of being rousted by security anyway. It was now midnight, and the shoot would begin in just a few hours – and suddenly Roxie's prediction about him spending the night at a casino table didn't seem that far off. He was tired from the drive, but figured that with ample coffee he could probably make it through to tomorrow, or rather today. He'd just have to limit himself to non-alcoholic beverages. Mostly.

Black parked in the mammoth lot and walked to the towering casino complex two football fields away, whose lights consumed enough electricity to power a Central American dictatorship with kilowatts to spare. He nodded at the doorman, dressed in garb that would have been a sensation at any Renaissance faire, who looked about as happy to be up as Black was. Inside, the casino hummed with activity as bells rang, sirens keened, chimes

126

trilled, jackpots blared, or at least that's how it sounded until Black realized that much of the cacophony was coming from overhead speakers, artfully placed to create the illusion of activity even with few people on the floor.

Black moved to the restroom and splashed water on his face, his eyes red from strain and allergies. An old man wearing a cardigan the color of moss and trousers so worn from casino chairs the seat was shiny brushed by him on the way to a stall.

"Bitch will steal it all, son. She's got no bottom to her well, boy. No bottom. Get out while you can," he croaked in a voice seasoned by decades of cigarettes and hard liquor. Black nodded, wondering what the appropriate response to that declaration was, but decided it didn't matter as the man slammed the metal door closed with a groan all too familiar to Black's ear. He dried his face and beat a hasty retreat, leaving his new friend to his penitence.

A scantily clad cocktail waitress who looked like she could have taken Black in three rounds approached as he sat at one of the slot machines and asked him what he was drinking. The best of intentions gave way to familiarity, and he ordered a Jack and Coke, rationalizing that the caffeine would offset the effects of the alcohol and help him stay awake. As he waited for his drink, he fed five bucks into the machine and had lost all but fifty cents of it by the time she returned three minutes later. He tipped her a dollar, earning a courtesy smile, and he returned his gaze to the machine, whose blinking lights dared him to show it who was boss. Two more spins and he was cleaned out, his appetite for chance sated. The bourbon tasted cheap and watery, which was about what he expected for the price.

He rose and wandered around the casino until he came to a cordoned-off section near the rear exit. A bored security guard leaned against one of the posts to ensure that the area remained unoccupied. A system of railings was suspended from tall iron scaffolding the likes of which Black was familiar with from rock concerts, and steel cables hung from above like ferrous spaghetti in the dim light. Black approached the man and stifled a yawn.

"This where the shoot's at this morning?"

"What's it to you?" the man replied.

"I'm with the crew."

"Then you'd know, wouldn't you?"

Apparently Vegas wasn't the place to come if you were hoping for a warm welcome. Black moved off toward the exit and walked outside, placing his drink by a slot machine near the doors. Two large trailers had been positioned nearby and four semi-rigs hulked next to them, no doubt to accommodate the scaffolding and lights. Black slid his phone from his suit pocket to check his messages, and confirmed that Gunther had sent instructions on the point person to contact – his old friend Jeanie from Cabo again, he was relieved to see. At least he'd recognize her, sparing him the need to guess whom to talk to in order to get a security badge.

As the hours dragged by, one drink led to another. By 3:00 he was feeling that strange sleepless sense of being both tipsy from the booze and jittery from the Coke. His better judgment finally kicked in as he went in search of the inevitable 24-hour diner somewhere in the far reaches of the casino, where he would be surrounded by kindred spirits who'd lost everything and were hell-bent on winning it back before they had to go to work or home to explain what had happened to the rent.

The restaurant was everything he'd imagined and more, having spent enough time at its twins around town on prior pilgrimages to practically know the layout of the menu by heart. Large breakfasts featuring slabs of tough steak or rubbery ham graced the photos at the tops of the pages with prices in kitschy starbursts, as though nothing went better with booze and cigarettes and imminent destitution than a farmhand breakfast with extra everything. A woman on the wrong side of a hard forty, whose makeup had the brittle sheen of polished plaster, wearing a Hollywood rendition of a fifties diner uniform, took his order – a number three, which euphemistically called for "flapjacks" instead of pancakes and "spuds" instead of hash browns, crowned with "three pigs," which he presumed to be sausages or bacon but was afraid to inquire about.

After woodenly shoveling heaping mouthfuls of congealed carbs slathered in sugar into his maw he felt somewhat better, and on his third cup of strong black coffee he believed he might make it after all. He toyed with the idea of taking a nap in his car – or even less appealing, locked in one of the bathroom stalls – but dismissed it. With his luck, he'd sleep through the shoot or be jostled by hotel security in the bathroom just as he finally nodded off, his legs going quietly numb. Instead, he elected to play a hundred dollars at the two-dollar blackjack table, practically fulfilling

Roxie's prophecy, only needing a cigarette dangling from his mouth to finish the tableau.

He was up sixty dollars when he saw Jeanie making her way from the hotel entrance to the staging area. Nodding to the dealer, he cashed in his chips and followed her over.

"Morning, Jeanie. Long time no see," he said, smiling in what he hoped was an engaging manner.

"Mr. Black. I got a message to expect you. I see you take your work seriously. Five o'clock and on deck. I'm impressed."

"Early bird gets wormed," he said.

"Right. Come on back to the trailer. The badges are inside. Makeup and wardrobe will be there in ten minutes, and the girls a few minutes after them. We're supposed to start shooting at 6:15, and as usual, it's my job to make sure we make it."

"Lead the way."

"Catering will be here at 5:30 if you want coffee or breakfast," she called out over her shoulder, already moving at a good clip toward the exit. "When did you get in?"

"Last night."

"You're lucky you got a room. Town's ugly right now."

"I'm always lucky in Vegas."

Two women were already waiting by one of the trailers when they walked outside, and Jeanie greeted them as she unlocked the door. "This is makeup. Wardrobe's the other trailer. Dressing rooms, outfits. Off limits to men, though. This is a female-only area."

"Good to know. How long have you been here?"

"Since yesterday. We had to get everything erected and do a rehearsal with the models. We needed to make sure it all worked and they understood the drill."

"What's with the cables?"

"Oh, we're doing an angels and demons theme. The girls will be hanging over the casino machines and tables. Very high concept."

"Who dreams this…stuff…up?"

"I know. They get paid a lot of money to storyboard this. Talk about a great job."

"How long will the shoot take?"

"Three hours, tops. Then we have to start breaking it all down again. You don't want to know what this place costs per day to close off. Seriously expensive."

"I can only imagine."

Black got his badge as sleepy models began arriving for their hair teasing and primping.

"How many on this shoot?" he asked as he clipped it to his lapel.

"Models? Nine. All told? Thirty-something. Photographer, crew, makeup, wardrobe, technical…"

"So another big production."

"Not huge by any means. We had double that in Cabo. But for one company, yes."

"So this is all Demille's talent?"

"Yup. He's got a strong relationship with the client, and he's done their last two campaigns."

"What do they sell?"

Jeanie smiled. "Does it matter?"

Black laughed. "I guess not that much."

"The girls will be scantily dressed angels and demons. The shoot's after sexy fun with a sense of humor. Wry, the creative director called it. So we'll have half-naked women suspended from the ceiling to create a 'wry' effect. With a price tag that could buy a house in Bel Air."

"Be glad they didn't ask for irony or whimsy."

Jeanie winked. "That's next year."

Black got coffee, watched the new arrivals, and recognized Hailey with the ever-present Trish by her side. Trish spotted him a moment later, and nodded in his direction as they brushed by. Hailey looked very much like a groggy fifteen-year-old roused from sleep too early, and a small part of him felt pity for her. He wondered what she made for a shoot like this, and decided it must be a lot. Not movie or TV star a lot, but still, a lot. Certainly more than most teenagers made unless they were drug dealers or pop stars.

A technician fiddled with the towers and double-checked fittings, and the crew foreman climbed up and inspected the suspension mechanisms, checklist in hand. Four uniformed Las Vegas police showed up just before 6:00, which Black suspected was the result of some sort of a union rule, as was the presence of most of the heavyset riggers standing around doing little but drinking free coffee and wolfing down breakfast pastries, paid a king's ransom to carry the gear from the trucks into the casino and set up the scaffolding.

A thin black man wearing a prominent rapper's tour jacket and a ski cap took up position by a DJ station and twisted knobs, and a hip-hop beat began pounding from two stacks of speakers on either side of the restricted area. A small crowd of spectators had gathered along the perimeter as the crew had gone about its errands, and Black saw Demille's distinctive profile outside the exit door, speaking with a lanky surfer type with long hair and a two-week-old growth of beard. Jeanie walked by and he stopped her.

"Who's that with Demille?" he asked.

"Aston. The photographer."

Demille entered with the photographer and the DJ increased the volume. Then Aston took control and began issuing instructions to his helpers, who ferreted in nearby road cases and held up cameras for his approval. Black edged nearer to Demille as the first models appeared in the doorway, robes over their outfits, followed by wardrobe personnel who fussed over them like mother hens. Hailey was among the first group, and Black offered a wave. She stared straight at him and then looked away, no sign of recognition in her dull eyes, completely at odds with the girl in the photos and on the beach, who had seemed larger than life – a presence.

Aston directed the models to their positions and they shed their robes. A small man with heavy black spectacles and a black turtleneck sweater connected the cables to each of their harness clips fitted beneath their lingerie, and gave the rig a strong pull before nodding and moving to the next model. On Aston's signal, winches whined, and the first three models rose into the air, suspended twenty-five feet over the gaming equipment. A fussy heavyset woman with a headset quickly guided a dozen tuxedo-clad male models to the tables, where they took up position, appearing to be gambling as the girls hovered overhead.

"Won't they see the cables in the photos?" Black asked Jeanie.

"They'll remove them in touch up. Photoshop. Makes it all much easier these days."

"Ah."

"Same for bags, wrinkles, augmenting cleavage, adding contour…"

"Who knew?"

Aston directed the scene with the confidence of a master, moving among the gamblers to get the shots he wanted. This was the demons round, the girls wearing horns, their makeup accentuated, and Black mused that maybe hell wasn't such a bad place to be, if there was any accuracy at all to the depiction. He watched for a few minutes and sidled up to Demille, who didn't seem to register his presence until he was alongside.

Demille turned his head toward Black. "So, Mr. Black. We meet again."

"Yes. Daniel asked me to stop by."

"I know. I've been instructed to submit to your interrogation."

"I'm not sure I'd call it that. Friendly questions, nothing more."

"You've gone to a lot of trouble to ask some questions."

"You'll find I'm nothing if not persistent."

"I'll grant you that. Let's get together after the shoot. We should be done by 9:00."

"Plan on it."

Trish approached them and Black sensed Demille's body stiffen. Black didn't know why there might be friction there, but it was unmistakable. She stood next to Demille to watch the shoot, and seemed to be working up the courage to say something to him.

Gasps suddenly arose from the crowd as a snarling figure barreled at Demille. Two of the police rushed to restrain the assailant as a security guard moved to stop him.

The man was yelling almost incoherently. "You miserable bastard. You think you're so much better than–"

His diatribe was cut off as the guard got his arm around his neck and choked him. Black stepped back as the assailant swung at Demille, who dodged most of the blow. Black heard the sound of skin striking skin, and recognized the attacker even as the first cop reached them and brought his billy club down on Zane's shoulder. Zane fell forward, a dazed expression on his face, and Black smelled the sour stench of hard liquor as Zane clutched at him for support.

"Zane! What the hell do you think you're doing?" Demille exclaimed, holding his jaw, blood trickling from the corner of his mouth.

Zane glared hate at Trish with bloodshot eyes as she backed away, and returned his focus to Demille.

"You miserable piece of shit. You ruined my life. I'll kill–"

The second cop had arrived, and cut Zane's threat off with a burst from his Taser. Zane's legs buckled beneath him, and he fell to the floor quivering as the voltage short-circuited his nervous system. Everything around them had stopped, and for a moment that lasted a year Black saw the tuxedoed faux gamblers frozen in a montage of slicked-back hair and perfect jawlines, the female demons suspended overhead with shocked looks on their faces, 50 Cent blaring from the speakers as the bystanders watched in horrified fascination.

And then everything seemed to accelerate to real time again. The other two police officers arrived, cuffed Zane, hauled him to his feet, and dragged him to the exit and the waiting squad cars. Jeanie rushed to Demille with a tissue in hand and dabbed at his lip. He pushed her away gently, and after probing his jaw for tenderness, shook his head.

"Do me a favor and get some ice for the swelling. It's not bad. He mostly missed me," he said.

"Are you sure?"

"Just get it. Let's not make this a big deal. It's over. And we have a shoot to finish." Demille clapped, summoning his group's attention. "Everyone. Don't worry. It's nothing. A drunk. I'm fine. Carry on. We've still got two more groups to go before we're done."

Aston gave him a long look, and then nodded and called out to the assembly. "Come on, everybody, focus. Time's wasting. Let's do this!"

The DJ cranked the music again and Aston went back to work, the incident seemingly forgotten as the overhead slings moved the models over different sections of the playing tables in response to Aston's instructions.

Jeanie returned with a plastic bag holding some ice, and Demille held it to his cheek, watching the shoot.

"That wasn't just any drunk. That was Zane," Black said softly.

"As far as I'm concerned, it was just any drunk. He's nobody. An angry kid who can't hold his liquor."

"I wonder what he was doing here?"

"It's a free country. He probably heard from one of his old modeling buds that there was a shoot. Got wasted, as usual, and decided to set me straight. He's got a real problem with alcohol and drugs. As you saw firsthand. Maybe a few nights in jail will straighten him out. It's not my problem anymore."

"I'd say it's safe to say he blames you for his problems."

"Drunks and addicts always blame someone other than themselves. They're always victims."

The first inning of the shoot drew to a close as Hailey and the other two models were lowered from their lofty positions nearly three stories above the casino floor, and everyone took a breather as the next group got into position. Aston called a five-minute break, and Demille excused himself to go check on his condition in the men's room. The ice had arrested the swelling, as far as Black could see, and Demille wouldn't suffer any ill effects – Black had been hit more solidly by angry girlfriends.

Black got another cup of steaming coffee from the breakfast bar near the exit and watched the spectators ebb and flow as their early morning interest waned and they moved off to other pursuits. Demille emerged from the bathroom and moved to rejoin him, but paused when he saw an unexpected familiar face – Gabriel Costa, outside the glass doors, talking to Hailey and Trish. Black tried to think of any good reason Costa might have for being at an out-of-town, exclusively Demille shoot, and nothing came to mind. Except...

"What the hell?" Demille exclaimed as he stormed through the exit, and Black realized that Costa hadn't been invited. A new set of models entered and proceeded to the cables as the DJ began playing some old school Snoop Dog and Dr. Dre, and Demille elbowed through the doors to confront Costa.

"What are you doing on my shoot?" Demille shouted, obviously furious, Black could tell, even from his vantage point inside.

"Tom. Please. Let's not create a scene," Gabriel said, his voice calm.

"Too late. Start talking."

"Mr. Demille, Gabriel's here because we asked him to come," Trish began, her voice steady. "We've been meaning to talk to you, but you're always so busy..."

"Talk to me about what?" Demille spat.

"Hailey and I have discussed things, and we're not comfortable re-signing with the Demille agency now that it's going to be sold to DNA. We've decided to go with Gabriel's firm after her contract runs out...after the next shoot in Tahoe. I'm sorry. I really am," Trish announced.

Demille was seething. "What? How dare you. I discovered Hailey. I've invested a fortune in making her a star."

"Which we appreciate, and you've certainly done well representing her. But things have changed, and we're not comfortable with a large outfit like DNA. It's nothing personal..."

Demille was glaring at Gabriel. "Gabriel. How could you? Poaching my talent at my shoot. Does it get any lower?"

Gabriel shrugged. "It's just business, Tom. I was going to touch base with you to talk it over. But then Trish called and suggested I come out and finalize everything–"

A scream and a crash interrupted the tussle. Black spun to where the crew and spectators were frozen, staring in shock at one of the models sprawled on the top of a roulette table, twitching. Aston and two of his helpers rushed to her, and then the photographer glanced around with a wild look and called to Jeanie.

"Get an ambulance. Now."

Jeanie came running over, horror written across her face. "Oh, my God. What happened?"

"The harness must have broken. She dropped two stories. Get help," Aston's assistant said.

Jeanie hurried to the police, and one of the officers called it in as the others tried to establish order. Black saw a spreading pool of blood on the green felt table top, and realized that the model must have been partially impaled on the roulette wheel, in addition to whatever damage she'd sustained from the fall. Her beautiful face was white from shock, her angel wings crushed beneath her. Black turned away. He couldn't look. He'd seen enough injuries to know that this was a bad one.

Demille burst through the exit doors, an expression of incomprehension slowly transitioning to panic, and then another model screamed at the technicians manning the winches.

"Get me down. Get me down!"

Aston barked orders and technicians scrambled to comply. The girls were lowered, the shoot obviously over as everyone tried to give the police a wide berth. Sirens howled from the street outside, and Black scanned the men and women in the vicinity, looking for anyone out of place. Because even as more security personnel trotted over, he knew in his gut that the model's fall was no accident, and that whatever twisted bastard had targeted Demille's talent had struck again.

Chapter 17

The detective heading up the investigation methodically interviewed everyone who'd been present at the shoot, asking a standard list of questions as the crew and models waited their turn. Black recognized him – Martin Grimm, ex-LAPD, a colleague of Stan's who'd moved to the high desert two years earlier for better pay and less stress than Los Angeles afforded. Black called Stan on his cell, catching him at home, and explained what had happened and what he needed. Stan agreed to do his best to help before he hung up, not particularly chatty first thing in the morning.

An hour later it was Black's turn to meet with Grimm, who had the sad look of a bloodhound and the yellowish complexion of a hard drinker. Grimm nodded to Black and invited him to join him at the breakfast bar as he refilled his coffee.

"Hey, Black. Fancy meeting you here."

"Yeah. How's desert living treating you?"

"Like shit. Crime's skyrocketed since I got here, and the captain thinks it's directly related to my coming aboard."

"But other than that? Gets pretty hot during the summer, doesn't it?"

"It's a dry heat," Grimm said, his tone bitter at some inside joke he didn't find funny.

"How's the girl?" Black asked.

"In real trouble. Ton of internal injuries and bleeding. She's in the OR right now. Might not make it. And even if she does, sounds like she'll be paralyzed. Admissions gave us a synopsis, and it's ugly."

"This was no accident," Black said flatly.

"I know." Grimm looked around as he sipped from his steaming cup. "You never heard this from me, but it looks like somebody sabotaged the girl's harness."

"How?"

"Cut the screws that hold the eyelet that the cables connect to. Left only one intact, or I should say relatively intact, and glued the screw heads back into the other three holes so it would look untouched."

"So no question about premeditation."

"Zero. Forensics is looking at the final screw to see if it was deliberately weakened. My guess is yes."

"That explains why the tech didn't catch it. I watched him hook everyone up and give each cable a firm tug."

"Which wouldn't have been enough to break it. But once they were suspended and moving, it was just a matter of time."

"You better seal off the wardrobe trailer. That has to be where the harness was sabotaged."

"I already have, and that's part of my questioning. I'm focusing on who could have had access yesterday or last night."

"How long would it have taken to do that?"

"Only a few minutes if you came prepared. A screwdriver, bolt cutters, super glue. Maybe a Dremel or a file to weaken the final screw. Probably not all that long." Grimm shook his head. "Stan called and said you're investigating some other related events?"

Black told him about the acid and the suspicious deaths. When he finished, Grimm stared at the waiting group. "Sounds like you've got your hands full with this, buddy. It's definitely attempted murder. With a high degree of likelihood to be murder one if they lose her on the table. You got any hot tips for me on who could be behind it?"

"There was an arrest here this morning, at around six. Zane Bradley. I'd take a hard look at where he was yesterday. He assaulted Demille, the modeling agency owner, right in front of me. Out of his mind on something stronger than beer, and he's got a grudge against not only Demille, but some of the models – he looked like he wanted to kill one of the stage moms. And that guy, over there, in the white slacks and silk shirt? His name's Gabriel Costa. A competitor of Demille's who's been stealing his talent for his own agency. I'd focus on when he got to Vegas. He was in L.A. as of two o'clock yesterday. Oh, and talk to Jeanie, the event coordinator. She can fill you in on who had access to the wardrobe area, who's got keys, and so on." Black hesitated. "I also haven't written off Demille yet. If I were you I'd give him the third degree. And Jeanie, too. She had access, if no obvious motive."

Grimm nodded. "You know, if they'd positioned the trailers facing the opposite direction, the wardrobe entrance would have been on the exterior security cameras. But as it is, no love there."

"That's a crappy break."

"Tell me about it. So far a bad morning." Grimm studied Black's rumpled suit. "How's the PI thing working out?"

"You're looking at it. When there's work, it's not a bad gig. But the job isn't steady, so it's tough a lot of the time."

"Everything's tough a lot of the time. All right. Let's head back and get your statement on record so you can get out of here."

"Thanks for filling me in. I owe you."

"No problem. But you never heard any of it from me," Grimm reminded.

"Any of what?"

Black was finished with the interrogation in another five minutes, and spotted Demille talking to Jeanie outside as he moved away from the holding area. Black walked toward them and took up a position nearby, waiting for them to finish. Demille said something to her and she nodded, then brushed past Black on her way into the casino.

Demille's face was slightly swollen, and part of Black hoped it was painful. He didn't like the man's arrogance or dismissiveness, and he was convinced Demille wasn't on the level. He wasn't sure about what, but he believed himself to be a good judge of character, and Demille just struck him as...wrong.

"Mr. Black. There you are. I hope you don't take this personally, but with everything that's gone on, today's a lousy day for your questions."

"Seems like no time is the right time."

"If you'll excuse me, I think having one of your models almost killed right in front of you qualifies as a pretty good excuse for not being up to it."

"Mr. Demille. You've been stonewalling me for a while. Now's the only time we have. I don't mean to be difficult, but I need some answers. So get used to the idea that you're going to have to talk to me. Or do you want me to call Daniel?"

Demille grunted. "Fine. What are your questions? Let's get this over with."

"Let's start with New York. What was your relationship with Daria?"

"My relationship? She was one of my models."

"Was she anything more?"

Demille's eyes narrowed. "Why would it be any of your business if she was?"

"Put simply, were you sleeping with her?"

"Next question."

"The way this works is I ask, then you answer. We don't skip the ones you don't like."

"Mr. Black, I'm trying to be civil, but nothing gives you the authority to interrogate me about my personal life. Not your mistaken sense of duty, not Daniel buying my company…nothing. My private life is my private life. Understood?"

"I need to know everything I can if I'm going to have a clear picture."

"Then invent whatever scenario in your head you think fits. That I was sleeping with Daria, or not. It's of no concern to me."

"Anything you say will remain confidential," Black promised him.

"Sure it will. Next question?"

"The model who got the acid. What was your relationship with her?"

"Same answer. None of your business."

"I think it is."

"Now we're back to where you can think whatever you want."

"And Clarissa?"

"Do you have any questions that are actually relevant to the merger or the attacks? I thought Daniel hired you to keep the talent safe and prevent any more disasters. How are you doing so far?"

Black tried to resist rising to the bait, but couldn't help himself. "I've been observing your company for, what, a week? Tell me – how much consulting did you do with me before scheduling this shoot? What professional security systems did you put in place? What precautions were there to protect the talent, or anyone, for that matter? Elmer Fudd with a baton inside? I'll ask you, as the man at the helm of your company, what precisely have you done to prevent anything but me getting straight answers to my questions?"

Demille studied him as if he was an errant child, then shook his head. "I don't see this as being helpful."

"Mr. Demille, you aren't being asked what you think about it. You aren't being asked anything but questions that I, as the only security professional working with your group, have deemed important, which you've dodged and stonewalled. You're losing models faster than I change socks, yet you're acting as though your approval is required for anything I do or say. Here's a newsflash. I work for DNA. They pay me to give them my input. Right now my take is that you're about as uncooperative as imaginable, and that if I were doing this deal, I'd walk away. In fact, that's what I'm going to tell Daniel as soon as we're done."

Demille glared holes through him.

"Mr. Black, this little discussion is at an end. I've suffered enough of your insulting innuendo. Tell Daniel whatever you want. As far as I'm concerned, you've contributed nothing, and you're a bumbling fool – and that's being charitable. That's my report to him. Good luck collecting your final check. I wouldn't pay you, personally."

Black smiled humorlessly. "If you misjudge all your negotiations this badly, it's no wonder you're broke and your company's falling apart. I'd be jumping ship too. Sounds like Hailey's just the latest in a long list that's going to get a lot shorter. Good luck with that. I'm done here." He turned and began walking away.

Demille grabbed his arm. "How dare you. Who do you think you're talking to?"

Black shrugged off Demille's grip. "Mr. Demille. If you ever lay a hand on me again, you'll have a lot of broken bones. I'm not one of your models, and you don't have the stones to go up against me."

Demille visibly struggled to contain the rage playing across his features. Black watched the show dispassionately, wondering if his face would crack from the strain. After a few seconds Demille's customary imperious sneer replaced the conflicted expressions, and he sighed.

"I'll answer any questions except those that intrude in my private life. As I said, they're none of your business, and you're crossing a line with them. I don't want anything to happen to my models, and maybe you're right, I should have called you in to look over things for this shoot. But that's over and done with. Let's try this one more time, and see if we can both walk away from it with what we need."

Black debated telling him to pound sand, but relented when he considered the dollars in the balance. It was always possible that Daniel would fire him rather than backing him against Demille, citing a personality clash, and hire one of the countless other PIs who would jump at the chance to make two-fifty an hour watching modeling shoots. That might have been crumbs to the Daniels of the world, but right now it was the only thing standing between Black and the street, and he'd gotten kind of used to indoor plumbing and electric lights.

Black drilled him on every aspect of the business he could think of, including countless details about the various shoots, where he'd been at different times during the suicide and overdose, what time he'd flown in yesterday, whether he'd been in the wardrobe trailer. The answers were direct, but left nothing resolved, and after forty minutes of peppering Demille, both men were tired of the sight of each other. Black had recorded the entire interaction on his phone without telling Demille, so he could review the answers at his leisure, checking for inconsistencies.

"Are we done here?" Demille asked when it was obvious Black had exhausted his questions.

"For now. I'd ask that you make yourself available in the future if I need to ask you anything else."

"Fair enough. But Mr. Black, I get the impression that you suspect I might have something to do with today's tragedy, and I can assure you that if you pursue that as your best lead, you're going to have more bodies on your hands. I had nothing to do with any of this nightmare."

"My approach is to presume everyone guilty until I can prove to myself they aren't."

"A cumbersome way of doing it, but I'm not going to try to tell you your business. I will say it's astounding to me that you saw Zane attack me, and you watched Gabriel poaching my talent, and yet you still like me for the bad guy. At the risk of being obvious, I think you're allowing your bias against me to color your reasoning. I just hope that doesn't cost some poor girl her life."

Demille spun on his heel and walked back into the casino, where he would be talking to the police for some time, Black was sure. Demille's words stung, but only because they contained an element of truth. He didn't like Demille one bit and it showed. But it was also unprofessional to formulate a theory based on personalities. Demille was right – Black was trying to make the case fit Demille, which was amateur night, and beneath him.

The ride out of town was a breeze compared to the prior night, hardly any congestion as he barreled west at midday, the top down, the temperature perfect, his stereo blaring Stevie Ray Vaughn to the pale blue sky. Once over the first row of mountains he pulled off the highway at the tiny hamlet of Baker to top up his tank and use the bathroom. His stomach growled as he stood by the pump, watching his wallet drain into the car. Pulling out of the station, he spotted a restaurant nearby and put the top up, the sun's warmth now oppressively hot in the Mojave Desert, and dialed Roxie as he entered the dining room.

"Black Investigations," she answered.

"Roxie."

"I saw something online about an attack at a casino. I'm guessing that was you?"

"It happened at the shoot. Sabotage. The model is in critical condition. It was ugly."

"Where are you?"

"Driving back."

"Did you spend the night at the tables like I thought?"

"I'm not going to lie."

"That's a yes, I take it."

"Correct. But no cigarettes."

"Really?"

"You owe me ten big ones."

"You never took the bet."

"Damn. Why do you always have a comeback?"

Roxie ignored him. "I've been digging into Gabriel's company. Did you know he doesn't own it? Or I should say, he isn't the majority owner."

"Really? I wonder why?"

"Could be that he had to borrow money to start it, and the lender wanted a majority position."

"Who's the majority owner?"

"That's where it gets tricky. It's owned by another corporation."

"And who owns that?"

"If I knew, I'd just tell you who the other owner was. Assuming it's just one person."

"Oh."

"Right. And it gets harder, because that other corporation is a Nevada corporation, and the shareholders are private."

"What does that mean?"

"It means that it's not part of the public record."

"So where does that leave us?" Black asked.

"I'm trying a backdoor way to see if anyone slipped up."

"Dare I ask what you're doing?"

"Don't worry. It's legal. Mostly. Somewhere."

"I don't want to know."

"Probably best if you don't. I'll tell you when and if I get more info."

"All right." Black hesitated. "How's the German going?"

"Not bad. But it's like they have a different word for everything."

"Inconsiderate of them."

"I know. It would be way more helpful if everyone just spoke English."

"There are some who think that would work well here in the U.S."

"Good point," Roxie conceded.

"I should be back by quitting time. Will you call me if you come up with something?"

"Sure. Or I'll email you."

"Either way."

Black ordered the combo plate, which in this case was a variety of home-cooked Greek delicacies he prayed wouldn't turn him into a human yogurt machine halfway home, and he decided to take prophylactic measures by having a beer with it. Lunch turned out to be delicious and seemingly fresh, and soon he was tearing down the freeway, cars flying past him even though he was doing eighty, eager to get back home before rush hour clogged the roads and added hours to his travel time.

Lady Luck was riding on his shoulder, because he was back in Los Angeles by 3:45. He stopped at a gas station and was filling up again when his phone rang.

"Mr. Black?"

"Yes. Who is this?" Black asked.

"Gunther. From Daniel's office."

"Ah, Gunther. What can I do for you?"

"Daniel wants you to come over as soon as possible. He's back in town."

"Right now? I'm just returning from Vegas. I had to drive."

"He was very specific. Now would be good."

Black breathed heavily, a dull ache having started behind his eyes about a hundred miles into the drive. "I can be there in half an hour. Tops."

"I'll let him know."

Black had a bad feeling about being summoned to the client's office, but knew there was no way he could decline. Daniel had obviously heard about the morning's disastrous shoot and felt that a powwow was a good idea. The problem being that Black had no idea who was behind the attack, and was no closer to figuring it out than he had been when he'd been boozing in Cabo on the company dime.

When he entered the DNA lobby the receptionist wasted no time, and Gunther was leading him to Daniel's office seconds later. Daniel sat behind his desk, a headset on, speaking quietly. He terminated the call when he saw Black.

"What happened in Vegas?" Daniel asked by way of small talk.

"The police haven't made it public yet, but they're confident that someone sabotaged the model's harness. It was deliberate."

"I just spoke with Demille's assistant. The model's out of the operating room, but it's touch and go. She'll be paralyzed from the waist down. I don't need to tell you what a disaster this is for the agency."

"I was there. Believe me, I have a very clear idea of how bad it is."

"Did you know there's already footage up on the internet? Somebody was filming from off to the side when she dropped. And it's going viral. Of course."

Black didn't say anything.

Daniel exchanged a glance with Gunther.

"What exactly am I paying you for, if you can't keep the talent safe?" Daniel asked.

"All due respect, nobody consulted me on security. I was told to get to Vegas and do what I could. There's no way I could have known that someone had sneaked into the wardrobe trailer, probably the day before, and rigged the harness. I'm good at what I do, but I'm not psychic," Black said, feeling the heat rising in his face, less able to contain the anger after running on no sleep for almost two days.

"I'm paying for results, not excuses."

Black sighed and sat down. "I spoke with Demille this morning. Finally. He gave me the same line, only slightly different. I'll tell you what I told him: that there was no way I could safeguard anything if I hadn't been consulted. That's the truth. Nobody asked me. And now both of you are acting like I was negligent in some way. I'd strongly suggest you take a hard look in the mirror if you want someone to blame. Because I'm getting pretty tired of being used as a punching bag when one of you gets frustrated, and it's not doing anything to protect the models or catch the perp."

Daniel held his stare for a few seconds, then looked away. "We're all tense. This is a public relations nightmare. Never mind the lawsuits…"

"Look. If you want me to run security for a shoot, that's fine. I need at least a week's notice, complete control over all aspects, and veto power if I think something's too dangerous. And while I'm doing that, I won't be able to mount an effective investigation. It's a matter of bandwidth. I can only be in so many places."

"Frankly, Mr. Black, I'd hoped to have you more proactive on this case, based on Bobby's description of your abilities."

"You need to decide what you want me to do. If you want me running security and rooting around, that's fine. I'll bring in a pro to handle the security aspect while I run the investigation. Or you can hire someone for security yourself. However you like."

Daniel flipped a manila envelope at him. "Get whatever resources you need. There's a shoot in Tahoe in three days. First snow's fallen, so it's a winter shoot. I want you up there. Investigating. If you need to hire someone to take security precautions, do it. But we can't afford another mishap."

Black opened the envelope and studied the information. "Three days isn't enough time to guarantee anyone's safety. I need at least a week."

"We have three days."

"Remember that I went on record saying that's inadequate."

"I heard you the first time."

"I'll need complete control."

"Then you'll have it."

"I'll also need you to be prepared to cut a check to one of my colleagues who specializes in security."

"Just tell Gunther and he'll make it so. I'll be back in New York. I leave tonight."

"When will you return?"

"Next week, when we're supposed to finalize the merger. Assuming there's anyone left to merge with."

"Are you having second thoughts?"

"The value of the firm to me is its reputation, its contacts, and its talent. Right now its reputation with clients is still wonderful, but that can change. Its contacts are intact, so those are still of value. But we're experiencing significant talent drain, and that must stop, or I'm paying far too much."

"That's between you and Demille," Black said, but in the back of his mind he was thinking that if he could find any real dirt on Demille, Daniel would be the first to receive a full report. "I'll stick to what I understand, which is figuring out who done it."

"And preventing them from doing it again. Don't forget that part."

On the way out of the building Black telephoned Bill Rawls, one of his friends who ran a private security firm, and after a long discussion, got him to agree to take on the Tahoe shoot. Black gave him Gunther's number and told him to arrange for a check to be cut so he could start working on it immediately. Bill voiced the same timing concerns and had similar misgivings, but he was willing to do his best – which would be far more than had been done to date.

In the garage, he dialed Sylvia, who sounded out of breath when she answered.

"Hey. I'm back in town."

"Oh. How did it go?"

Black told her. When he was finished, silence hung on the line like the pause before a terminal diagnosis.

"That's horrible. You sound beat."

"I am. Watching young women get mangled does that to you. But I'll be fit as a fiddle after a few hours of sleep. You want to grab dinner somewhere?"

Sylvia hesitated, and when she answered, sounded…distant. "I'm pretty tired too. Maybe not tonight."

"Are you still angry because I had to go to Vegas?"

"No," she said unconvincingly.

"Listen. There's another shoot in Lake Tahoe in three days. I have to go. But I really want you to go with me so you can see what I've been doing."

"Tahoe? Isn't that up by San Francisco?"

"Inland a few hundred miles. But close enough."

"I have things I need to do here."

"Come on, Sylvia. We can turn it into a road trip. We can leave the day before and stop in Berkeley and see my parents. You seem to enjoy watching me squirm. That'll more than do it."

"Has your mother been calling again?"

"Always. I'm a bad son because I have to stay in town and earn a living. You've heard it all before."

"Well, I've never been to the Bay Area…"

"With the added bonus of staying in my parents' haunted house."

"Is it really haunted?"

"I just made that up."

"How long would we be gone?"

"Maybe three days. One up, one in Tahoe, one back."

"I suppose nothing I've got to do can't wait a few days."

"That's the Sylvia I know. You sure I can't talk you into dinner?"

"No. I really am tired. It's been a long day," she said, her voice softening. "And you sound like you could use some rest. Let's plan on it tomorrow night, and then we can leave early in the morning."

"That's perfect."

Black's head was still pounding when he made it home, and after a quick shower, he fell into bed, never happier to be in his crappy apartment than at that moment. He shut his eyes and willed the sound of cars on the street outside away, eager to finally get some sleep after yet another long stint without. The last thought he had as he drifted off was a vision of the model in Las Vegas lying on the table, mouth working like a beached carp, blood seeping around her like a crimson halo as all her hopes and dreams died with her ability to ever feel her legs again.

Chapter 18

The following morning began calmly enough. Black was now fully rested and felt as chipper as he ever did. It was unseasonably warm when he slid open the door that led to his small balcony to gauge the weather, so he dressed more casually than on a typical workday, opting for a vintage Hawaiian shirt from the fifties, left untucked so it would conceal his belt holster, and a pair of butter-colored linen slacks. He was quite sure Roxie wouldn't mind since she delighted in bagging on his wardrobe, and he wasn't planning on seeing any clients – not that he had any other than Daniel at the moment.

Stan called during Black's drive to the office to discuss the plan to catch Ernest faking, and Black filled him in on exactly how he wanted to handle things. When he was done, Stan was chuckling.

"I can't wait to bust him. I mean, I'm actually having fantasies about it," Stan said.

"Is he wearing pants?"

"You know what I mean."

"Are you?"

"Right now, or in the dream? Why, are you feeling lonely today?"

"I don't think I'll ever get that lonely. I'd buy a dog first."

"Probably best for us both. But poor dog. Living in that rat trap."

"Hey. It's not so bad."

"For a family of boat people being held at gunpoint, maybe. When are you going to move?"

"When I win the lottery."

"Hey, don't try to tell me you aren't making bank on this modeling thing."

"I'm doing all right, but I have a feeling it's going to come to a screeching halt at any moment...and I'm not going to be getting any glowing references."

"At least I don't have to worry about that in my line of work. Dead men don't give references."

"Tell you what, when I get back from Tahoe, we can implement my scheme to nail Ernest, okay? Call it three days. Can you get the notice printed up by then?"

"They have this new technology, Black. It's called the computer and the laser printer. They run on electricity. Amazing stuff. I could have it knocked out in an hour."

"Then you know what to do."

"I'll be ready when you get back. Everything will be set to go."

"Thanks. By the way, did you ever get anything more on that Tasha woman I asked you about?"

"Yeah, but no signs of foul play. She was drunk, hit her head, game over. In this case, the butler didn't do it. There's no 'there' there."

"All right. That's one item I can cross off my list. Hey, could you call Bill and see what happened with Zane Bradley?"

"What did he do?"

Black told him an abridged version of the story.

Stan was amenable. "If Demille pressed charges, he's probably still in lockup, unless someone bailed him out. Although if he's a serious suspect in the attack, they might hold him as long as possible while they debate charging him."

"I didn't get the impression they thought so. But could you find out?"

"You betcha. For my man Black? Anything, baby, anything."

Roxie was beaming when Black entered the office. Black studied her, unsure of what she was so happy about, and waited in front of her desk with an expression of puzzlement as his silent query.

"Did you get my email?" she asked.

He closed his eyes and shook his head. "Damn. Sorry. I spaced. I was out of it."

Her shoulders sagged. "I figured out who owns most of Gabriel's company."

Black did a double take. "Well?"

"The company in Nevada was a dead end. No way to get the shareholder info. So I started probing around his website. And it turns out that the same person who paid for the website for the Nevada corporation, who owns most of the company, also paid for Gabriel's site."

"The Nevada corp has a website?"

"Just a one-page placeholder. But it was enough."

"I'm not going to ask you how you got payment info."

"You probably don't want to know."

"I figured. Well? Who is it?"

"Does Mugsy look thinner to you?"

"Roxie. Come on. Give."

"Gabriel's company's website was paid for by Arapaho Holdings."

"Super. And who's that?"

"Arapaho Holdings, unlike the Nevada Corporation, is a California LLC. Which I was able to get records for."

"Roxie, is this going to take much longer?"

"Fine, Mr. Grumpy. Suck all the joy out of it. Arapaho Holdings is a hundred percent owned by none other than Thomas Demille."

∼⚬∽

Gabriel looked up from his desk at Black, who had barged into his office, a sheet of paper in his hand. The fussy man at the reception desk hadn't moved fast enough to keep Black from proceeding to Gabriel's door, and he appeared behind Black three seconds later.

"I'm sorry, Mr. Costa. He got by me before I could stop him..."

Gabriel eyed Black and waved the receptionist away. "That's all right, Jacob. I'm sure Mr. Black won't be here very long."

Black approached Gabriel's desk and took a seat in front of it. "Not very long at all," he said with a dry smile.

The receptionist hesitated in the doorway before departing with an exasperated hiss of breath. Gabriel leaned back in his chair, and Black was again struck by how perfect his features were.

"Well? What do you want?"

"I know you don't own your agency."

If Black had tossed Gabriel a live grenade he couldn't have gotten a more shocked look. Gabriel's face literally fell, as though made of melting wax, and his demeanor seemed to collapse in on itself. He tried to stammer a denial, but Black cut him off.

"And I know who does."

Black allowed that to sink in. Outside the picture window behind Gabriel's desk, a rust-colored pigeon strolled along the stainless steel rail mounted along the base, its head jutting forward with each precarious step. It stopped and peered in at the two men sitting motionless inside, and then alighted with a sudden flap of wings.

Gabriel tried to parry Black's accusation, but it was a feeble attempt. "There's no law against that, is there?"

"That depends. I'm quite sure a case for fraud could be made. And of course, murder and mutilation are frowned upon, whatever the circumstances."

Black held Gabriel's gaze, unblinking, waiting for him to say something. It took a while, but when Gabriel finally reacted, it wasn't the way he'd thought he would. His eyes welled up with moisture, and then he closed them and began sobbing.

"I told him this wouldn't work. Somebody would find out. I knew it. I just knew it."

"Gabriel? Look at me. Stop that, and look at me."

Gabriel reached for a package of tissues and dabbed at his eyes, then took several deep breaths. Black waited patiently as Gabriel composed himself.

"It wasn't my idea. It was Tom's."

"I kind of figured that for myself. The question is, why?"

"You can't guess?"

"Sure I can. But why don't you tell me? I hear confession is good for the soul."

"Isn't it obvious? Tom's selling the agency. He's strapped for money. For real money, not a few thousand here and there. DNA has a non-compete in the agreement that locks him up for two years. But he wants to have his cake and eat it too, which if you know him well, is so typically him." Gabriel paused. "When he started getting serious about doing the deal, he had me start this company. The idea was that I'd get his best faces during the lockup period, and then when he could leave, he'd join me here. Where his stars were waiting."

"That would be the fraud part."

"I don't know anything about that. I just did as he asked."

"And you didn't suspect what you were doing was wrong?"

Gabriel frowned and waved his hand. "Please. We live in L.A. Look around. Are you for real with your right and wrong act?"

"You helped Demille defraud DNA. Did you tell the models he would be coming to work here once he was done with his contract?"

"Models are total gossips. It's just between Tom and me."

"And then he started killing them. You realize you'll be viewed as an accessory to murder, don't you?"

"No! I don't know anything about that! Besides, why would Tom want to hurt any of his models? That doesn't make any sense."

"Maybe they had something on him? They found out?"

"Are you nuts? How? And do you really believe Tom would do something horrible like at the casino? Or the acid? He's greedy, not psychotic."

"Then who's behind it? Zane? Another ex-model? One of the current ones?"

"How would I know?"

Black debated accusing him directly of being behind the attacks, but then thought better of it. He had no evidence and no motive. Although he now had enough to hang Demille, as far as Daniel would be concerned. The question was, when to present it to him?

"Gabriel, I'm going to give you some advice. Don't tell Demille that I know about his little charade. I'll decide when and how I confront him, do you understand?" Black rose. "If you do as I say, you might be able to walk away from this relatively clean. I have no desire to hurt anyone here," he said, stretching the truth – he absolutely had a reason to take Demille down a few notches, not the least of which would be the huge bonus Daniel would be willing to pay for the information so he could get out of the deal that was going south by the day. Demille had embarked on a dangerous game, and if he was going to risk it all to cheat one of the biggest players in his industry, then he'd have to deal with the fallout. "You're under no circumstances to even hint to Demille that anyone knows. Are you with me?"

"It's not like I even see him much anymore," Gabriel said glumly. "He only calls when he wants something."

A burst of insight flashed in Black's mind. "Which wasn't how it was supposed to be, was it, Gabriel?"

"No."

"This was a chance to spend more time together. To do something important together. To build something, wasn't it?"

"That was the idea," Gabriel answered in a small voice, and Black understood everything.

"Well, don't feel too badly. Sometimes things don't work out as planned," he said, thinking about Nina and his own betrayal. "Just hold it together, Gabriel. I'll deal with Demille in my own way when the time is right. If I can keep you out of it, I will. I have nothing against you. It sounds like you're just caught in the middle of a bad situation."

"How do I know I can believe you?"

"I'm here, aren't I? I could have just gone to the police and Daniel, and you'd be getting cuffs put on you," Black answered, exaggerating so Gabriel would cooperate. "But I didn't. So count yourself lucky, don't ask questions, and just go about your business."

"Like nothing's wrong."

"Exactly."

Black kept the stereo off as he drove back to the office, wondering at Gabriel's gullibility at getting sucked into Demille's scheme. It was obvious to him that Gabriel was still enamored with Demille – the handsome, powerful older man who had at one time been his everything. Demille had played on that weakness to offer a future where they were together, embarking on a new enterprise, and conquering the world side by side. Only that wasn't how Demille rolled. Gabriel was just a means to an end, someone to be used for his pleasure and cast aside when his usefulness was over. He recalled Sima's allusions to Demille's reputation and thought they were certainly deserved. And Gabriel was the only one who didn't seem to have figured it out.

When he returned to the office, he told Roxie how his meeting had gone. She listened attentively, for once not staring at her computer as he talked.

"Then he's doing it all for love. Poor bastard. And Demille's playing him," she said.

"That's how it seems to me."

"But then, who's after the models?"

"That's the question, isn't it? I kind of like Demille for it. But I don't have a motive."

"And this Zane character?"

"Also a contender. He's certainly bitter enough, and has a lot of anger."

"Sounds familiar."

"What?"

She looked over at the couch. "Mugsy seems angry. I think that's why he acts out like he does and is so destructive."

"Mmm. Mugsy. And what does he possibly have to be angry about?"

"We don't know what kind of life he had before we took him in."

"We know he never missed a meal."

"That's not what I meant. He might have been mistreated. Abused."

Black shrugged. "Could be. But he does look thinner."

"You're just saying that."

"Am not."

"I know you too well. You're blowing smoke."

"Maybe I'm telling the truth. I just look like I'm always lying. It doesn't mean I'm actually lying."

"Right."

"Really. I'm aware that I could look like I'm lying, and that you might think it's possible I'm lying, even though I'm not. So I get a guilty liar look on my face even when I'm telling the truth."

"Sure thing, Dr. Freud."

"The point is, I look like I'm lying because I recognize the possibility that I could be lying, even though I'm telling the truth."

"Uh huh."

Black spent the rest of his morning going through his email and signing the paperwork and checks Roxie had laid out for him. Stan called back on his cell, and it was bad news about Zane.

"Demille wound up not pressing charges. Said he was too distraught over the shoot. So that didn't leave anything to hold him on. He was released this morning, after spending yesterday sobering up. Best they could manage was public drunkenness, which the DA won't want to take to court. Which means as of now, he's at large and free as a bird."

"The system at work. Poetry in motion, isn't it?"

"Hey, I'd have just shot him. It's not my fault the Vegas cops are pussies."

"Good to know."

Black puttered around the office for another hour, bored, nobody returning his calls, and decided to put his time to better use and stake out

Ernest in case he caught a break. Although his plan to ensnare him was brilliant, he thought. He'd read about it online – where the police would send out notices to all the bail skips, posing as an appliance store or a car dealership that was giving away merchandise in a sweepstakes they'd won, and when they showed up to claim their prize, arrested them. If that could work on perps, it could work on Ernest. The idea was to mail him a notice that he'd won a flat-screen TV, and when he came to collect it, nobody would be available to help him carry it to the car. If he was a greedy faker, he'd haul it himself, and that would be that. It was really perfect – unless he was truly hurt, in which case all bets were off.

Black settled in across the street from Ernest's house, resigned to spending a solid six to eight hours there, and was surprised when after twenty minutes Ernest emerged from the house, collar on, and made his way to his car. Black followed him at a safe distance. First he stopped at a hardware store and emerged a few minutes later with a small bag. Next stop was a dry cleaner's for two shirts – hardly incriminating.

And then Fate smiled upon Black at Petco.

Black trailed Ernest inside the massive store, recalling Roxie complaining that she needed to get Mugsy a travel crate. He figured he could kill two birds, and keep an eye on Ernest while currying favor with Roxie. He eyeballed the selection of travel containers, chose the largest one available for cats, and then reconsidered and went in search of a small dog crate. Ernest was in the dog food aisle, staring at the large bags of chow. Black held his breath and removed his phone from his pocket, palming it expertly, and began filming as Ernest pushed his cart nearer the racks and then hoisted a forty-pound bag of dog food into the cart with the ease of a toddler lifting a pillow.

Black couldn't help but smile to himself, and decided to celebrate by stepping up and getting Mugsy a cat treat and a toy in addition to his portable prison. He was whistling as he followed Ernest to the cash register and stood in line behind him.

"Beautiful day, isn't it?" Black said conversationally as the cashier rang Ernest's dog food up.

"If you say so."

"What happened? Car accident?" Black asked, pointing to his neck. "I got whiplash once. That was a real bitch."

"Something like that."

"Well, good luck with it. You need some help with that bag? Getting it into your car?" Black asked, with as creepy a smile as he could muster.

"Uh, no, I got it. Thanks, though," Ernest said, hurrying to get out of there and away from the overly friendly Black.

"You sure? Just have to ask. We could get coffee or something after. I know a cute little place near here."

Ernest had heard enough, and practically ran with his cart to the exit. Black dropped a hundred dollar bill on the counter, waited for his change, and then hurried to the doors. As he'd hoped, Ernest was loading the bag into his car, which Black filmed as he approached him.

"Here, let me help you," Black cooed.

"I told you, I don't need no help. I got it," Ernest snarled, and lifted the bag into the back seat of his sedan in a fluid motion, his powerful arms exhibiting no strain.

"Ooh. You must work out," Black said, and then decided to stop tormenting the man.

Stan howled with laughter when Black called and told him what he had on tape.

"Dude. You're absolutely the best. You know what? Let's hook up. Download the video, put it on a flash drive, and I'll trade you the footage for a fifty-inch TV. Brand new. I'd say you earned it."

"Really? You don't have to."

"No problem. Besides, it's not like I can take the TV back. It might be a little…warm. You know?"

"I have no idea what you're talking about, but appreciate any gifts you feel like making."

"That's my boy."

Chapter 19

The Eldorado ate up the miles as it hurtled north up I-5, only a few miles now from the turnoff that led to the East Bay and Berkeley, where his parents were waiting for their imminent arrival with the anticipation of hunters for the first season's buck. Black's mother had been ecstatic that they were coming, but that had quickly turned to disappointment when she'd learned that it was only for the night. Black had studiously ignored her passive aggressive disapproval, and promised only that they would be there by mid-afternoon.

The Gypsy Kings crooned and strummed from the stereo, a compromise with Sylvia from his usual guitar-driven hard rock. She'd put her foot down somewhere north of Hanford and switched off ZZ Top's wailing riffs. Black had acquiesced to her wishes, determined to make the trip as enjoyable as he could, and they'd settled on a safe neutral ground of rollicking acoustic guitars and soaring harmonies. The drive had gone faster than he'd expected, the other vehicles on the freeway averaging ninety, and the big car effortlessly keeping pace.

Berkeley was a stark contrast to the farmland they'd been driving through. Lush fields gave way to tree-lined streets and hulking Victorian homes once they passed the downtown and made it into the hills. When they pulled to a stop in front of what Black would always consider to be the new house, Sylvia's eyes widened at its size. Luxury vehicles lined the street in both directions, and Black fleetingly wondered why the area was so crowded – the last time he'd been there it had been a ghost town.

"Only two people live here?" she asked. The home sat on a double lot that stretched far down the hill.

"I know. They fell in love with it when they saw it and had to have it. They're very impulsive like that."

"More like a hotel than a house."

"With none of the positives. Come on. Might as well get this over with," he said. They moved to the trunk and retrieved their bags, which Black carried to the front door.

"Do you hear that?" Sylvia asked, her head cocked, a puzzled expression on her face. A rhythmic thumping sound drifted from down the hill, below the house.

"I do. But I have no idea what it is," Black said, equally mystified.

He rang the doorbell and regarded the exterior of the oversized dwelling, noting that its wooden shingles could use some maintenance, and wondered how long it had been since anyone had performed any. Knowing his parents, not since they'd bought it.

The front door creaked open and Black's mother, Spring, stood gazing at them, clad in some sort of a tie-dyed shift, her pink-sock-sheathed feet ensconced in obligatory Birkenstock sandals, her untamed gray hair cascading over her shoulders like a wild animal had taken up residence on her head.

"Artemus! You made it! Let me take a look at you. And Sylvie! Welcome!"

"It's Sylvia, Mom."

"Well, of course it is. Artemus. Have you put some weight on?"

"I don't think so."

"Well, that's what happens as you get older. You'll see. Gravity has its way with you."

Black hugged her, determined to ignore her snipes. "I'm pretty sure gravity doesn't have to do with gaining weight except in a measurement sense."

"Hello, Mrs. Black," Sylvia said as the older woman embraced her in turn. "It's nice to see you again."

"Please. It's Spring."

"What's that noise? Did Dad start a band?" Black asked, the pounding louder inside the house.

"Oh, no, silly. It's Chakra's drum circle, out in back. They get together once a month. It's a male bonding thing. Polyrhythmic. Cleansing. Trance inducing – a way of connecting to a higher power."

"It sounds like a bunch of chimps beating on a hollow log."

"It's not about what it sounds like."

"Then what's it about?"

"The experience of being part of the circle."

"Huh. And what do you accomplish, banging on drums in a circle? What's produced besides noise pollution?"

"It's different for everyone. Stress relief. Letting go of anger and negative emotions. Finding your inner rhythm…"

"Why can't it stay inner? I thought living in the hills was all about peace and tranquility."

"Not on drum circle day."

Spring led them into the expansive living room area, furnished with hand carved pieces made by a friend of theirs who lived in a trailer and spent months making chairs and couches from driftwood. Outside, a dozen older men were pounding away at their various instruments, each with its own timbre and tonal characteristic. Black and Sylvia watched in amusement, and Black turned to his mother.

"Wait a minute. That guy next to Dad looks kind of familiar. That's not Larry Elli–"

"Oh, Larry's a hoot. He owns some technology company. Very funny guy. But he can go on and on about sailing. It's a big thing for him. Everyone else kind of plays along," Spring said. "Let's go upstairs to the family room. It'll be quieter there."

"And is that Michael Milk–"

"They don't like to use last names. Everyone calls him Mikey. Or the Mikester."

The din receded as they climbed the wide stairs to the upper floor, where a massive family room separated three guest rooms. Black tossed their bags into the largest of them and returned to where Sylvia was sitting with Spring on an overstuffed couch made from a patchwork of different colored fabrics, admiring some photographs on the bookcase of Spring and Chakra standing among pine trees.

"Where's that?" he asked, taking a seat on a beanbag chair that was easily ten years older than he was.

"Oh, that's up in Mendocino. We went to a retreat there about three months ago and absolutely adored the energy in the place. It's a magical area."

"I've been there. It's mainly redwoods and rednecks," Black added helpfully.

"Not anymore. It had an almost holy feeling to it."

"Holy?"

Spring nodded. "Enchanted. We're thinking about opening a getaway there of our own. Something far from civilization."

"A getaway? For what?"

"Drumming. Dancing. Yoga. Meditation."

"Isn't that kind of what Berkeley's been built on?"

"We want something remote."

"Ah. I see. Sort of a place for the two of you to camp out?"

"Something like that."

Spring chatted about the neighbors and her work with the local pet shelter and how expensive tea had gotten over the last year, Sylvia listening attentively as Black sneaked glances at his watch, already restless, dreading when the conversation would inevitably turn to him. His mother was nothing if not predictable, and she didn't disappoint.

"And you, Artemus? How's your company going?"

"Great. I've got a big case right now. That's why we're here. I've got a fashion shoot near Lake Tahoe tomorrow morning."

"Oh, my. A fashion shoot! I thought you were a detective. When did you become a photographer?"

"I'm not a photographer, Mom."

"Spring," she corrected. "Well, with the extra pounds, you're not modeling, so what are you doing there if not taking pictures?"

"I'm handling security for the shoot."

"Like, as a guard? Do they make you wear a uniform?"

"No. I'm directing their security efforts."

"Oh, sweetheart, I'm so happy for you. I know half the people with kids in Hollywood say their children want to be directors. I can't wait to tell the girls."

"That's a different kind of director. Hey, did I tell you that Sylvia sold a bunch of paintings the other day?" Black asked, changing the subject. He knew his mother had a chronically short attention span – probably a function of too much marijuana.

"Did you! That's fabulous. Is there really a business in that?" Spring asked.

"There can be. But the sales are few and far between some months," Sylvia said.

"Well, look at the two of you. An artist and a director. What exciting lives you lead. And Artemus. Didn't you tell me you were in Mexico? I read about the cartel shootings there and was so afraid for you."

"Like I said. I was already home when I told you I'd gone. So there was nothing to stress over."

"Still. A mother worries."

Black nodded. Of course she does. Never mind there was nothing to worry about, and the place in Mexico he went had far lower crime rates than their own town, much less L.A. Rather than bait her, he let her continue, determined to put a brave face on the visit even as his stomach churned with bile.

"What's that?" Sylvia asked, pointing to a metal-topped glass tube on a steel base.

"That? It's a lava lamp," Spring said.

"A lava lamp?" Sylvia repeated, unsure that she'd understood the words.

"Yes. They were really big back in the sixties. What a fabulous time that was. Anyway, here, let me show you how it works." Spring stood and moved to the lamp and switched it on. Long gelatinous tendrils of color drifted languorously through a clear, viscous fluid. "This one oscillates and blinks. I designed it with one of my friends."

"You designed that? Why?" Black blurted, almost afraid to ask.

"You know me, I get bored. And I was thinking back to when we first arrived in Berkeley and I met Chakra. We had a lava lamp in our room. In fact, Artemus, you were conceived near that lamp. There are a lot of good memories for me involving lava lamps."

Black didn't want to hear any more. "Mostly, though, people sat around staring at them when they were whacked out of their skulls on acid. Their popularity faded as that population eventually had to stop doing drugs every day and go out and get a job," he explained to Sylvia, ignoring her warning look. "Everywhere except Berkeley, that is."

"Anyway, I teamed up with a friend of mine who's a sculptor, and we made a few of these lamps. I have Ruth selling them down at her store, and so far, they're doing okay."

"Wait – you started a company to make these?" Black asked.

"Not really a company. He's making them as time permits, more as a hobby than anything."

"Didn't your last hobby…wasn't that the candle business?" Sylvia asked.

"Right. But that's gone now, so I wanted to keep busy. Between that and the retreat…"

Dawning awareness registered on Black's face. "Mom. Tell me you didn't buy a piece of land up in the middle of nowhere."

"It's Spring, honey. And don't worry. Everything always turns out all right. You just need to let the positive energy in. It's all around you."

Black bit back the urge to demand whether she was insane, and instead affected a Buddha-like calm. "I'm sure you're right. What time does the drum circle finish up?"

"In a few hours, at dusk. They go at it all day. Very determined. I get a kick out of it."

Black changed the subject. "What are we doing for dinner?"

"Oh, there's a new macrobiotic place that specializes in organic, non-dairy quiches made with tofu and soy. We figured we could go there as a treat."

"Great," Black said, his smile never fading as he wondered where the nearest store he could get a Snickers bar was.

"And their wheat grass smoothies are to die for, I hear," Spring enthused.

"They don't happen to put vodka in them, do they?" Black asked.

"It's not that kind of place."

"Of course not."

Dinner turned out to be a misery, with his parents insisting on regaling them about his ex-wife Nina's latest accomplishments – a sold-out world tour kicking off, a twentieth anniversary release of new material featuring the old band – sans Black, of course, who only wrote every hit they ever had – and a televised New Year's special on VH1 where Bono, Elton John, and Madonna were slated for guest appearances along with a special surprise performance by the Rolling Stones.

When they politely inquired about Sylvia's art there was an uncomfortable pause, and an even longer one when Chakra asked what they had planned for New Year's Eve – which they hadn't even discussed, as it was still six weeks away.

"I don't know. We're probably just going to hang around and problem drink, and then go shoot up the neighborhood at midnight," Black said, wishing a triple shot of Jack would somehow miraculously appear on the table in place of his water glass.

Spring clapped her hands together. "You should fly to London to see Nina's show! I know she'd be delighted to see you. We were thinking about it. Just say the word and I'll book two more seats! Imagine! How fun. New Year's Eve together as a family!"

Sylvia and Black exchanged nervous glances. "That's an idea, Mom. But let me get back to you about it. I have a lot going on, and so does Sylvia."

"That's right. The holidays are a whirlwind for me," Sylvia agreed.

Spring squinted at Black. "Is it my imagination, or is your hair getting thinner?"

"I prefer to think of it as my scalp getting more prominent."

Once home in bed, Black's arm around Sylvia as they snuggled, he shook his head at the night's events. "I know they don't mean anything by it, but they drive me nutty. And always talking about Nina. This is the woman who divorced me, cheated on me, and destroyed my musical career. And it doesn't occur to them I might not want to fly to another country to watch her be adored by millions – with my girlfriend in tow."

"You can go alone, if that's the problem," Sylvia said.

"Does it seem that I'm in any way interested in going?"

She eyed him distrustfully. "You could be faking to see how I react."

"Even I'm not that good. I'd rather be dragged behind the Cadillac through broken lava lamps."

"While a drum circle plays on."

He closed his eyes. "They're insane."

She shifted her head on his chest and closed hers as well.

"There's a lot of that going around."

Chapter 20

The road to Lake Tahoe wound through the Sierra Nevada Mountains as they climbed. The Eldorado's big engine labored as the altitude increased, the air growing thinner and colder as they ascended the pass. Black passed another bus grinding along in the slow lane, on its way from California to the nearby casinos in Reno and Lake Tahoe, and wondered at the number of passengers who chose to travel by that lowbrow method rather than fly.

Sylvia grabbed his arm and pointed off to the side of the freeway. "Look. A deer."

They'd awoken at 5:00 and scarfed down coffee and muffins in the kitchen, peering out into the still dark sky with Spring keeping them company before they hit the road, anxious to get underway. The trip would take three hours if the roads were clear, but Black didn't want to be late for the shoot, which was scheduled to start at 9:00. He'd spoken with Bill multiple times and was confident that security was as tight as it could get, but still, Daniel had been clear that he expected Black to be there, and since Daniel was paying the freight, he would get what he wanted.

"We're in God's country now, that's for sure." Black had given her a running travelogue as they'd driven through gold country on the way to the mountains. He combined what he could remember of the actual history of the area with pure invention, which she seemed not to notice. "Up ahead is Donner Pass. A group of settlers got stuck there during the winter a hundred and fifty years ago, and wound up having to eat each other to make it through to spring. Fortunately, there were some tasty ones in the group."

She swatted at him. "Is that true?"

"We don't really know how tasty they were. I did hear that they tasted kind of like spam, though."

"I honestly think that you're messing with me most of the time."

"I'd like to mess with you most of the time. But sometimes you have a headache."

"If we break down, we could just eat your calf. That would last us a few days."

"Seems reasonable. I'm not really using that left one much anyway."

Sylvia watched the pine forest whizz by. "I wonder how they knew which ones would be tastiest?"

Black grinned. "Oh, baby, you just know."

As they passed the snowline the ground turned white, the first snowfall of the season having hit two weeks before. They went from verdant green to a winter wonderland within the space of twenty minutes, and Sylvia pulled her coat around her as they neared the summit.

Black turned off at the resort exit and slowed, mindful of ice on the road and not wanting to turn his car into a giant convertible sled. At the end of a long road they approached a guard gate, which was empty as they drove past it – not a great sign from a security standpoint, but also not necessarily indicative of anything but the personnel being on a bathroom break. Once on the resort grounds, they followed a small map Daniel had emailed until they arrived at the staging area for the shoot. It was relatively small compared to Cabo or Vegas, with only five models working and eighteen support staff. All the talent was being provided by Demille, who had flown into Reno the night before and arrived at the shoot early that morning.

They parked near the wardrobe trailer and stepped out of the car, their breath steaming the air. They made their way to Jeanie, who was on her ever-present radio, listening intently as someone spoke between bursts of garbled static. Her eyes widened in recognition and she ended the discussion with a terse instruction, and then held out a gloved hand in greeting.

"Well, if it isn't Mr. Black."

"The one and only."

"Your buddy Bill has been making my life miserable. But he's thorough, and he definitely works long hours. I have to say I feel better that he's helping here," she said.

"That's good to hear. Jeanie, this is Sylvia. Sylvia, Jeanie. She runs the show at these shoots. A regular drill sergeant," Black said.

"Hardly. More of a gofer and bottle washer than anything," she replied, shaking Sylvia's hand while appraising her.

"How's it going? What's on the schedule?" Black asked.

"They're setting up a shot over on that far bridge by the edge of the lake. Only one model in that one. Then we go up on the ski slope for a group shot with three, and we round it out with some outside the chalet over there. We already did all the interior shots in the lodge – lots of lounging around in après-ski apparel."

"What are they modeling?"

"Winter garb by a new brand being launched for one of the big snowboarding companies that's trying to expand and leverage their reputation into winter wear. We did a shot for them a month ago or so in Canada, and they liked it so much they hired us to do another."

"Where in Canada?"

"Banff. Lake Louise."

"Nice. You really get around, don't you?"

"So far this year I've been to eleven countries, with two more to go by year's end. So yeah, my passport's pretty full." Her radio screeched and she held it to her ear. "Will you excuse me?"

"Sure. Where's Bill?"

"I saw him over by the bridge. You want me to find him for you?"

"No, no need. That's a long haul. If he's there, he's working. I'll see him when I head over to check things out."

Black and Sylvia wandered to the wardrobe trailer, where the staff was working busily to keep the outfits straight. Black gave Sylvia a quick tour and did the same in makeup, where only one model remained – Hailey – the others having already gotten their outdoor faces done. Black introduced Sylvia to Hailey, who seemed typically subdued, and when they left the trailer Sylvia pulled close to Black.

"I see what you mean. Not exactly Miss Congeniality, is she?"

"She's been like that every time I've talked to her. And yet when the camera's on her, she transforms into a different person."

"Okay, that's officially weird."

"I know."

They moved back into the parking lot and stopped near the area where the big rigs parked. A loud diesel generator clattered nearby, providing power for the trailers.

She took in the semi rigs and the busy crew marching around with earnest looks, arms full of cases and bundles of cables.

"It's a big production."

"This is nothing compared to Vegas or Cabo."

"Still, it's interesting to see."

"I agree. Listen. If you don't mind, let's get you situated in the lodge, where it's nice and warm. It's freezing out here, and I need to get over to the bridge."

"Trying to get rid of me while you rub mittens with the models?"

"I'm an open book, aren't I?"

"Just be careful. I'll bet there are some pretty hot ski instructors here."

"Aren't all ski instructors hot? I don't really know. I don't ski. But I imagine it's like being a tennis pro. Hotness is just part of the job description."

"Leave me at your peril, Black," she teased.

"Come on. Let's get some coffee and I'll scope out the lodge to ensure you aren't attacked while you're waiting for me."

"By anyone but ski instructors."

"Just tell them you're poor. They hate poor people."

"Elitist swine."

"That's more like it."

Sylvia was the only customer in the lodge, with three service staff for company, and after bringing her a steaming cup of hot chocolate Black departed, eager to reach Bill and hear the latest. He found his way back to the trailers and stopped by the nearest, holding his cell phone up to confirm he had a signal. It was weak, only two bars, which he hoped would be sufficient. He pressed a speed dial number and held it to his ear.

"Black Investigations."

"Roxie. It's me. I made it."

"Super." Nothing more. Roxie wasn't particularly talkative, and he could hear her fingers flying over her keyboard in the background. No doubt sending personal messages on company time.

"Listen, I've been thinking about this. I want more on Zane. Pull his credit report. Phone records. Credit cards, if you can. I want to know if he was in Cabo when we were."

"Does it bother you that what you're describing is totally illegal?"

"Really?"

"Uh, yeah. We've had this discussion before. Does the word 'felony' ring any bells?"

"If you can't do it, say so. Maybe Stan can."

"I'll have it for you by the time you get back. But I swear, if I get caught, I'm totally ratting you out and playing dumb."

Black resumed walking, eying the bridge a half mile away. "I'd expect nothing less."

When he hung up, he did a quick estimation and figured he could make it to the bridge in ten or fifteen minutes. Not seeing any transportation, he resigned himself to a long slog and set out for the lake, his hiking boots crunching against the icy snow as he moved off the pavement and onto the trail that led to the bridge. The snow crackled underfoot with each step, and his feet were already freezing after five minutes of walking.

A snowmobile roared by Black as he made his way along the lake. Black saw strands of long hair blowing from under the passenger's helmet as the contrivance pulled past him, and then another snowmobile eased to a stop beside him.

"Sorry I can't give you a ride, stranger," Jeanie called from the back. The driver turned his goggled face and stared at Black before giving him a shrug. "But if you want, I'll radio for another snowmobile."

"Nah, I can use the exercise. I gather Demille's on the bridge with the crew?"

"You know, I haven't seen him for a while. I don't know."

"Go do what you need to do. I'll be along in a few minutes. By the time someone gets out here on one of those things to haul my fat ass over there, I'll be at the bridge."

"Okay. And for the record, I've seen fatter."

The snowmobile rumbled away, leaving a cloud of snow and exhaust in its wake. Black put his head down and pulled his jacket tighter, his hands in his pockets, and continued onward, wishing he'd thought through how cold it was going to be when packing for the trip.

As he neared the bridge he could see bright lights focused on it from either end. Four figures held reflective plates to better train the lighting on the model standing in the center of its span, one hip cocked out, a bright red jacket and goggles her concession to the winter weather.

Suddenly an explosion sounded from behind him, a deep boom that echoed through the valley, causing Black to start. A high-pitched whistle reached his ears, and then the center of the bridge detonated in a bright orange ball of flame, vaporizing the model instantly and sending huge pieces of the wood and iron sailing through the air. Black stood, stunned, unsure what had just happened, and then screaming reached his ears as the terrified crew reacted to the unthinkable.

Snowmobiles and a heavy truck rumbled toward him from the lodge and flew past him, filled with grim men racing to try to help. Black was frozen in place by the enormity of what he'd just seen, his brain refusing to process the unthinkable. Jeanie's snowmobile came racing back with her gripping the handlebars, the original driver nowhere in evidence.

"Jump on. I don't have much time. One of the crew is wounded. They're doing everything they can, but I need to coordinate getting a helicopter up here to airlift him out."

Black swung his leg over the saddle and they lurched off, the growl of the motor deafening as she goosed the throttle, his thoughts racing as they bounced along. When they reached the edge of the parking lot, she stopped and he leapt off. Sylvia had come over from the lodge and was standing on the periphery of the small crowd that had gathered, horrified expressions on the spectators' faces, murmured speculations drifting on the breeze as he approached. Sylvia ran to him and studied his wind-burned face.

"What happened?"

"I don't know. It sounded like a...like a big gun. Artillery. But where would anyone get an artillery gun up here?"

Jeanie stepped around them. "They have howitzers for avalanche control," she said simply and jogged off to the lodge, her radio glued to her ear.

Black took in the scene and spotted a face he hadn't been expecting. He pushed past Sylvia and through the crowd to where the tall figure was in a hushed discussion with one of the crew members.

"Demille! What are you doing here? I thought you were on the bridge."

"I came back to use the can. What the hell happened?"

"The bridge is gone. We think it was one of the howitzer shells."

"Howitzer? What in the name of God are you talking about?"

"Apparently they have them here to trigger avalanches."

"And someone fired at the bridge?"

Black held Demille's stare. "*Someone* obviously did."

Jeanie returned, followed by Trish and the wardrobe woman.

"What about Hailey?" Demille asked Jeanie, his voice lower.

Trish looked confused. "Hailey? She's not in this shoot. She's in makeup."

Demille shook his head and walked away.

Trish grabbed Jeanie's sleeve. "What? What happened?" Trish demanded, her voice now tinged with panic.

"Demille changed models for the shoot. Hailey was on the bridge, not Veronica," Jeanie said.

"What does that mean, she was on the bridge? That's impossible. She was just here."

Black looked over at the smoking wreckage of the bridge in the distance and couldn't meet Trish's eyes. When she collapsed in a heap, he barely caught her, preventing her from hitting her head against the hard asphalt. The realization that her pride and joy was dead, coupled with the altitude, proved to be a cocktail too strong to stomach.

Chapter 21

The trip back to Los Angeles was subdued. Sylvia sat beside him in silence, the stereo on low, any joy in the air sucked from it by the image of the smoking crater where a promising young talent with her whole life ahead of her had been extinguished like an errant cigarette butt. Black had phoned Daniel but it went to voice mail, and he decided that he wouldn't take it personally when he fired him. He got a call back three hours later from Gunther, who explained that Daniel was in the air, on his way to Argentina for trout fishing in Patagonia with his entourage for several days, and would likely be in touch when he got back, there being no cell service in the wilds of South America.

A beige blanket of smog welcomed them back to the City of Angels as Black pulled over the Grapevine and into the San Fernando Valley. Black wondered how it must have been fifty years earlier when it was largely farmland, like much of Orange County. No smog, that was certain, with just a few people, the dense crush having not yet begun, the final push to the sea still to come. It was evening by the time they made it over the hill and into L.A., and neither of them was in the mood for company. The road had left a film of dust and fatigue, and the explosion had destroyed their peace of mind along with the bridge.

Black dropped Sylvia at her place and stopped at the liquor store on the way home, this time not even trying to resist the siren song of amber relief in pint bottles, or the allure of carcinogens that would lay waste to his lungs just as the memory of Hailey's disappearance in a blinding orange flash had savaged any belief in a reasoned or fair universe.

He sat out on his shabby little terrace, taking long pulls on the liquid fire and belching smoke at the heavens like an angry dragon, and wondered how he was going to catch the callous murderer who was targeting the models. He could still see the hysterical absence of reason in Trish's eyes when she'd come to, the denial of the truth, the unwillingness to believe a reality that had robbed her of the only thing she held dear. It hadn't surprised him when he'd spoken to Jeanie, halfway to L.A., and been told that Trish had been sedated and hospitalized, rambling and incoherent, the trauma of her loss too much for her brutalized psyche to endure.

His phone rang at ten. He held up the bottle, barely an inch remaining, and punched the call button on.

"Are you still awake?" Sylvia asked.

"Yep."

"Drinking?"

"How'd you know?"

"I just know."

"Ah."

"Is it helping?"

"Some. Not really."

"Thank you for taking me."

"Welcome."

"Stay out of the shower, okay?"

"'Kay."

"Good night, Black. Get some sleep."

"You too."

Morning came too early, bringing with it the too-familiar pounding in Black's temples, the cotton mouth and fetid breath that promised a day of misery. He forced himself to rise even as he coughed up a piece of something he hoped wasn't vital and staggered into the bathroom, the air feeling thick as he moved through it, his lungs laboring greedily, every nerve ending seemingly a pain receptor designed specifically for his torment.

And yet, through it all, he felt no remorse. He'd done it to himself, knowing full well the price he'd pay, a sort of chemical self-flagellation, an ethanol penance that was as avoidable as it was agonizing. The shower head sprayed warm needles at his skull, each one the accusatory finger of an angry god, and yet some part of him felt good that he had the familiar discomfort to contend with rather than being forced to focus on the prior day's debacle.

He managed to keep a muffin down at the coffee house, and the second cup of Costa Rican Christmas Surprise actually had him feeling somewhat human. He considered going into the office but decided that he was in no shape to deal with Roxie, who would take one look at him and make it her life's mission to torment him. Instead, he'd go by Eric's tattoo parlor and see if anything had changed. Now that he was effectively unemployed again, awaiting a confirmation from Daniel that was purely a formality, he had nothing but time on his hands, and dozing in front of Eric's shop was as good a way to waste his time as any.

He texted Roxie a terse missive about being out for the day getting his car worked on and set out for the tattoo parlor. When he arrived, the shop was still dark. He checked his watch and then strolled down the street to verify the operating hours. On the door was a hand-scrawled sign advising customers that he would be at the convention center in booth number 2760, today and tomorrow. He belatedly realized that Roxie had told him about the show, and time had simply slipped away from him.

Black had never been to a tattoo trade show, but he couldn't think of any reason not to go – he had the time, and there was always the chance that Eric would slip up publicly, emboldened by the crowds. It was a long shot, but he didn't have any other options, so he returned home, pulled on a pair of jeans and a black long-sleeved concert T-shirt, and headed for the hall, feeling suitably disguised. The chances of a narcissist like Eric remembering him at all were slim, but without his trademark fedora and suit, Black could have been invisible.

The convention center was sparsely attended, the tattoo crowd apparently not as compelled to participate as the event organizers might have hoped. Black bought a Harley Davidson baseball cap inside the hall and kept his sunglasses on, further increasing his resemblance to most anonymous white males wandering the aisles, with the exception that he didn't have tattoos crawling along his hands or up his neck, or piercings distorting his features and plugs distending his earlobes.

He easily found Eric's booth, a humble affair like countless others in the lower-rent section of the show, manned by Eric and his new friend from Berlin, who Black had to admit looked fetching in a tube top and lacquered-on black jeans that revealed her body art in all its glory. He moved by the booth without either of them noticing him and continued to the end of the aisle, where there was a seating area for attendees with scattered chairs and tables.

Black took a seat and read though the pile of brochures he'd collected as part of his cover, and was amazed at the number of products being offered – more so that anyone would want to pay to have any of the procedures performed, than that someone was manufacturing products to aid in the process.

Eric didn't move from the booth for an hour, and as it approached lunchtime, Black's hangover built to epic proportions. If the ravaging his body had taken processing the alcohol wasn't enough, the cigarettes had been icing on that toxic cake, and he was more than paying for it today. His attention was attracted by movement from the front of the booth, where the Berlin tattoo artist was walking toward him, her gait drawing the admiring gaze of many of the gathered males in the area. Black waited until she'd moved past him and then followed her at a discreet distance.

She entered the bathrooms and returned a few minutes later, and then headed to the food court, where she bought two lunches consisting of greasy pizza slabs and sodas. Black decided that nourishment seemed like a reasonable idea and did the same, doubling up on the six-dollar pizza slices in deference to his resource depletion from the night before. He ate quickly at one of the Formica-topped tables, surrounded by a collection of humanity that would have been at home in the bar scene in *Star Wars*, inked in every possible area of their bodies, some including their faces and shaved heads.

Upon his return to the seating area adjacent to the booth, he spied Eric slipping a pint bottle of bourbon to his German friend, who poured half of it into each of their soda cups after glancing around to ensure there were no security guards patrolling the aisle. Black felt a pang of envy and wished he'd had the forethought to sneak in a little headache remedy to spice up his Coke. As it was, demons danced the tarantella in his skull, and he hadn't had the presence of mind to bring so much as an aspirin. He fumbled his phone from his pocket and checked his email, expecting the message from Daniel to be in his inbox, and was surprised he still hadn't been canned – no doubt due more to the lack of cell phone tower investment in rural Argentina than Daniel's acknowledgment that he'd been warned about Black not having enough advance time to guarantee anyone's safety.

He glanced surreptitiously at the booth. The Berlin artist was giggling at some joke, and Eric had his trademark punk smirk plastered on his face as they toasted with their soda cups and finished their cocktails. He felt a stirring of hope at the woman's body language as she touched Eric's arm and played with her hair as she laughed, but that was dashed when two lanky teens dressed entirely in black, with dyed black hair and elaborate piercings and tattoos, stopped at the booth and began a discussion. Black cursed inwardly and wished death upon them, to no effect, and they continued chatting with Eric and the artist while Black's dreams slowly faded.

Then they moved along to bore the next exhibitor, and Black's optimism returned. Ten minutes later the artist went to the bathroom again, and when she returned, she grabbed Eric's hand and dragged him from the booth. Black watched out of the corner of his eye, his breath quickening – he'd been dragged like that before, and he had a pretty good idea what it meant.

He let them get a fair distance ahead of him and watched as they moved into the unlit conference room area, where there were at least twenty meeting rooms for presentations – not a big draw at this kind of a retail-oriented show, but heavily used for trade shows. Eric's comely friend tried the doors until one opened, and after peering inside, she switched on the lights and pulled Eric in after her.

Black took photos of them entering the room, but that wasn't going to be enough. He needed something concrete if he was going to sway Roxie. He waited five minutes before approaching the door, wary of any sign that they were exiting. When he didn't hear anything, he carefully depressed the door lever and cracked it open.

Eric and the artist had apparently been in a rush, and he was able to get more than adequate shots through the gap of Eric taking his new friend from behind, her pants around her ankles and her exposed, tattooed breasts leaving little to the imagination. He got a few that perfectly captured the sneering look of contempt on Eric's face as he drove home his point, and made a mental note to consider getting that one blown up to poster size for the office.

Black eased the door closed again and moved back to the hall, but not before stopping one of the bored security guards and telling him he'd seen some suspicious characters skulking around conference room C, and believed one of them had a gun. As the guard hurried off, calling on his radio as he bee-lined to the room, Black smiled to himself for the first time that day. With any luck at all this would be an adventure Eric wouldn't soon forget, even if no charges were pressed.

The sun was shining brightly as Black moved down the steps in front of the convention center and out onto the pavilion alongside. He watched as a kit of pigeons marched in bobbing lockstep across the square before being chased into the sky by a toddler shrieking with glee at her power over the birds. He checked his watch and yawned, and after thumbing through his new photo collection with a satisfied grin he made for his car, his good deed for the day done, to be rewarded with a long and deserved nap.

Black stopped at the market on the way home and treated himself to a large bottle of Gatorade, his resentment of the container no deterrent to its contents. Once inside he washed down two aspirin and closed his blinds, his eyes already drooping at the thought of a nap and an easing of the relentless pain that had been his companion all day. He stripped off his clothes, crawled into bed, and had a final look at his compilation of snaps from the show before he drifted off, his mouth open. A rattling snore echoed through the room as the ceiling fan spun lazily, a long strand of dusty spider web trailing from it like white smoke as it circled in its endless orbit.

Chapter 22

Gabriel looked through his office window at the street below. Headlights illuminated the darkened thoroughfare as twilight faded into night. He passed a hand over his face and rubbed his eyes – it had been a long day, made more so by the stress created by Black's warning. He'd had a difficult time focusing on anything since the meeting, and had been noticeably on edge with his staff since the infernal investigator had threatened him.

He wasn't cut out for this sort of high-stakes duplicity. Maybe Demille was – he'd always been a schemer and an alpha, whereas Gabriel had a more gentle personality. Which was part of the problem. Gabriel still had strong feelings for Demille, even though he realized that for the modeling mogul he was a disposable convenience, just one in the long string of romantic dalliances that had characterized his career. In Demille's world, it was all about Demille, all the time, and everyone else was just a satellite to his solar presence.

Gabriel rolled his head, trying to get the stress kinks out of his neck. He'd reached for the phone countless times since Black's visit, wanting to confide in Demille and find out what to do. But he had enough self-preservation instincts to realize that if he did that, Demille would gladly take him down with him, and that he could expect no mercy from Black. Gabriel didn't know for sure that the subterfuge with the agency was criminal, but there was no question that if Daniel found out, he'd make it his life's mission to ruin him. So now his future depended on the discretion of a thug in a fedora – a state of affairs that couldn't continue.

He slid his center desk drawer open, removed a prescription bottle, and shook out a pill. His psychiatrist had given him Xanax for panic attacks, and he'd been gulping them like PEZ just to hold it together.

A sound reached his ears from the front office – the entry door opening.

"Hello. We're closed," he called, listening for a response.

Nothing.

Gabriel stood and moved to his doorway. "Hello…" He stopped when he saw who it was, and smiled. "Well, this is a surpr–"

His grin froze on his face as a razor sharp KA-BAR knife blade plunged through his ribcage. He fought to breathe, but his lungs suddenly wouldn't obey. His legs lost their strength and he dropped to his knees, the knife handle protruding from him like a new appendage.

Puzzled pain flashed from his eyes and he tried to scream, but it was as though someone else's body was now supporting his head, a foreign form that refused his commands. His mouth formed one word, which came out as a wheezy mewl.

"Why?"

His assailant pulled the knife free and stabbed him again and again in a frenzy. The crimson blade flashed in the cold fluorescent office lights, the only sounds a muted thumping as the hilt slammed against him and the wet splatter of blood droplets on the walls.

When the police arrived with a forensics team and the coroner's van five hours later, after the cleaning crew discovered Gabriel's mutilated form and called 911, they counted thirty-four stab wounds, and eventually determined that Gabriel had died after the fifth. Unfortunately, the building had no security cameras, and by the time footage from the traffic cams had been pulled and checked for anything suspicious around the time of the attack, the trail had gone cold, and it was too late.

ॐঔ

Knocking from the front door jarred Black awake. The pounding continued, so he rolled off the bed and pulled his bathrobe off a hook on the back of the door before moving into the living room to see what the ruckus was all about.

"Yeah?"

"Black. It's Jared."

Black blinked and twisted the doorknob. Jared, his landlady's nephew, was a slacker who'd taken up residence on her couch while he waited to be discovered by the Hollywood machine and made a star.

"Yeah, Jared. What's up? Is Gracie okay?"

"She's fine. She just sent me up here to remind you that you still owe her half the rent from the first."

"Crap. She's right. I totally spaced on that with everything else going on. Come on in and I'll cut you a check."

Jared entered and Black closed the door and got his checkbook. He sat down at the kitchen table and began writing, and then glanced up at Jared.

"You want a beer or something?"

"Hard to turn down free beer."

Black went to the refrigerator and returned with two cans, popping the tops with a hiss. "There you go."

"Thanks."

Black signed the check and handed it to Jared with a flourish. Jared slipped it into his shirt pocket as he eyed Black.

"What's wrong, are you sick or something?" Jared asked.

"Not particularly. Why?"

"The robe at eight o'clock at night…"

"Damn, is it already eight? I took a nap. Had a late stake-out…"

"Oh. I didn't think about that."

"All part of the PI game."

"Who were you staking out?"

"Some bum cheating on his girlfriend. I got him red-handed on camera, but I'm not sure how to break it so it's public. I'm not really very tech savvy."

"You can always upload it anonymously and create a photo album in Flickr, and then send whoever the address with Twitter…"

Black took a pull on his beer. "That might as well have been Swahili, Jared."

"It's not that hard."

"Maybe not for you." A light bulb went on in Black's head. "Say, maybe you could help me. Could you create the photo album and see if you can find the person on one of those sites? It'd be worth some money to me."

"Did you say money?"

"As in cash. Cold, hard cash."

"How much?"

"You said it was easy. So…twenty?"

"I was thinking a hundred's a nice round number."

"So's twenty."

"It'll still take some time. Make it fifty and we have a deal."

"Done."

"Fine. You have the photos?"

"On my phone."

"Let me see it. I'll send them to my email and upload them from my laptop. What's the GF's name?"

"GF?"

"Girlfriend."

"Ah. I see. Because whole words are exhausting. LMFAO. Isn't that what the kids say nowadays?"

Jared stared at him stonily. "So do you have her name?"

Black wrote down the information and handed it to him. "Let me know when you do it."

"Where's the fifty?"

"What? I'm good for it…"

"Then I'll do it when you give it to me."

Black nipped into the bedroom and returned with two twenties and a ten. He slid them across the table to Jared, giving him an evil glare. "I can't believe you don't trust me, after all I did for you. And look – I even gave you a beer."

"Sorry. Business is business."

Black eyed him. "You've learned a lot since hitting town. You'll go far, young man."

Jared chugged the rest of his beer and emitted a loud burp before rising. "Gotta run down more deadbeats, my man. No offense."

"None taken. You thinking you'll get it done tonight?"

"In an hour or so."

"And then all hell will break loose," Black said with a smile.

"It's nice to see a man who enjoys his work."

Black was exiting the shower for the second time that day, this time in considerably more stable shape, when another knock sounded from his door. He groped for a towel and wrapped it around his waist.

"Who is it?"

"Police," Sylvia's voice called from outside.

He pulled the door wide and she regarded him, his hair sticking up at all angles, water tricking from his hairline and down his legs onto the carpet, and held up a white plastic bag with two containers inside with one hand and a bottle of budget Australian Shiraz with the other.

"I thought you might be hungry after a long day fighting crime."

"You know me like you know the beating of your own heart," he said, stepping aside so she could enter.

"Sorry I got you out of the shower."

"I was just thinking that you could make it up to me by joining me."

She set the food and wine down and smiled. "Before or after dinner?"

Chapter 23

Demille finished stretching in the lavish living room of his hilltop home and gazed out at Los Angeles laid out before him like a tapestry in the morning light. He loved this time of day, just after dawn, when life seemed filled with possibility. That would quickly change once he went into the office and had to field countless worried calls from clients, deal with insurance companies looking for reasons to stiff him, and talk his models into staying aboard, he knew; but for a short while, the universe seemed in balance, the world at tentative peace.

Fallout from the Tahoe debacle had been severe, which wasn't unexpected given the circumstances. The police were stymied trying to figure out who the killer was, and the papers were having a field day with the sensationalistic murder of a semi-famous model. Every paper carried a headshot of Hailey, and she'd become a staple on the news circuit as the networks milked the combination of sex appeal and tragedy for all it was worth.

Demille did a set of ten knee bends and pulled a lanyard with his house key dangling from it over his head in preparation for his morning run. Every day, regardless of the previous night's excesses, he ran five miles without fail, which contributed to his lean good looks – which he believed were still at least five years younger than his chronological age. Of course the surgical augmentation, the nip here, the tuck, lipo, and Botox there, had also helped, but it was mainly diet and exercise. He'd been eating almost exclusively high-protein for a decade and swore by it, to the annoyance of his few steady friends, all of whom were experiencing the middle age spread that seemed to be an essential part of moving from their forties into their fifties. But not Demille. He still fit into the same jeans he'd been wearing twenty years ago, and was as rigid in his calorie intake as with his exercise routine – a carryover from his modeling days.

He stepped outside and looked up at the trees surrounding his home. The cool air smelled of dewy grass and privilege. After three deep breaths he trotted to the end of his drive, where he turned right and slowly picked up the pace. Down the street a gardening van crawled up the grade, the undocumented aliens inside of it accustomed to the early hours their employer demanded, and Demille hugged the shoulder as the tired vehicle passed him. It pulled to a stop across the street and the crew tumbled out of the doors. Demille could hear the leaf blowers fire up as he wound his way around the corner on his customary route.

He barely registered the roar of an engine behind him, hurtling down the hill at increasing speed – and then he was flying through the air, tumbling head over heels in a limp mockery of a back-flip before bouncing against the pavement like a rag doll, his skull splitting open with a sickening crack. He rolled four more yards and lay still near the gutter. Blood pooled beneath his head as his last few breaths burbled in his chest. The rising sun's golden rays caressed his face while he convulsed violently, his hands curling unnaturally before he stiffened and lay still.

The driver continued down the hill, unobserved by the sleeping neighbors, safe behind their faux Tuscan walls in a neighborhood where money insulated them from the ugliness of the outside world. A man walking his dog discovered Demille's battered corpse fifteen minutes later, by which time his blood had already coagulated in a rust-colored puddle as his body cooled. In the pocket of his jogging jacket Demille's cell phone trilled, with nobody to answer it ever again, or to retrieve the shocked, sobbing message from Gabriel's sister.

ॐ∘ॐ

Roxie's eyes were red and swollen when Black made it into the office toting a chai for her and a half-drunk drip coffee for himself. Her heavy mascara was blotchy, as though hurriedly applied. Mugsy purred loudly in her lap as she hugged him to her chest. Black envied the corpulent cat for a moment and then shook off the inappropriate thought as she snuffled and reached for a tissue.

"What's wrong? Allergies?"

"Something like that."

Black stopped. "Something? What's wrong?"

"Eric and I broke up," she stated flatly. "He was cheating on me. Again."

"What?" Black exclaimed, taking a seat on the couch across from her station, careful not to sound too shocked. "What a piece of shit."

"Yeah. I never should have given him that second chance. But I thought he'd changed…"

"You're better off without him. If he doesn't know what a good thing he had going, he's an idiot," Black said, and meant it.

Roxie told him about the anonymous Twitter account that had sent her the URL for a photo album containing explicit photographs of Eric *in flagrante delicto* with his new friend from Berlin – his new very good friend, judging by her expression in three of the shots.

"Wow. So someone got him on camera? What a moron. I don't really follow all that tweet stuff, but that's the end result, isn't it?"

"That's right. I keep forgetting that you still think phones have rotary dials."

"Hey. I'm learning. I can check my email from my cell now."

"After how many years of not knowing you could do that? Hello."

"For me it's progress."

"So anyway, we had a big fight last night and I told him to leave for Berlin early, because I was throwing his lying, cheating ass out."

"Good for you."

"I'm not going, by the way."

"I read between the lines on that."

"Yeah. Besides, I've been following the weather online. Who would want to live there?"

"Lying, cheating scumbags?"

"At least one. I hope she's got a big enough pad to accommodate him. Probably lives with her parents. Serves him right. I hope he winds up sleeping on a park bench in the snow."

"Well, I know you probably don't want to hear this, but it's probably for the best. You don't need that crap. You deserve better."

She sniffed. "I know. It's just…it's hard."

He nodded sagely. "Of course it is."

She eyed him. "You look relieved."

He rose, trying to force his poker face back into place. "I am. Now I don't have to worry about how to explain there's no big bonus."

"I knew it."

"But that's water under the bridge. Did he move out yet?"

"Yeah. I own everything but his clothes, so it wasn't hard."

"Did you get the locks changed?"

"Late last night after he left. Cost a fortune, but hey, with such a generous boss, I figured I could afford it."

"Put the receipt into the company folder and write yourself a check."

Black was just settling into his office, satisfied after a job well done, when Roxie called out from her position in the outer sanctum.

"Boss. Did you see this?"

"See what? I haven't seen anything."

"Come out here. It's Gabriel."

"What about him?" Black asked as he approached her desk.

"He was murdered last night. It's on the local news page."

"Murdered?" Black's face froze as he processed the information. "Where? How?"

"Says here in his office. Stabbed to death. Police will issue a statement later. Blah blah."

"That bastard," Black muttered under his breath.

"Who?"

"Demille," Black said, and ran back into his office for his cell phone. He pressed a speed dial button and Stan picked up.

"Stan. It's me. I just saw the news. Last night one of the guys involved in this modeling case I'm working got offed in Santa Monica. Stabbing."

"Yeah? I got my own problems. Good morning, by the way."

"The reason I'm calling is because I think I know who did it."

"Really? That'll make things a lot easier. Who?"

"Thomas Demille." Black quickly explained the relationship and the scheme to defraud DNA.

"And what's the motive?"

"To shut him up. Or maybe it was a lover's tiff. How would I know? But that's who did it. I'd bet money."

"Really? How much?"

"What? What do you mean, how much?"

"A hundred?"

"Stan. What's going on?"

"I typed in Demille's name while we were talking, and he just turned up dead outside his home. Hit and run."

Black was speechless. "Oh, God."

"No, still Stan here. But you can call me whatever you want…"

"Stan. Listen. Then it has to be Zane. Zane Bradley. Look up that name."

Black heard rapid typing. "I always wondered what kind of parent names their kid something like Zane. Guaranteed to mess with their head…"

"You got his record?"

"Yeah, I see the DUI and a pending in Vegas. Oh, that's right. He's your Sin City boy."

"And he's also who killed Demille and Gabriel. And the models…"

"You wouldn't happen to have any proof, would you?"

"Pull him in and sweat him. He won't have an alibi for last night or this morning."

"I can't just pull him in with nothing but your say-so."

"Come on, Stan. You know you can do anything you want."

Stan sighed loudly. "I can swing by his place and ask him a few questions. No promises, though. You're lucky Demille's death will land in this office. Otherwise I'd have no authority."

"Stan, you're a Godsend."

"Yeah, yeah. Assuming he's even at his place or his work. I hear a lot of mass murderers tend to take the day off after a big spree. Tiring, I guess."

"Damn. You're right. He could still be out there…I need to go."

"What? Where?"

"There's somebody else he's really holding a grudge against. She could be next." Black told him about Trish.

"Dude. Slow down. You're going into overdrive, and you don't even know if the guy was in church this morning or something. You really think he blew up the daughter and is now going after the mom?"

"Stan, trust me. Go get him. He's your man. I'm headed over to Trish's house. Call me once you know something."

"All right, Kemosabe, but I think you're off the reservation on this one."

Black didn't wait to hear more. He hung up and went into his office, opened the safe, and removed his gun. Roxie watched from the doorway.

"You think Zane's gone frigging nuts?"

"Yup. He snapped. Or he's doped out of his mind. Who knows? It's the only thing that fits."

"But why is he killing everyone?"

"Oldest motive in the world. Revenge."

Black sped out of the office and took the stairs two at a time to the street. He called Trish's home number as he jogged to the car, but it just rang. After glancing over his shoulder to ensure there was no traffic he did a quick calculation as he pulled away – he could be at her house in half an hour if he didn't mind breaking a few laws.

The drive over the hill went quickly, and fortunately for Black, there were no Highway Patrol cruisers monitoring the stretch of road he was on. When he pulled off the freeway he exhaled in relief, and realized that his stomach was a knot of tense muscles. His phone rang as he eased to the curb in front of Trish's house. Her truck sat in the driveway, no sign of anything amiss. He answered, tapping his ear bud to life.

"Hey, buddy. Thanks for nothing. You just had me waste half an hour I'll never get back," Stan's voice boomed in his ear.

"What happened?"

"He was at the fur shop, which, by the way, is a little weird, but hey. Anyway, I drilled him, and he's got an alibi."

Black shut off the engine, thinking. "Impossible."

"Yeah, that's what I thought you would say, so we're checking it out. But if he's telling the truth, it's back to square one. Listen. I've got to go, here. Call me later. I'll do the same if I hear anything."

Black stepped away from the Cadillac, lost in thought. None of it made any sense. He looked up at the sound of Trish's front door opening. She walked out hefting two heavy travel bags, her purse over her shoulder. She spotted him and froze, and then her face broke into a smile.

"Why Mr. Black. What are you doing here?" she asked.

"I...I thought there might be a threat to you, Trish. By the way, I'm sorry for your loss."

"Thank you." She looked over his shoulder, then back at him. "A threat?" she asked, sounding puzzled.

"Yeah. Turns out I was...wrong..." Black's eyes drifted over to the truck, whose steel front bumper and passenger side fender were crumpled. "Going on a trip?"

"I can't stay in this house anymore. It's too much. Too many memories," she explained, setting the bags down.

"I can understand that. Trish – what happened to the truck?"

"The truck?"

Black nodded as he unbuttoned his jacket.

Trish shrugged. "Oh, that's nothing."

Neither of them said anything for a moment that stretched uncomfortably long. Black began walking toward her, his hands held open just in front of him, like a tightrope walker trying to balance.

"Trish. Don't do anything stupid. It's over, okay?"

Their eyes locked and she tensed. Time seemed to slow as she reached into her purse and ducked into a crouch. Black got his Glock free and chambered a round as she whipped out an ugly-looking pistol and drew a bead on him. He fired a split second before she started shooting, and he threw himself to the ground as he continued firing, squeezing off shots as fast as he could pull the trigger.

Trish jerked back as a round caught her in the torso. Another hit her in the chest, and she dropped her weapon with a grunt and collapsed. Black lay on the sidewalk, gun trained on her, and fought for breath as he assessed whether any of her shots had hit him. He knew from his army days that often the wounded didn't realize they'd been hit until after the shooting stopped.

He got unsteadily to his feet, the barrel of his pistol never straying from her, and slowly moved to where she was lying on the porch, twitching spasmodically. Her gun was lying near the smaller of the bags and he toed it out of reach as he gazed down at her.

"I told you not to do anything stupid," he whispered. Her face was pallid. Her lips trembled, and blood trickled from the corner of her mouth. A bubbling, sucking noise emanated from the wound in her chest as she breathed, and he knew enough to know that sound wasn't good. One hand clutched at her abdomen, and her eyes fluttered open at his words.

"She…she wasn't…supposed to be…on the…bridge," Trish managed, the last word ending in a groan that ended in a wet cough.

"Why, Trish? Why?"

Her eyelids drooped closed as she spoke, her life running out of her onto the hard cement slab, nothing anyone could do to stop it. "Other…girls…in Hailey's…way…"

"Why Demille?"

"He...he and...my...baby..."

Black dialed 911 and described the scene in precise terms to the operator, and promised to stay on the line while she sent help. He set his pistol on the walkway so he wouldn't be shot by an overzealous officer and waited for the squad cars to draw near. A seagull, too far from the ocean, seemingly lost above the concrete sprawl, wheeled overhead before flying west, back to a distant shore where fish awaited and the water was cool. A warm breeze stirred Black's hair as he slowly sank to the ground and watched Trish pass from this world into the next, carrying with her the stain of her deeds as sirens wailed their approach to a sky the color of wet cardboard. A front had moved in from the ocean, bringing with it the cool first rain of winter.

Chapter 24

Black stared at his beer bottle, sweating next to the empty shot glass on the scarred wood table top of the Calypso Queen's bar – a dark dive that perfectly matched his mood after the shooting that morning. Steel drums and acoustic guitars provided the background music, and haggard men with lean, hardscrabble faces etched with disappointment lines and stained with nicotine and despair, the company.

Stan finished his shot and elbowed Black. "Come on. Let's get a table. Your date's here."

Black turned to where Sylvia stood at the entrance, a slab of mahogany fashioned from an old sailing schooner's door, and grunted. They rose, and Stan held up two fingers to the bartender and pointed at their drinks. He nodded, his face permanently cast in a frown, and turned to the rows of bottles as they made their way to one of the small tables along the periphery of the gloomy room.

Sylvia approached, kissed Black on the cheek, and then took a seat next to him.

"Nice places you boys hang out in."

"We're classy guys. What can I say?" Stan offered.

"How are you?" Sylvia asked, putting her hand over Black's.

"Not so great. I hear shooting a woman on her front porch will do that to you," he said, not slurring yet, his voice gutted of emotion.

"She pulled a gun on you, boss man," Stan reminded.

"That she did. And I killed her."

The bartender arrived, and Sylvia looked at the bottles and smiled. "I'll take one of those beers, please." She returned her attention to Black. "She was trying to kill you. She killed all those people. Her own daughter. I'm not saying you should feel great about it, but I'm glad you're the one left standing and not her."

190

"She said that Hailey wasn't supposed to be on the bridge. So she was trying to kill one of the other models," Black said.

"Which is completely insane, in case you don't realize it," Stan said. "As is putting acid into makeup or any of the rest of it. Big sale on crazeee on aisle five. I see it all the time. A mom drowns her baby because it won't stop crying. A husband kills his wife of forty years because she keeps leaving the bathroom door open when he's asked her a million times to close it. Some people are just nuts. And those people, when they pull a gun on you, need to be put down like mad dogs."

"I know that. But it still sucks, killing a woman."

Sylvia studied his face. "Is that it? Because she was female? Okay, so would you still feel the same way if it had been a two-hundred-pound gang banger?"

"Well...maybe not."

Stan shook his head. "Black. She was a mass murderer. She killed Demille this morning. Went berserk on Gabriel last night. You should've seen the photos of that one. Looked more like hamburger than a human body by the time she was done with him. Trust me, there has to be a lot of rage built up inside you to do something like that. You did the right thing, buddy. So have another shot, understand that's how it is, and move on."

"I wonder why she killed Gabriel?" Sylvia mused.

Black shrugged. "Who knows? Maybe she discovered he was really working with Demille? That's not the kind of secret that stays a secret forever." Black paused. "You know, something she said as she was dying...I think Demille...was banging Hailey."

"What? She was just a child," Sylvia said. "He was, what, fifty?"

"Forty-something. But it doesn't matter. It's still sick. Maybe that's why she was so...muted," Black said. "What's even worse is that Trish obviously knew about it, and was willing to let it happen. At least until the end. Makes you wonder what else she turned a blind eye to – how many boyfriends she had over time who might have...I don't even want to think about it."

"I pulled her CV. Trish was in the Army for four years. Artillery corps. Which explains how she knew how to work a howitzer," Stan said. He downed his latest shot in a gulp and washed it down with beer.

"What kills me is that I thought Zane was completely guilty," Black said quietly. "I couldn't have been more wrong."

Sylvia squeezed his hand. "It's over. Nobody else is going to die. You did it."

"Hey, don't say that. My job depends on people dying every day, young lady. You want to talk me out of a career?" Stan said.

"Sorry. Didn't mean it that way."

"That's better."

Stan cleared his throat. "What about the model who overdosed in Mexico? Do you think she was behind that?"

"We'll never know, but if you ask me, she was. I have no idea how she got into her room – I'm thinking Clarissa had a date with someone and left the door open, and when Trish saw that, she acted impulsively and went in. If Clarissa was out of it, that was probably too sweet an opportunity for Trish to pass up. That's my hunch."

"And the New York suicide?"

"Again. No way of knowing. But I could certainly see her scheming to get Daria alone and then pushing her off the building. Remember she was in the Army. She could have coldcocked her and dumped her over the rail. The trauma from the fall would have erased any evidence of a blow prior to her death."

They sat for a quiet moment, listening to the slightly out-of-tune music and the dull hum of conversation from other patrons in the background. Black looked around as though waking up from a dream.

"It's too dark in this damned place. What time is it?"

"Nine," Sylvia said. "You getting hungry yet?"

"A little," Black conceded.

Stan waved for the bill. "Dude, I'm not going to say you'll be singing in the rain tonight, but you'll get over this. It's perfectly natural that you feel like hell. You should. If you can shoot someone and not feel bad, you're part of the problem, not the solution. But this was a clean kill. You warned her, she drew on you, and you defended yourself. That's pretty straightforward. Cut and dried. The only thing you're guilty of is being a decent shot. God knows how you pulled that off. You never go to the range."

"I also have a lovely singing voice."

"I'll take your word for it. So here's my advice, for what it's worth. Go have a nice dinner. Have another drink or two, but not too many more. Enjoy each other's company. Make love, create something good and honest, cry if you want to, but put this behind you. It's just another shitty thing that's happened to you. There'll be plenty more. Focus on the positives, not the negatives, because the world will rain those down on you plenty more times before you take the old dirt nap." Stan finished his beer with a long swallow. "I've been there. More times than I like to think about. I know what I'm talking about. Beating yourself up about it won't change anything, won't make you a better human being, and is basically just wallowing in self-pity. So knock it off. Thus spake Stan Colt."

Black hiccupped. "Sorry." He regarded Stan. "You should do motivational speaking or something. You missed your calling."

"I've been told that. I also write poetry and cry when I watch Meg Ryan movies."

"She's not that bad."

"Kind of hot, actually."

Black shook his head. "You're a pig. You've got a Meg jones?"

"Hey. Let me at least have that, okay? Don't kill all my dreams."

Sylvia smiled. "Black, your friend is a wise man. I say we take his advice. Eat, drink, and be merry. Maybe roll around and pull some hair. Sounds like a plan."

Black brightened. "I like the hair part."

She patted his hand. "I figured that would get your attention."

Black eyed Stan. "What happened with Ernest?"

"Let's just say that the hot dog empire is back on track, and Ernest won't be pulling that stunt anymore. On anyone."

"You didn't…do anything rash, did you?"

"Nah. I filed a copy of your cinematographic debut with the disability boys, who take a dim view of being defrauded by scumbags. I also showed his attorney the footage and played him the part of the recording where he assures you he can handle the food bag when you offer to help. Which, by the way, you were a little too convincingly creepy at, no offense. I would have punched you."

"Maybe he was curious?"

"Or maybe he thought you were cute," Sylvia suggested.

"What do you mean, thought? I am cute. In a ruggedly handsome, he-man kind of way."

"Come on. Let's get out of here. Too much testosterone in the air for me," Sylvia said, standing.

Black gave Stan a wan smile. "You heard the lady. Thanks for listening, buddy. I kind of needed that."

"Any time, my friend. Any time."

Chapter 25

Black lowered the top of the Cadillac and smoothed his hair in the cool morning light before setting his fedora firmly on his head so it wouldn't blow off. He turned on the stereo and blared Little Caesar as he wrenched the steering wheel left and gave the big ride some gas. He eased onto the leaf-blown street as he reviewed his mental checklist on the way to the office.

He stopped at his favorite coffee bar for his morning shot of wake-up, and noted that his nemesis, the smugly arrogant barista, was holding court, smirking at his customers' orders as he repeated them back in a tone that was both insulting and superior. Black locked eyes with him from over the shoulder of a short, older woman muttering on her cell phone in front of him in line, and steeled himself for the ordeal to come.

He stepped up to the counter and a wave of calm flooded through him, a transcendental peace like he was sure Samurai attained as they prepared for battle. After a brief study of the board, he cleared his throat and ordered a venti cup of the drip coffee of the day. The young man paused, as if savoring his possibilities, and then called the order back to his associate without engaging with Black.

"Will there be anything else?"

"A large chai," Black said.

"You mean a grande?" the server asked, stressing the last syllable, making it sound French or Italian.

"Sure. One of those."

"Excellent. Have a nice day." The plastic smile was patently phony, but there was nothing to fault the barista on. He'd taken the order without drama, and was already looking at the next person shuffling forward in line. Black felt an odd sense of letdown, prepared for another in a long string of scuffles with the punk, and only as he stepped toward the cash register did he realize that this was what it was like to have things go his way – no drama, just his cup of steaming hot coffee delivered quickly and efficiently.

He'd become so accustomed to defending himself from the threats in his environment he felt disappointed when they didn't manifest, and wondered at what his life had become, where even the purchase of a morning beverage was a call to arms.

Roxie was at her station when he arrived at the office, Mugsy lying on his back on the couch, all four paws in the air, snoring happily. Black set the chai down in front of her like an offering and took in her new hair color – platinum blonde with pink tips. Her outfit was, as usual, completely inappropriate for work: a green leotard top and a pair of ripped jeans with generous expanses of skin showing through the gaps in the fabric, and her beloved knee-high biker boots, the silver side buckles undone, as though purely ornamental.

"Hey. Look who brought you some tasty chai! How about that?" he asked.

"How did you know it was my birthday?"

Black's eyes betrayed his confusion for a split second – long enough. She snorted and shook her head. "You don't even remember when it is, do you?"

"Your birthday?"

"No, the anniversary of the bombing of Pearl Harbor."

"I'm pretty sure that was in February."

"Uh, December seventh. Even I know that."

"Right. I was testing you."

"Sure you were."

"How about a 'thanks, boss, you're the best for bringing me chai this morning' instead of looking for reasons to bag on me?"

"If I was looking to bag on you, I'd just go for your outfit."

"What's wrong with it?"

"You look like a low-rent tango dancer or something."

"I'll have you know this suit was expensive."

"Maybe in the nineteen twenties."

Black sighed. "I suppose it's silly to ask if anyone called?"

"Actually, someone did. Gunther, from DNA."

Black's pulse pounded in his ears. He'd been wondering when they'd call to fire him, and had already prepared a final accounting.

"Ah. Good. Payday's coming up."

Roxie hesitated and her tone softened. "I saw the news about the shooting. How're you doing?"

"Fine. No sweat. Just another day in the PI game."

"Uh huh. You sure?"

"Positive. But thanks for asking."

"No problem. I'd say if you need to talk, I'm here…but I wouldn't be able to manage it with a straight face."

"I wouldn't want to put you through that. You might pull something and hurt yourself."

"And sue you."

"Exactly."

Roxie handed him a message slip with a phone number scrawled on it. "He called about twenty minutes ago."

"Probably thought I'd be working during business hours."

"Think he'll pay you, or am I back to shopping for ramen for dinner?"

"You like ramen."

"Yeah. Rat tail soup with noodles. My favorite."

"Don't talk about food. You'll wake Mugsy." Black entered his office, flicked the lights on, shrugged off his jacket, and hung it on the door hook. He went to his chair and noted Mugsy still hadn't eviscerated it, for which he was grateful every day, and set his half-full coffee cup down after removing the plastic lid. DNA's receptionist answered the phone on the second ring, sounding constipated as usual, and after a twenty-second wait, Gunther came on the line.

"Mr. Black."

"Gunther."

"Daniel would like to have a conference call. Could you hold the line while I get him on the phone?"

"Sure."

Some insipid pop anthem droned in his ear as he waited, and then Daniel's voice joined the call with a slight echo.

"Black. I heard about the shooting. Gunther filled me in. It's a shame about Demille. Must have been an ugly day all around."

"It was. Are you still in Argentina?"

"Yes. I'll be flying back to New York tonight."

"I have news for you about your merger you may find interesting." Black told him about Demille's scheme with Gabriel to steal talent.

"At this point in my life I'm not sure anything surprises me, but that's all ancient history now. I intend to make Demille's estate a token offer to purchase the company in light of your revelations and his untimely death, and if they refuse, I'll wish them well and simply hire his agents away from the firm. It will be out of business in a matter of months if they decline, so I'm not worried. With no viable alternative, I have a feeling the estate will take the offer."

"That could well be. I don't know much about business."

"Which brings us to the conclusion of our engagement. I believe we owe you some money?"

"I've prepared a statement. I can shoot it to Gunther in a few minutes. It'll bring us current, through yesterday afternoon."

"Very well. I have to say I've been surprised and pleased by your diligence in this matter. I think most would have waited for instructions once Demille was killed. To follow through and pursue the killer, as you did…well, color me impressed."

Black didn't see any point in correcting his misapprehension. "That's what you hired me for."

"Yes, well, you can expect positive referrals from me. Even if we had our differences over your handling of the affair, I have to say that in the end, you delivered."

"That's why I require autonomy when taking a case. I have my own methods, which are usually effective, even if it's not obvious at the time."

"I won't argue with that. Bobby was right about you."

"I'll send the invoice to Gunther. Feel free to contact me if you have any questions."

"Thank you, Mr. Black. Will do."

Black punched the line off and returned to Roxie's station, where she was giggling over a video of funny cat bloopers.

"Hard at work, I see," he said. She ignored him. He put the statement on her desk. "I ginned this up at home. Add another grand to it – four more hours. Might as well charge for my time with the cops yesterday."

She turned and looked at the sheet and her eyes widened. "Are you sure this is right?"

"Lots of travel time in that. And interviews."

"You didn't add a zero by mistake?"

"Nope. We're fat and happy after they pay this. At least for a while."

"I want a raise. A big one."

"Because of all the back-breaking work you do around here?"

"I figured I might as well ask."

"I'll consider it. Take it under advisement."

"Sure. I'll start looking at condos on Melrose."

"I don't see you there."

"Not working here, that's for sure."

Black went back into his office. So far the day couldn't have gone better. He considered buying a few lottery tickets, but thought twice about it. The way things had been going up till then, he'd get hit by a car crossing the street from the market. Better to keep his head down and count his blessings.

He heard a shredding sound from his office sofa and peered over the desk. Mugsy had waddled in and was tearing at the corner of the black vinyl like there was catnip hidden inside. Black stood abruptly and spilled his coffee all over his desk, drenching the papers and checkbook.

"Roxie!" he called, surveying the damage as warm fluid dripped from the table top. Mugsy, interrupted by the ruckus, sauntered back out to his throne in the outer office, his important work there finished, offering Black his backside in salute before disappearing around the door jamb. Black took in the sopping paperwork and ruined couch and sighed.

Things had gotten back to normal all too quickly.

Roxie poked her head in. "What?"

"The fat bastard tore up my couch."

"Oops. Sorry, boss. Maybe he's upset at you for some reason."

"I swear I'll stick him in the microwave this time. Only he probably won't fit. That's the only thing that's saving him."

"Think of this as an opportunity to work on your anger issues. It's just a sofa."

"Keep him out of here."

"You left your door open, not me," she said, and then disappeared. Black stared at the doorway, speechless, and then shook his head as he moved to get a roll of towels from the cabinet in the corner. He heard the phone ring and Roxie answer, and then she called out from her station.

"It's your mom. Line one."

He stared at the coffee pooled on the table. "Tell her I'm...busy. I'll call her back."

"You never do. I told her you'd be with her in a second. Nothing on your schedule, all the time in the world. She was worried she might be interrupting something. Said she called yesterday and you didn't answer. She's worried about you. Don't be a dick."

Black shook his head, and considered saying something nasty, but thought better of it. He moved to his desk, a wad of paper towels in his hand. He felt something warm on his thigh and looked down at his trousers. A brown stain ran from his crotch to his knee from where some of the coffee had gotten him. He studied the damage and shook his head.

Back to normal.

To be alerted to new releases, sign up here:

RussellBlake.com/contact/mailing-list

About the Author

Russell Blake lives full time on the Pacific coast of Mexico. He is the acclaimed author of the thrillers *Fatal Exchange, The Geronimo Breach, Zero Sum,* The Delphi Chronicle trilogy (*The Manuscript, The Tortoise and the Hare,* and *Phoenix Rising*), *King of Swords, Night of the Assassin, Return of the Assassin, Revenge of the Assassin, Blood of the Assassin, The Voynich Cypher, Silver Justice, JET, JET II – Betrayal, JET III – Vengeance, JET IV – Reckoning, Jet V – Legacy, Jet VI – Justice, Upon a Pale Horse, Black, Black is Back,* and *Black is The New Black.*

Non-fiction novels include the international bestseller *An Angel With Fur* (animal biography) and *How To Sell A Gazillion eBooks (while drunk, high or incarcerated)* – a joyfully vicious parody of all things writing and self-publishing related.

"Capt." Russell enjoys writing, fishing, playing with his dogs, collecting and sampling tequila, and waging an ongoing battle against world domination by clowns.

Visit Russell's salient website for more information

RussellBlake.com/

CPSIA information can be obtained at www.ICGtesting.com
Printed in the USA
BVOW05s1418080614

355673BV00002BA/115/P